Dead Men Do Tell

Becoming a doctor's wife was **Rose Marie Castle**'s way of obtaining the beautiful life she wasn't born into. But after being jilted at the altar by Mr. Prominent Plastic Surgeon, this aging beauty stumbles braless and pantyless out of her fortieth birthday and into a murder investigation.

Dr. Pierce Carver is Austin's very own smooth-talking, fast-living, upwardly mobile, womanizing...murder victim. And with his three ex-wives, widow, stepdaughters and estranged sons crawling out of the woodwork, it can finally be revealed just how many lives one man can lead.

Rosie's sexy high school crush **Michael Nash** still remembers the time they spent together under the palm trees in Mexico. As the acting homicide detective on Rosie's case, he just can't agree with her on who derailed whose life. But with so much blame to pass, why not share it?

Now this nurse turned premature (yet never matured) grandmother has a coming-of-middle-age journey to take and a whodunit to unravel. With a rough-cut Texan police officer on her trail, Rosie snoops to find her fairy-tale ending behind the lies where the beautiful life loses its luster.

Once, all she desired was Dr. Pierce Carver's head on a silver platter, and everyone knows it. Too bad her dreams *do* come true.

THE SECRET LIVES OF DOCTORS' WIVES

ANN MAJOR

MIRA®

ISBN-13: 978-0-7783-2346-4
ISBN-10: 0-7783-2346-3

THE SECRET LIVES OF DOCTORS' WIVES

www.MIRABooks.com

Printed in U.S.A.

This book is dedicated to Tara Gavin.
She contributed the title and
much more, as always.

ACKNOWLEDGMENTS

I need to thank Kimberly Huett for her help.

Prologue

Austin, Texas

He remembered the flash of the blade, the slender hand in the dark. His screams had been followed by eerie silence. Too late he recalled that this house had a history of tragedy.

The dying man could barely hear Rose Marie Castle's flying bare feet on the sculpted stone staircase. Besides her shoes, she was missing several intimate garments that, doubtless, the police would find later.

Run, run as fast as you can....

His hands were bound together with Rosie's silky black bra. Her paring knife was lodged firmly in his Adam's apple. The security cameras would capture incriminating images of her escape, but he would be dead long before she was brought to justice, which could be slow, even in Texas.

The deathblow had been savage. Delicate vertebrae had been smashed, his spinal cord nicked or severed. He'd had no sensation of falling as he'd crumpled to the white carpet, his blood staining it a vivid crimson.

He'd been a fool, ensnared like a stupid fly in a web. Because of her—the bitch.

He was cold to the marrow of his bones.

Downstairs, Rosie let out a panicked little cry. She began to pound on the door with her fists. When it finally opened, and she stumbled outside, the prisms of the chandelier above the grand staircase tinkled.

He thought of his mother and father. Of the old life and its false promises; of all the bitter years when he'd longed for vengeance, which would have been his—except for her.

Down the hill, the big engine of her Beamer purred to life. When she sped away, his useless body convulsed. As his eyeballs rolled upward, he heard the wind in the branches of the pecan trees outside. She must have left the door open in her haste to escape.

The harsh music of the cicadas joined the sweeter chime of the chandelier that she'd imported from Paris.

Paris, France; not Paris, Texas. What grand ambitions she'd had before the wedding.

Run, run; you can't catch me….

Like hell.

She'd pay. She deserved to pay.

His body convulsed one final time.

He thought about her dreams of being a grand lady in Austin society, married to the eminent plastic surgeon Pierce Carver. She'd wanted to live down the poverty and shame of her childhood.

Was there enough money or fame to heal such wounds?

The dying man almost felt pity for Rose Marie Castle as he died.

But not quite.

One

Austin, Texas

"Oh my God! More blood?" She'd thought it was only a nick.

Rosie couldn't believe what had just happened. Pierce had gotten angry so quickly. He'd seemed weird, strung out, not himself at all.

Her every breath was a harsh, tortured rasp as she grabbed a tissue and dabbed at her cut finger and the steering wheel. She didn't want to think about her former fiancé, or their quarrel, or how quickly the violence had escalated.

Perspiration drenched her, not just because it was a hot, sultry August night or because of the champagne she'd drunk with Pierce before the evening had gone wrong. Or because today was her fortieth birthday and maybe she was simply having an early hot flash.

She rubbed her head. Her scalp hurt where Pierce's watch had caught her hair. He hadn't cared that he'd hurt her. In fact, he'd smiled.

She wrapped the tissue around her finger and applied pressure. When the Beamer's tires squealed, rounding a sharp curve, she gripped the wheel. It wasn't like her to mistreat her car by driving too fast. She was *that* anxious to get away.

Well, at least she was finally over him. No more wisecracks to the other nurses about wanting revenge, to salve her wounded ego because they knew he'd dumped her for Anita.

For what it was worth, tonight Mr. Prominent Plastic Surgeon hadn't paid her a dime of the money he owed her, either. Big surprise. She still didn't know why she'd snapped. But for sure, she had bigger problems now than the money he'd owed her.

What had she ever seen in Pierce? He was a gifted doctor, and being a nurse, she'd admired that. She'd been having a hard time accepting her grown daughter's lifestyle, so maybe he'd come along when she'd needed to feel successful in other areas of her life. Being seen on the arm of a handsome plastic surgeon had made her feel good.

But even before he'd dumped her, the romance had taken a dark turn. Like a lot of Rosie's boyfriends—and there'd been a lot, way too many in some people's opinions, such as her mother's—Pierce had developed the knack for punching the wrong buttons. He brought out the Bad Rosie, just like her mom, Hazel, did sometimes, which was why Rosie should have been delighted when he'd jilted her for a younger woman right before their wedding day nearly a year ago.

Okay, so Rosie hadn't been delighted or acted mature, despite her "mature" age. Okay, so maybe that was partly because she'd been feeling romantic about being a bride again, and partly because she'd seen Dr. Pierce Carver as the ticket to the sparkling train car.

Rosie's least favorite movie scene of all time, and of course it had to be the one that haunted her, was the opening sequence in Woody Allen's *Stardust Memories*. In the scene, poor Woody sat in a dark, dirty train car with a bunch of other pathetic losers. Unfortunately, he had looked out the window just in time to see a sparkling train car filled with happy, glamorous people drinking champagne streak by him, and he had despaired.

There'd been a lot of times when Rosie would have sold her soul to be in that sparkling car.

Pierce had come into her life just when she'd been feeling superguilty about Carmen dancing at The Cellar and neglecting her five-year-old daughter, Alexis, to the point that Rosie had had to take Alexis under her wing. Pierce had seemed glamorous and caring and sure of himself, when she'd been feeling vulnerable because she was getting older and didn't have enough to show for it.

When he had jilted her and she'd had to face reality again, she'd had to see a shrink for a while to reclaim her sanity—on a weekly basis, as a matter of fact.

So—okay. Okay. Okay.

Rosie really had thought she was over Pierce, until he'd called tonight. He'd flattered her and said he was tying up loose ends. He'd promised to pay her the money he owed her, and she'd agreed to give him a new key to the warehouse where he stored some medical records.

Now she was racing down the curving, narrow road in Westlake Hills that led through sweet-smelling juniper-covered, limestone hills, away from his mansion.

Rosie lifted her gaze to the rearview mirror. She caught a glimpse of one blue eye and her coppery-red curls. She adjusted the mirror and saw her shoes on the back seat.

As for her bra and panties... Her heart began to beat fast. She did not want to dwell on missing underwear.

Damn. Damn. Damn.

She couldn't believe he'd made her feel so vulnerable and lonely. Why else had she started stripping for him and...

He'd said she was beautiful, and maybe she was...for her age. She was slim. Her legs were long. Okay, so maybe she was a little worried about her neck at times. Just as she lifted her chin to check it in her rearview mirror, her cell phone vibrated on her lap.

Damn. No way could she talk to anybody.

But when she picked up the phone, she saw Yolie's name highlighted in brilliant blue. Yolie had let her and Alexis move in when Rosie's house had burned not long after Pierce had jilted her. Alexis was home with Jennifer, who was just a teenager. A responsible one, but still a teenager. Yolie was supposed to go to her ranch tonight.

What if there was a problem? Rosie had to answer.

"Where've you been? Celebrating your big birthday with a lot of sex and sin and alcohol, I hope," Yolie said in that crisp, in-your-face voice she usually reserved for the managers of her various fast-food Taco Bonito restaurants.

No way was Rosie admitting the truth. That she'd gone to Pierce's. That she'd almost… Not to Yolie, of all people! Yolie, who, among her many identities, happened to be one of Pierce's ex-wives.

Yolie had totally agreed with Nan, Rosie's shrink, when she'd advised Rosie not to date for a while, so that she could confront the psychic wounds of her childhood. Whatever.

They both said she'd obsessed about Pierce for too long. They'd been the first to quit laughing when she'd joked about having vengeful fantasies, although Yolie had enjoyed her saying she'd have Pierce's head on a silver platter if he kept refusing to pay her what he owed her.

Alarmed that Yolie, who hadn't gotten rich in the

fast-food business by being the dimmest bulb in the kitchen, might somehow hear the quiver in her voice and suspect something, Rosie tensed.

"Oh...I was at my house—you know, painting with Harry...so that someday—sooner rather than later—you'll have your mansion back to yourself." *Not exactly a lie.*

Harry's main job was to run her rental properties, which included houses in her old East Austin neighborhood, as well as the warehouse where Pierce stored some of his stuff. Of late, Harry had been the contractor on her house.

"Really? Until midnight? I just got back from your place. Harry was smoking grass in that portable potty your nosy, next-door neighbor, Mirabella, is always in such a snit about. Would you believe Mirabella was actually up and that she and her dog watched me from her kitchen window? Does she ever mind her own business?"

"She makes a career of running me down to the entire neighborhood."

"When I knocked on the door of the portable potty, I almost got high myself on fumes when he kicked it open. Harry was pretty fuzzy headed, but he did say he thought Jennifer called you around 11:00 p.m., maybe about Alexis, because you sure peeled rubber when you left."

Busted. Rosie swallowed. She'd been only too happy to let him think it was Jennifer, her favorite babysitter.

But had she actually said she was going home to check on Alexis? No. Did she have to account for her actions to Harry, of all people? Definitely—no!

"I…" With Yolie, who was way smarter than Harry, sometimes the less said, the better. "So… what's up?"

"I was on my way out the door, late as usual, to go to the ranch, when Beth called. In fact, I just left Jennifer and Alexis, who are fine, by the way. Beth sounds frantic. Says she's been calling you for over an hour…."

Beth was an R.N. in the I.C.U. at Brackenridge Hospital, where Rosie worked. Beth had been sick earlier in the week, and Rosie had had to pull double shifts. Not fun, since she needed every spare minute to clean and paint her burned-out mess of a house because Harry's progress on the job had been so slow and her neighbors, stirred up by Mirabella, were bugging her about the unmowed brown grass and the awful orange portable potty in her front yard.

"Beth?"

"She said to call her at the unit ASAP." Yolie paused. "Oh, and before I forget, I left you a teeny piece of double-fudge, Italian-cream chocolate cake in the fridge for your birthday."

"You swore you wouldn't—" Rosie stopped herself.

There was no point in arguing with Yolie, who was a larger woman, who loved to cook, and who ate whatever she wanted. She wasn't neurotic about her butt size or her jean size or even the fact that her next big birthday would be fifty. She had a thing for younger men, too. Her current hottie was Xavier, her gardener, of all people. He was ambitious. Yolie was always helping him with his English. He was going to school, and he worked for Taco Bonito, too. The one condition she'd made when Rosie had moved in was to leave Xavier strictly alone—or she'd teasingly threatened to turn her into taco meat for her restaurant chain.

Of course, Rosie had promised to leave the yardman to his clipping, but that was before she'd seen Xavier, who had a head of thick black hair, a body of sleek dark muscles and a lopsided smile that reminded her too much of the first man she'd ever given her heart to, under a palm tree in Mexico, no less.

"I swore I wouldn't make brownies, but didn't say anything about Italian-cream cake," Yolie said. "Life is far too short and much too cruel to live without chocolate. You're only forty once, sweetie. Enjoy…that is, if you ever get home tonight."

Before Yolie, who no doubt had time to talk, went on to press her for details about where she'd been, exactly, Rosie hung up and dialed Beth.

"I'm sorry to bother you…but I really really need you to come in," Beth began. "Just for an hour—it's an emergency."

"It's after midnight. Can't a supervisor pull a nurse off another floor? I can't just…"

"Please."

"I'm out. I'm a mess." She couldn't very well say, "You think you have problems? This has been the most terrible night of my life! I'm braless and panty-less and so totally mental after losing it with Pierce and Pierce losing it with me that there is no way I could take care of patients."

Aloud she said, "Why don't you get Margaret to find somebody?" Margaret was their supervisor.

"I can't. I just can't." Beth, who wasn't one to give details about her personal life, and who was usually very stoic, started in with broken sobs.

This was bad.

"I am not coming in!"

Two

In the mock Tuscan villa down the hill from Dr. Pierce Carver's four-acre lot and mansion, Amanda Jones, who was a light sleeper, especially when Ralph was out of town on business, was awakened by the faint but persistent sound of her neighbor's car alarm.

She sat up and listened.

When it didn't stop, she grew frightened and went to the window. Pierce was anal about his Porsche.

No matter how hard she squinted, she couldn't see much of Carver's property through the thick cedar and oak. Suddenly, two black figures burst out of the darkness from the direction of the Carvers' house and raced down the strip of road that wound in front of both their houses.

Since she wasn't about to turn off her own house alarm and go out in the dark and investigate, or even step out onto her upstairs balcony, which had such spectacular views of the sparkling city far below, she went back to her bedside table and called Pierce's place. When his answering machine picked up on the first ring, she hung up without leaving a message. Then she dialed 911.

Michael Nash had a bad case of brain fog. Not great when you're Homicide and you've got a body upstairs with a paring knife in his Adam's apple, and two punks in black with blood on their shoes handcuffed to a tree in the victim's front yard.

The body was probably that of Dr. Pierce Carver. Who the hell else could it be?

Funny, the rich jerk just happened to be somebody Michael had something in common with—namely a woman. Rose Marie Castle, to be exact. Nash knew Carver was a prick because Rose Marie had told him so and quite heatedly—after Michael had ticketed her for stalking the bastard with her Beamer last year. Apparently, Carver had dumped her for a younger model, Anita Somebody from Guatemala. Rosie never had taken failure well.

Not that Michael wanted to think about Rosie or *that* night ever again because, as usual, she'd twisted him around her little finger and had made a fool out of him.

Carver and she had probably deserved each other. Rosie was trouble, always had been and probably always would be. She'd cut Michael's heart out on more than one occasion. Just not with a paring knife.

Hell, maybe he should count his blessings.

But murder? Rosie couldn't have anything to do with this. Still, she'd been royally pissed at the guy.

Michael glanced up from his notebook and said a silent prayer for the dead man in the house. Not that he was sure there was anybody up there to listen. Still, his mother had taken him to church when he was a kid. Old habits died hard.

Michael glanced at the punks handcuffed to the tree and then at his watch. It was late, nearly 2:00 a.m. He lacked the energy to deal with their lies.

Liars! He hated liars!

Too bad, Nash. Everybody lied to cops. The murderers lied because they had to. Witnesses lied to cover up all sorts of minor peccadilloes that as often as not had nothing to do with the case. Everybody else lied just for the sheer joy of it.

His head was pounding as he approached the punks again. His eyes felt grainy. On top of that he was sweltering out here even at this hour.

Michael needed to share a cold beer with Ronnie Bob at The Tavern before heading home, where he would've loved to zone out channel surfing. Maybe watch a tiger eat a zebra or a rattler pounce on a mouse before he passed out on his couch.

Instead, he forced himself to concentrate on the shifty-eyed kids in the faded black T-shirts and ragged jeans, slouching against the tree trunk. Talk about being in the wrong place at the wrong time.

Even though Michael didn't think they had a damn thing to do with the murder, the older kid had a prior for car theft. No, they'd been after the Porsche and had set off the car alarm that had alerted Amanda Jones down the hill.

"You just got out of a detention center for stealing cars," Michael began. "Am I right—Paulo—"

"Pablo." The kid spat the name.

"Sorry." Feeling the kid's hatred, Michael scratched through the *u* and jotted a *b* on top of it. "Pablo."

"We was joggin'." This from Raul.

Michael's thick, black brows shot together in a lethal frown. "Right. And you two live...where? Eight miles from here? East Austin. My old neighborhood."

Rosie's, too. Not that she liked to admit it even now that it was becoming rather gentrified.

"It's a free country," Pablo spat.

Michael was lifting his head to stare at the kid again when Ronnie Bob Keith's florid face appeared at the front door. Keith's smirk was a mile wide as he waved a plastic Baggie.

Michael loped toward his partner.

"Raul dropped his wallet. They were up there, all right. Their bloody footprints are everywhere. Talk about contaminating the scene!"

Michael returned with the evidence. Clenching the Baggie, he eyeballed the older kid. "Pablo, my men just found your little brother's wallet in a pool of blood by a man with a knife in his throat, and you don't know nothing?"

"Right."

"How about you—Raul?"

Raul started shaking and refused to look up from the ground.

Michael continued to stare at Pablo. The youth was too tall and too skinny for his large frame. He wore a dirty red bandana. A greasy dark braid hung down the middle of his back. He shoved his hands deep in his pockets and eased his weight from one foot to the other, his soulless eyes gazing anywhere but at Raul or Michael.

Michael wanted to know what the kids knew, what they'd seen, but he was going to have to take them downtown and separate them.

Sweat dripped from his brow onto his notepad as he sucked in a long, exasperated breath. "Kid, we're getting nowhere fast."

"I told you all I know."

The fog in Michael's brain thickened. He held up the wallet again. "You're going to change your bullshit story before I'm through."

Pablo stared at his dirty athletic shoes.

"Damn it! You were all over the house! Did you see anybody else? Hear anything?"

"Man, I don't have to take this. I'm only sixteen."

"Kids like you get tried as adults all the time. You think about that—Paulo."

"*Pablo!* You think I'm just a kid, but I know my rights. We don't have to talk to no cop without our lawyer."

"All right. Have it your way." Michael left them and headed toward the house.

"Hey! You! Come back here! Let us go!"

As their screams grew louder, Michael took the stairs beneath the brilliant chandelier two at a time.

To hell with them!

Finally, Beth had made it back to the hospital.

Maybe it was the late hour, maybe Rosie was just exhausted, maybe she'd seen too many scenes on TV where women got assaulted in parking garages, or maybe it was aftershocks from her ugly run-in with Pierce—whatever, Rosie had a bad case of the jitters as she climbed the concrete stairs to the fourth floor in the hospital parking garage. She was nearly to her Beamer when her cell phone rang.

Climbing faster, she dug for it in her purse, and for her keys, too, only to panic when she read Yolie's home phone number in the little blue window.

It was well after two-thirty. Jennifer and Alexis were home alone now, since Yolie had driven to the ranch.

Rosie pushed open the door to the fourth floor. "Jennifer?" Her voice echoed in the dimly lit garage.

"Alexis is gone!" the teenager shrieked without preamble. "I've looked everywhere!"

Seeing her Beamer, Rosie raced to it. "She can't be…gone. She's hiding or something."

"No…I've looked everywhere."

With shaking hands, Rosie unlocked the car and got in. "Did you check the pool?"

"I turned on the pool lights and the floodlights and everything…. She went to bed with Blue Binkie not long after Yolie left. My boyfriend called, and I was on the phone for a while. Then I went up to check on her. I swear, she was fine, but now her bed's empty. I checked every door and window. They're all locked. Your bedroom's empty, except for Lula."

Lula was Yolie's huge, white poodle.

Rosie couldn't believe anything else could go wrong—even if it was her birthday. Alexis gone?

Rosie squeezed her eyes shut and fought panic, not for the first time tonight. As she started the ignition, she thought about their mysterious break-in two days ago. That had been so strange…just as Pierce calling her tonight had been strange. Looking back, the break-in felt almost like an omen.

Yolie's security company had phoned her and said the alarm was going off. When they'd checked it out, the kitchen door had been unlocked, but shut. Oddly, Lula had been locked in an upstairs bathroom without food or water, barking her head off. When Rosie had gone up to let her out, Yolie's favorite pink bath mat had been nothing but bits of rubber and pink fuzz.

Other than that, there had been no signs of an intruder. Nor had any valuables been missing.

So, who had unlocked the door and set off the alarm? Who had locked Lula upstairs? Lula had a bad habit of biting postmen and pool men, but she'd let herself be locked in the bathroom without shedding so much as a drop of blood on the white wall-to-wall carpet.

"Shit happens," the security guy had said, as if that explained it. "Or you have a mystery intruder. Somebody who's got a key. Somebody your doggie knows. Or you've got a glitch in your system somewhere."

"Check the system," Yolie had said.

"I'm so scared, Ms. Castle," Jennifer whispered now, cutting into Rosie's thoughts.

Me, too, Rosie thought.

She wound her way down the parking garage ramp and soon was speeding west on Martin Luther King, Jr.

"The house is so big and dark…. And there's all these spooky sounds. I've been hearing them ever since Yolie put the garage door down and drove away."

"Then call 911! I'll be there as fast as I can, but I'm at least ten minutes away!"

Oh, why hadn't Yolie installed cameras?

The break-in had seemed so insignificant. It was odd how the small moments and the casual decisions could turn out to be the most important ones of all.

What if…Rosie simply hadn't gone to Pierce's tonight?

She forced herself to concentrate on her driving and getting home safely so she could find Alexis. Darling precious Alexis.

Alexis had to be all right.

A distant light switched from green to yellow to red.

Rosie slowed, looked both ways; then she stomped down hard on the gas pedal. She prayed that Michael wasn't nearby in his radio car, ready to pounce again, like he had that night a year ago when she'd seen Pierce jogging and had decided it was time to confront him about the rent.

No sign of a radio car.

Rosie shot through the light.

Michael was worrying over his report in his unmarked four-door Crown Vic in front of Carver's mansion.

The scene, the punks, the victim, all felt wrong. Why? What was he missing?

Keith was leaning back in the passenger seat smoking while Michael went over the facts one last time. Suddenly they caught a call about a missing little girl on their radio.

The name Alexis Castle meant nothing to Michael. The name Rose Marie Castle charged through him in a soul-searing bolt.

Castle. His old girlfriend, Rosie. Carver's girl-friend, too.

Her grandkid missing tonight? That was a helluva

coincidence. What was going on? He had to make sure Rosie and the kid were okay.

"We're not taking another damn call." Keith's eyes flashed in the dark as he sent a smoke ring toward the ceiling.

"The grandmother's the victim's ex-girlfriend."

"Shit." Keith blew another smoke ring and settled back in his seat.

Michael was glad Keith decided to give him the silent treatment instead of pumping him with questions. He wasn't in the mood to discuss Rosie, whom he had no desire to see ever again.

Still, he couldn't stop himself from thinking about her.

A year ago, Michael had caught her on the rebound from a bad relationship with the dead man. And damn it, as always, they'd ended up in bed.

So what else was new? He'd been her first back in high school, but then she'd dumped him, married, had a kid. Not that his own life had been any less complicated. Last year when he'd run into Rosie, he'd been separated from his wife, Marie.

Funny that her name was Rosie's middle name.

Not so funny.

Michael's mouth thinned at the memory of Rosie's long, honey-gold legs wrapped around his on that hellishly hot Sunday, the morning after. They'd cuddled all night long, but come morning, she'd turned on him.

Why was it that, with a little alcohol on board, two former lovers feeling the need for a little TLC could take up right where they'd left off?

It had been a pretty amazing night. He might have been well on his way to falling in love with her again, but the next morning she'd taken one look at his black head on her pillow and had started throwing things at him—first his shirt, then his jeans and then his boots. When she'd gone for the lamp and handcuffs, he'd locked himself in the bathroom.

Good thing, too. She'd smashed the lamp against the door. Next, he'd heard the handcuffs bounce off the wall. Then she'd run just like before, screaming, "You ruined my life—all over again!"

What the hell had that meant? She'd run out on him after high school. He'd called her a few times, but she'd always hung up on him.

When his wife had finally called him back, he'd stupidly confessed about Rosie, and that had been the final straw for Marie. Since their divorce, he'd been lonely as hell.

So, now Rosie's granddaughter was missing.

He hoped to hell Rosie wasn't connected to this murder. Or that the kid wasn't in the hands of whoever had cut Carver up.

Just the thought and his palms began to sweat. Gut instinct told him to get over there fast.

Without so much as a glance toward his silent partner, Michael started the ignition.

As he drove, he thought about the missing kid. When his marriage hadn't worked out, he'd been glad Marie and he hadn't had children. Still, deep down, not having them was one of life's big disappointments.

What if Rosie's granddaughter's life depended on somebody who gave a damn making the right decision?

Hell.

When he stepped on the gas, Keith swore viciously and flicked his cigarette lighter.

Three

The large windows of Yolie's mansion threw long bright rectangles of yellow out onto the dark lawn as Rosie pulled up. Red and blue lights blinking, cop cars were everywhere.

Alexis, please... Please be okay, baby.

Rosie parked the Beamer in the driveway, got out and ran stumbling up the dark sidewalk. Besides the radio cars, several cars she'd never seen before were parked on the narrow street in front of the house. Dark, shadowy figures moved about near the brilliantly lit pool house and pool.

Expecting the worst inside, she struggled with her keys and pushed the big door open.

"Jennifer?"

Her coppery curls bouncing and her blue eyes as bright as lasers in her olive-toned face, Alexis got up from the television set and hurled herself into her grandmother's arms, nearly knocking her down.

"You didn't come home when you said, Mimi!"

Rosie swallowed guiltily and tried not to think about why.

"So, I went to your bed! I crawled under the covers with Lula on top so I could hide and surprise you! I guess I fell asleep, and I didn't hear Jennifer when she called me! So, guess what? She called the nice policeman! But don't give me a time-out! Please don't!"

Rosie pressed the slim child close and drank in the musky fragrances of unwashed little girl, sweaty curls and peppermint breath. Her nose was running, too.

"You're okay? You're really okay! Oh, honey…" Relief flooded Rosie as she searched her purse for a tissue. Finally. Something good had happened since she'd turned forty.

"You're squeezing me, Mimi!"

As she hugged Alexis even closer, Rosie slowly became aware of the tall, dark, lean-hipped man writing something on a notepad.

The police! She was in no shape to deal with them. When he strode into the living room and stood over her, tingles of alarm coursed through her. Then her gaze climbed a pair of long muscular legs encased in rumpled black slacks.

Familiar long muscular legs.

For no reason at all she remembered the furious rattle of palm fronds, the sound of a Mexican xylophone, the salty air that smelled of the sea…and the sting of hot skin from that awful sunburn she'd gotten from lying on the beach in the shade too long with Michael.

It couldn't be him…. Not Michael Nash!

Michael wore a brown sport coat that needed an iron. His tie had been yanked loose at his throat. There were shadows under his long-lashed, dark eyes that hadn't been there when he'd fast-talked and fast-kissed and fast-petted her into riding off on the back of his motorcycle to Veracruz, Mexico, the day after they'd graduated from high school.

Michael. He had a tattoo of a cute little palm tree on his chest over his heart, which matched the one she had over her left breast. Thank God they were both clothed.

With a low moan, she stood up slowly and blew out a mortified breath. She'd dressed in such a hurry at Pierce's and then at the hospital again that she was sure she looked even more of a mess than Michael did.

Michael turned off the TV and shot her his famous football star grin that back in high school had made all the cheerleaders want to sleep with him. Okay, obviously she'd gone for it, too.

Alexis must've fallen for the smile because she ran over to him and lowered her lashes much too fetchingly for Rosie's peace of mind. And she was all of five.

Oh, my God!

Rosie watched in horror as he knelt. Oh, how she

hated how infinitely gentle his voice was when he spoke to the little girl. "You okay, sweetheart?"

Alexis nodded up at him. Holding her blue blanket, she twisted it to and fro shyly.

"Of all the cops in this city—you had to be the one to come." Rosie ran her hands through her wildly tangled hair. Then she snapped, "Alexis, it's time for bed!"

The child put her hands on her hips. Her jaw squared mulishly. "I'm not sleepy."

"I thought you were a homicide detective," Rosie said to Michael.

"So you remember?" His grin twisted. "I like it that you paid attention. Your babysitter called 911. I heard your name."

"So you volunteered?"

His eyes darkened, and she felt a little scared.

"Something like that." He lowered his voice, but not before she caught the edge in it. "Fond memories."

Why did he look so serious? Why was he studying her so intently with those cop's eyes of his? As if she'd committed a crime?

She tried not to think about Pierce. "Aren't there enough bad guys to keep you busy?"

"Maybe I prefer bad girls."

"I'm a good witch," Alexis said, and batted her lashes at him.

"Yes, you are, darling," Rosie agreed, glad of the distraction. "The best little witch ever to ride a broom with her very own Blue Binkie. But it's time for all good witches to go to bed."

As Michael continued to watch Rosie, his grin made her feel feverish and anxious.

She was forty, for heaven's sake. A grown-up. A *grandmother*. She was too old to get the chills because of him, of all people.

Michael shifted so that he faced her. She grew even warier of his penetrating gaze.

"I thought cops were supposed to be doughnut addicts with weight problems. When are you going to get fat and old?"

"You look good, too, Rosie. So good, you make me remember palm trees and…that night last year."

She flushed. "Don't!"

He grinned. "What are you—forty?"

She lifted her chin. "Don't remind me."

"Palm trees?" Alexis whispered eagerly. "Can we go to the beach, Mimi? I love the beach."

"Hush." She had to get Alexis to bed and Michael out of here fast before he grew bossy or inquisitive, or her hormones started acting up.

"I've got some guys outside making sure everything is all right," he said, in that deep, oddly tense, authoritative tone she'd never liked. "They walked Jennifer home. I stayed inside watching cartoons with Alexis to wait for you."

He glanced at his watch and then at her again. Maybe it was just her, but she thought his detective eyes glinted suspiciously. "So, where were you...so late?"

"There was an emergency. I'm a nurse. I—I had to go in to work," she said, finger-combing her hair as he continued to watch her, still in that too-assessing way of his.

"Your babysitter seemed to be expecting you much earlier. I think Alexis and she got nervous...."

"Jennifer knew I had to work." Rosie felt herself flushing guiltily. Then she bristled. What business was it of his? For a second or two she considered telling him about the break-in two days ago, but that would only prolong the encounter.

She glanced pointedly toward the door. "Well, Alexis is safe and sound now, so, again, thank you."

A beat passed.

He didn't budge. Not even when Alexis rubbed her eyes again.

"Look, I really do need to get her to bed," Rosie said desperately. "You know the way out."

He was still watching her in *that* way that so unnerved her when he said, "I called the hospital, and your supervisor said you were off all day and that you came in briefly around twelve-thirty...and that—"

Because of her fear and guilt, Rosie's temper blazed out of control. She felt her face grow hot. But instead of saying anything, she took Alexis's hand and hurried her upstairs. But as she ran, she was aware of him standing there, not moving, his keen gaze burning into her back.

In her bathroom, she strained her ears trying to hear the door close behind him. When she thought she'd heard it, she tried to forget him.

Not a chance of that! Not when Alexis turned to her, bright-eyed and curious. "Are you in love with him, Mimi?"

"*What?*"

"Are you?"

When she shook her head, Alexis, who was clearly in the midst of her first crush, smiled and then gushed in a confidential tone, "Good. Because I am."

Oh, God… Unwanted memories swamped Rosie— her arms laced around Michael's young, lean back as they roared toward Mexico, the wind gusting against their skin; his long naked body on top of hers at that secluded beach with the palms after he'd taken her virginity. Last of all she remembered the compassion in his eyes as she'd poured her heart out to him in that bar last year after he'd ticketed her. When she'd finished talking, she'd leaned across the table and kissed him as if he were the only person in her whole life who'd ever really mattered. His answering kiss had been equally tender and hot and all-consuming.

Nobody else had ever made her feel as if she was the *only one*.

Rosie yanked the brush through Alexis's hair and

then washed her face, but she was too tired and upset to bathe her.

"Tomorrow, first thing in the morning, after a night's sleep, we'll bathe together," she said, forcing a bright smile.

Alexis set Blue Binkie on the counter and squirted a blob of jewel-blue toothpaste on her brush, and for once didn't argue, so Rosie got to splash cold water on her own face in relative peace.

"I want to sleep with you," Alexis said when they were finished.

"Yes, I'd like that, too." Rosie wiped a bit of shiny blue off the corner of Alexis's mouth. "We'll have our very own slumber party." How Rosie had longed for such closeness to Carmen, Alexis's mother, when Carmen had been young. But it hadn't happened back then, and it still hadn't happened.

Someday.

When they closed the bedroom door, Rosie gently tucked the little girl, Blue Binkie, several books that she demanded, and three of her favorite stuffed animals under the covers of her king-size bed. When Alexis rolled over, hugging her blanket and shutting her eyes, Rosie tiptoed downstairs, intending to turn the lights out, lock up and set the alarm.

Instead, she nearly screamed when she saw Michael sprawled on the couch, writing in his little notebook.

"I thought you'd left."

He looked up, his eyes hard with suspicion.

"Cute kid," he said, forcing a mildness in his low tone. "Real cute. Reminds me of you. I envy you. I never had kids."

Quickly, she glanced at him and at her family pictures right behind him, and then away. Had he looked at them?

Deep breath. Deep breath.

"You have to go," she said. "Now."

"Why the hell are you so afraid of me?"

"Who's afraid? I was just worried Alexis might wake up and get scared."

"There's no need to be afraid of me, you know."

"Right. I'm not."

"Besides, I thought we kind of clicked again last year."

At the reminder, a ripple of tension raced down her spine. Maybe if she went on the attack, he would leave.

"Look, I was going through a rough time last year. You were pushy as hell. You took advantage. I made up my mind a long time ago...that you and I...weren't right for each other."

He slammed his notebook aside and sat up straighter. "Oh, right, blame me for what happened. Revenge fantasies cause you to chase your old boyfriend down with your Beamer, and then when I ticket you and prevent you from doing murder or whatever you intended, you reach under the table and grab—"

"Okay! I don't need a replay!"

"What was I—a revenge fuck?"

"Oh…! Is that what you told everybody you know—that I threw myself at you?"

"It damn sure would have been the truth. What about the revenge part? Is that why you did it?"

She marched toward him, intending to pound his wide chest. But as soon as she entered his space, she grew jittery and halted. Suddenly she was too afraid of his power and her own vulnerability after all that had happened tonight. Besides, anytime she saw him, guilt about the past swept her.

He lifted his hands in mock surrender. "Okay. Okay. I'm sorry I said that. And about what happened last year, I was a self-serving…er, pushy jerk… To let you feel me up right there in the bar. And then to kiss you back when you kissed me."

Just when her blood came to a rolling boil again, he paused.

"To let me?"

"Rosie, be fair. The sex was your idea. You knew how easy it was for you to stir me up in high school," he stated. "And you'd learned a lot since then. I was going through a rough patch with my wife, too."

"*Your wife?* You…you dog! I can't believe this!" Oh, yes, yes she could. After tonight, she could believe anything. Men were scum. "You were *married?*"

"*Was.*"

This was bad.

She gulped in a breath, almost strangling. She knew she should drop it, but she couldn't. "You should've stopped at that first kiss—or at least by the second."

"So should you. The truth is, you sort of pushed, too. I mean, your hands were doing all those things under the table."

"But *you* were *married*."

"Not anymore—thanks to you."

"What? You're blaming me? Oh…!"

"When Marie and I were making up, I'm afraid I told her about us."

"Marie? Her name's Marie, too? And what's this *us*? There is, I mean was, no us."

"I tried to explain that to her. Stupidly, I thought I should try to be honest when we started over."

"And you were dumb enough to tell her about us?"

"*Us*. There! You said it, too!"

Images of what she'd done with Michael sprang into vivid color in her imagination. This was a nightmare. She couldn't believe Michael had turned up the same night she'd seen Pierce again.

"How much did you tell her?"

"Too much."

Everything. He'd told his wife everything!

Why had she picked Michael to sleep with instead of some stranger? The point had been to reassure herself she was still even capable of sex after the number Pierce had done on her. Period. She'd wanted no attachments. Who better than a man she knew she *had* to be done with?

Strangely, the sex with Michael had quickly become a compulsion. After a kiss or two, she couldn't have stopped had her life depended on it. He'd made her feel too damned attractive, and she'd craved that after the way Pierce had discarded her.

A minute passed, and then another. The silence between them grew thick and heavy. Michael's eyes were so intense they were giving her a bad case of the chills.

"Last year you were so upset with that doctor, you wanted to kill him," he murmured. "You over the bastard yet?"

The question caught her off guard, and she spoke too abruptly and too defensively. "Yes!"

He was watching her eyes, reading her. "Ever see him?"

"No!" She forced herself to look Michael squarely in the eye.

"Ever talk to him?"

"No!" Her heart raced. But why was Michael probing so hard?

After a long moment of scrutinizing her, Michael's hard face relaxed again, and she decided maybe she'd pulled it off.

"Good," he said, his tone oddly controlled.

"Officer Nash, it's late," she stated.

"Michael," he murmured.

She went to the front door and opened it. She smiled when he grabbed his notebook and got up.

He glanced around. Fortunately, the family photos

didn't seem to attract his attention. But he'd had a lot of time alone with them in the den. Still, he had no reason to be suspicious. But if he looked at Carmen's pictures too closely...

"Nice house. Nice couch. And the pool. The pool's great. You always did like to swim. I remember when we ran away together, how you wanted to go to that beach with all the palms and skinny-dip."

She tensed again but said nothing.

"What about your art? You still draw everything you see?"

She shook her head.

"That's too bad. You were good. I remember how you wanted to be a famous artist."

His comment made her feel wistful. As a kid she'd seen her art as a way out of East Austin and the dead-end kind of life Hazel had led, just as Michael had seen playing college football as his ticket to success. Both of them had been through so much. First they'd blamed each other for their fathers' tragedy. Only with time had he seen that her pain was as great as his, and their mutual pain had caused them to form a bond. Then she'd gotten pregnant and made her decision.

Rosie felt the stirring of a vague, nostalgic longing. For what? It wasn't as if things could have ever worked out between them.

She'd done what she'd thought best, and now they both, him unwittingly, had to live with the consequences. Period. There was no going back.

Unable to read her mind, he grinned and changed tack. "I notice this house belongs to one of your ex-fiancé's ex-wives, Yolie Carver. The fast-food taco queen."

He'd emphasized the name Carver, and Rosie tensed again.

"You're not living with her just to cozy up to his family? You're not still stalking..." His eyes darkened.

"You were leaving," she reminded him, shakily. "Little girl found. Case closed." She tried to make her voice light.

"Right. Just curious. You always did want to live high, princess."

"Is that a crime?"

"Some things never change, I guess. Is that what you have against me? That I'm a cop? That I can't afford a house like this? If you weren't out for revenge, is that why you could bed me, but then be so anxious to get rid of me—"

"Why did you give up being a big pro football star?"

"You mean why'd I quit, just when I was set to rake in millions?"

"To become a cop?"

"You think I was a fool?"

"I didn't say that."

His daddy had been a cop. And he'd said he'd hated his daddy. Maybe being a cop was a calling.

Michael had moved up the ranks fast. She wondered if it was because he was good or because he knew the right people. Or because he was on the take like his daddy. Or maybe he felt he had to live down what his daddy had done.

"Why are you so damn set against me?" he demanded.

"Look, I don't need this," she whispered.

He pitched a business card onto Yolie's gleaming coffee table.

She felt a strange, aching disappointment that she didn't understand. As if her heart was breaking as it had all those years ago when she'd decided to dump him.

He'd ruined her life. Because of what had happened with him, she'd given up her art…and everything else she'd longed to have and be. Now she was a nobody, she, who'd been alive with ambition and so damned eager for a ticket on the glittering train car.

She picked up his business card and then set it down again.

"Well, you know where to find me, princess."

As he walked toward her, invading her personal space as only he could, his eyes burned her neckline. She blushed and became annoyed that he could upset her just by getting too close.

"I just broke up with my girlfriend. Maybe I could take you…and Alexis, too, to Zilker Park or something. Maybe teach her to throw a Frisbee. Maybe ride the little train…. You have my card."

"I don't think so."

He brushed past her and stepped outside. She

shot the bolt and leaned against the door, rasping in quick breaths as his brisk footsteps receded down the walk. For a long time, she just stood there, feeling as if she were melting on the outside but frozen in the middle.

He'd invited Alexis to the park. Why did that touch her? Had he felt some bond with the child? Did he suspect the truth, maybe, on some subconscious level?

Feeling a strange need to call him back, she rushed to her window and watched his lean form slide into a battered, blue Crown Victoria with a tall antenna on the trunk. Her heart caught. He looked so lonely out there in the dark.

Only after his engine started was she able to break the connection and make herself march to the kitchen. She was lusting for Michael, which meant she probably should indulge herself with some of Yolie's birthday cake. But when she opened the fridge and saw the huge piece of chocolate cake, the red candle on top of it spelled Forty.

Teeny piece. Trust me.

She pulled the awful candle off and licked the length of it.

De-licious! Sinfully so!

As she threw it in the trash, she imagined herself trying to zip her forty-year-old butt into her new spandex jeans. When she returned to the fridge, she pushed the cake plate behind the milk carton and grabbed an apple. She went to the drawer where she kept her favorite Kasumi paring knife, which Pierce had bought her on a trip they'd made together to Japan.

It wasn't there.

Frustrated, she dashed about the kitchen, jerking all the drawers open. Finally, she settled on a dull blade from Yolie's block. Then she sliced the apple into bite-size chunks and poured herself a glass of water.

The knife would probably turn up where she least expected it.

After putting her glass and Yolie's knife in the dishwasher, she went upstairs, undressed and got into bed with Alexis. She reached toward the lamp chain to switch on the light and then stopped herself. When her thoughts turned to Michael again, she felt weak and empty and strange.

Her heart pounded as she remembered how lonely he'd looked as he'd gotten in his car. He'd hit it off with Alexis. He'd wanted to take them to Zilker Park.

Feeling confused, she reached for Alexis and snuggled closer to her and tried to forget Pierce, Michael and her stressful night.

Forty. Life felt frighteningly too real. She wanted to be a kid again and believe she could have the fairy tale.

One thing was for sure.

She needed to put both her old flames in the past—where they belonged.

Four

When the phone rang at 5:00 a.m., Rosie's first weary reflex was to reach for Alexis to reassure herself that she was still there. Only after stroking the little girl's soft, warm shoulders and fingering her copper curls did she lift the receiver and turn on the light.

"Rose Marie!"

At her daughter's angry shriek, Rosie jerked to a sitting position, both hands shaking. Carmen, who was twenty-one—make that an immature, mixed-up and wild twenty-one—called her "Rose Marie" these days—to distance herself, she'd explained, and rather nastily. Carmen, who shared an apartment with two other dancers, never phoned her if she could avoid it. Obviously, this was an emergency.

Holding the phone, Rosie lay back, feeling groggy with exhaustion. How long had she slept? Two hours, maybe? She shut her eyes and tried to concentrate on whatever it was Carmen was saying.

"Hazel called me. She's out of her mind again. Only worse than usual."

Carmen had started calling her grandmother by her first name, too, which was really annoying to Hazel, especially since Rosie found herself doing it, as well.

"Why did Mother call you? Did she forget my number or something? "

"She says it was a bad birthday for you and she didn't want to make it worse, and that besides, she only wants me, that's she's scared of you."

Deep breath. "Scared of me?"

"She started hollering every time I started to call you. I couldn't call until the doctor came. He's in with her right now. She keeps saying you killed *him*."

"Killed who? Did I miss something?"

"Pierce. She says somebody killed him tonight. You haven't seen him or been around him lately, have you?"

A chill went through Rosie.

"Hey, Mom, please tell me you didn't catch him jogging on your way home, and lose it again."

She'd lost it all right.

So had Pierce. "That isn't funny," she whispered, her voice strangled.

Carmen heaved out a long sigh. "That's like a huge relief. Huge. With Hazel wicking out all the time, the last thing I need is a homicidal maniac for a mother."

"So, at least you still claim me."

"As if I have a choice."

"Excuse me?"

"If anything happened to you, who will take care of Alexis?"

"Where are you?" Rosie demanded.

"The E.R. Brackenridge Hospital. You've got to get over here. I can't take much more."

"Ditto." It would be an understatement to say that Carmen's many talents did not lie in the nursing field. "You'll have to take care of Alexis then. And that means being patient and nice and—"

"Fine! Just get here. Another hour and I'll be singing the loony tunes along with Hazel."

Except for her slack mouth, which she licked constantly, and her wild eyes darting everywhere, Hazel looked good. She'd had a lot of work, as Pierce used to say, and such good work, she looked years younger than she was.

She was clutching a stuffed cat and dressed in skintight black slacks and a black, long-sleeved shirt emblazoned with the message, Keep Austin Weird in red. There were red cats all over it.

Her mother—the Cat Woman.

Hazel's coppery-gold curls were bright and held back from her face with two red, sparkly, cat-shaped barrettes. She'd obviously had her hair and nails done recently, and her perfectly painted lips were the same bright shade as her nails and the cats on her T-shirt.

Like a lot of women of her generation, Hazel believed it was important to coordinate accessories. Maybe the lipstick and polish and the cats were a little too vivid for a woman her age, but then that was Hazel—a little bit gaudy—and into turning back the clock rather than aging gracefully, whatever the hell that cliché was supposed to mean.

So, why had Hazel snapped *this* time? Twice before she'd lost it after a bout of flu, coupled with sleepless nights.

"The date on my tombstone has to be March 2, 1945!" Hazel shouted from her gurney to no one in particular as Rosie pushed the door open, tugging a sleepy Alexis inside with her.

"That's your birthday, Mom. And don't shout. I'm right here."

"Finally!" Carmen snapped. Her dark eyes that were too much like a certain cop's flashed with irritation as she shot to her feet and yanked Alexis toward her.

"Stop it! You're hurting me!" Alexis fought to pull loose.

"Don't be such a whiny baby! We're outta here!"

"Hello to you, too," Rosie said. "And, hey, be nice to her. She's a little girl."

"I'm being way nicer than you and Hazel ever were to me! I'll park her in front of the TV. Will that make you happy?"

"Ouch!" Rosie said, feeling a guilt pang. She had

left Carmen with Hazel when she'd gone to college
and when she'd worked. But she'd had to.

"Murder," Hazel said. "I told you to kill that
arrogant bastard. It's about time you killed Carver!"

Still worrying about how Alexis would fare with
Carmen, Rosie sat down by the gurney. "Mom, Pierce
is fine, and I'd appreciate it if you don't talk about
him and me here…at the hospital. People might get
the wrong idea."

Hazel stared at the green walls. "When did I die?"

"You're not dead. You're going to be fine. You just
need to try to calm down and get some rest. That's why
you're here. When you're better, you can go home."

"You're still in love with that motorcycle guy. He's
Carmen's real daddy, isn't he? Your daddy shot his
daddy. It was an accident, you know."

Rosie covered her face. How much did her
mother know? She'd never told Hazel very much
about Michael.

*Families! Did all families share the obnoxious talent
hers had of being able to ferret out its members' best-kept
secrets and then broadcast them to the universe?*

"Where's the doctor?" Hazel demanded, frowning
in confusion.

"He's already seen you."

"When the TV said Pierce was stabbed tonight, I
knew right off who killed him. It's in your blood."

Rosie sighed, struggling for professional patience.
"Mom, Pierce is fine. I saw him earlier."

"You're twelve years old, Rosie. Mother committed suicide." Hazel's eyes rounded in fright and then in guilt. She gulped in a big breath and clamped both hands over her mouth. "Oops, I'm not supposed to tell that. She died in her sleep."

"Mom, please. Just don't talk anymore right now."

"You're still in love with that motorcycle guy. Is that why you stabbed Pierce?"

Rosie rubbed her brows with a sigh. "Mom, please…"

"Your father said murder's as easy as dog shit, and he would know, now wouldn't he? I'm who I am— I'm really me!"

Rosie popped her knuckles and stared up at the ceiling. She felt so helpless she wanted to scream. *Get me out of here!*

"It's me who's dead over there," Hazel said, staring wildly past Rosie and pointing out the door at a figure on a gurney. Her brow knitted into rigid lines, which meant she was late for her botox shot. Then Hazel slid off the bed and began to pace in small, tight circles. "I have to get over there—so I'll see you again."

Thankfully, the nurse came in, and Hazel went still. "We have a bed for her upstairs," the woman said in a kind, low tone. "Are you the sister?"

Grrr. "Daughter."

Hazel dashed behind Rosie and squatted down, using Rosie as a shield between her and the nurse. "Is she going to close the casket? Tell her not to close the casket!"

"You're not dead yet, Mom. You're just here for a little rest."

"Are you nuts? This place is a madhouse."

Five minutes later Rosie was sitting across from the admissions clerk, a middle-aged woman with a pinched mouth and piercing eyes, who kept handing her endless stacks of papers to sign so her mother could be admitted.

"That lady over there is pointing at you," the woman said, just as Hazel began to shriek again. "Is that your sister?"

"My mom," she said through gritted teeth.

Her mother's screams grew more frantic as an orderly wheeled her toward the bank of elevators at the end of the hall.

"I was a virgin and didn't know what the hell was going on," Hazel yelled. "Daddy had never had sex before, either. I was a nymphomaniac and screwed everything that came down the walk."

When Hazel suddenly spotted Rosie, her voice grew louder. "Rosie—do you know what's wrong with you? You've been frigid ever since you screwed that motorcycle guy! You need to learn about oral sex!"

"Mom!"

"My cats! Charlie and his friends! I've got to get home!"

"I'll feed Charlie, Mother."

Hazel struggled to get out of the wheelchair, but the orderly gripped her arm. At the use of force, Hazel's voice grew more hysterical.

"My daughter killed Dr. Carver! She stabbed him! Because I told her to. And because she's still in love with that motorcycle guy."

Shuddering Rosie covered her eyes with her hands. When she looked up and peered through her fingers, the admissions clerk's huge, magnified gaze was devouring her with what seemed to be excessive lurid interest.

Story of her life—being publicly humiliated by her family. Reason number one Pierce had dumped her for Anita and her girls, which he'd once described as aristocratic little ladies.

"I'm sorry," Rosie whispered. "There's not a word of truth in anything she's said. She's totally out of her mind."

"Not about Dr. Carver, she's not," the clerk stated in a conspiratorial whisper.

"What?"

The woman's thin brows lifted as she continued to study Rosie as if she were a microbe under a microscope. "I heard about his murder when I took my break. He's dead. It's a real shame, too. He had a lot of talent. We have lots of his patients here. He used to bring us candy all the time. Chocolate truffles. The best. Godiva."

Rosie blew out some air and then fought for her

next breath. The blood drained from her face. She almost felt as if she might faint. Pierce…dead?

He'd been horribly alive last night. He'd been his impossible, arrogant self. He couldn't be dead!

He'd better not be, girlfriend. What if you were the last person to see him alive?

"You…you can't be serious…about Dr. Carver…."

"He was stabbed in the face. Him, handsome as he was even at fifty. Multiple stab wounds. They say that except for the eyes, you wouldn't know him. His head was practically severed from his body."

Unconscious of the movement, Rose Marie sank her own head lower into her shoulders as if to protect it from being lopped off. "Oh, no. No. No."

"Crime of passion," the admissions clerk continued. "A woman did it, if you ask me."

"Why do you say that?"

Lowering her voice even further, she said, "Dr. Carver had a real reputation with the young nurses around here. I'd see him come in here, smiling at the prettiest women. He thought he was God's gift."

Oh, my God… What if I really was the last person to see him alive…I mean, besides the real murderer? My bra and panties!

What if the police found them?

Why did I have to tell everyone last year every vengeful fantasy I had about him, including joking about wanting his head on a platter?

"Be careful what you wish for," her daddy used to

say before the tragedy, back when she'd been a kid and they'd still been pals. "Because it'll come back and bite you in the butt. Every time, sugarbun."

What was she going to do?

Five

"There's damn sure no page-turner as good as reading about the vicious murder of your ex, is there?" Yolie said, fluffing her spiky blond hair.

Yolie's big white house was located in a posh, central Austin neighborhood. Todd, her seventeen-year-old son by Pierce, occupied the pool house when he was in town, which wasn't often, since he went to boarding school. Darius, her twenty-five-year-old stepson, Pierce's son from Vanessa, his first wife, who'd killed herself, stayed in the pool house as well on the rare occasions when he was in Austin. A college dropout, he did a lot of drifting.

The sun beat down on the pool as Rosie swam frantic laps. Yolie avidly read the newspaper in a chaise longue next to the pool house, which the maid was readying because both boys had called and said they would be arriving soon due to their father's demise.

Yolie looked up from the paper. "Hey, can you believe this? It says right here that Michael Nash is the detective in charge of the case. Wasn't he the guy you used to date, the hottie who gave you that ticket last year?"

Yolie tossed a section of the newspaper onto the ground and grabbed another.

At the mention of Michael, Rosie felt sick and faint as she emerged dripping from the pool. She toweled off before sinking back onto her own chaise longue. "There's something I've got to tell you."

"You damn sure got your wish. You should be a happy camper."

"What?"

"Pierce getting himself murdered and all. It's what you wanted."

"No. How can you say that?"

"You do remember telling everybody you wanted his head on a platter?"

"I was joking."

"Frankly, I loved the image."

"Yolie! Listen to me! I went over there last night. To Pierce's! And then Michael Nash…who must have already known about Pierce by then…answered the call about Alexis."

Slowly, Yolie set the paper down and stared at her.

"Pierce called me. Not Jennifer. I…I let Harry think it was Jennifer."

"You went over there? Were you out of your mind?"

"He owed me money."

"That is so lame. That's not why you went over there, and you know it."

"He was alive and furious at me, but he was searching the house for an intruder when I left him."

"What time did Nash show up over here?"

Rosie froze. "I…I think he already knew. I think that's why he came. He kept asking me if I'd seen Pierce…. And I lied."

"You should talk to a criminal attorney first thing," Yolie said in that maddeningly decisive way of hers— like there was no other opinion in the universe.

Despite the intense heat, Rosie shivered. "A criminal attorney?" She moaned. "But I didn't do anything!"

"But the police—that Michael guy—obviously thinks otherwise. You were *there* last night. Lucky thing Joe Benson's right next door."

Joe Benson was both a criminal attorney and the stepfather of Jennifer.

Rosie flung the last of the articles about Pierce she'd devoured earlier onto the litter of newspapers that lay between her chaise longue and Yolie's. At least there'd been no mention of a bra or panties being found at the scene.

Guilt struck her. She should be with her mother, not lying out by the pool under the leafy shade of the towering pecan trees, consumed with fear for herself.

How could all this be happening at once? Pierce

calling her? Going over there and stupidly quarreling with him when she should have just walked out? His getting himself stabbed? Michael being involved? Not to mention Hazel's having another breakdown?

Oh, God! This meant Michael would be back in her life big time. What if he found out about Carmen, too?

Rosie's nerves began to jump. Her inner thermostat went haywire. Suddenly she felt as if she was freezing.

"So, tell me, why do I need to see Joe?"

"For advice, sweetie. Just for advice."

"Which will cost a bundle."

"You'd rather have free room and board in prison?"

Rosie's chest went tight. "I really should go check on Hazel."

"Forget Hazel. She's got round-the-clock doctors and nurses."

"They are not her daughter. She wants me. Only me."

"You were the last person to see your murdered ex-boyfriend alive!"

"Except for whoever *really* killed him."

"What exactly happened at Pierce's?"

Rosie hissed in a deep breath. "Okay, like I told you, he called about eleven."

"And you just had to run over there."

"When I saw his name in the Caller ID window of my cell, I popped the rubber band on my wrist three times. I swear I tried not to answer. But Ticia Morgan had already told me Anita had left Pierce, and maybe I wanted to gloat a little."

Yolie nodded almost wearily. "Ticia? John's child bride?"

John Morgan was Pierce's new plastic surgery partner.

"Yes. So, Ticia called yesterday to tell me that Anita had phoned her. Apparently, Anita was telling anybody who would listen that Pierce was an obsessive-compulsive, alcoholic monster."

"Tell me something I don't know."

"Anita kept screaming that he'd threatened to send her daughters back to Guatemala because they wouldn't follow all his nit-picky rules."

"What did they do—wear their shoes in the house?"

"Yes, and they wanted credit cards, cell phones, driver's ed lessons, television sets, and cars, too."

"Hello? Why did he think *they* married him? Still, you should never have talked to Ticia. Or Pierce."

"I know."

"So, what did *he* want?"

"He wished me a happy birthday. He said he couldn't stop thinking about me. He said Anita was a mistake and that he wanted me back."

"He wanted you back? After you sent him that painting where you made his Mr. Willie look like a shriveled peanut, and his entire staff laughed when he opened it? He wanted you back? And you bought it?"

"Well, not at first, but he was totally sober."

"You could tell that over the phone?"

"He said he wanted a new warehouse key. And I said he'd have to pay the rent. He said he would pay it."

"This from the man who won't pay for his wife's kids? And you went over there?"

Rosie nodded miserably.

"And?"

"We drank some champagne."

"Not good. How much?"

"He kept my flute full while he gave me a tour of the house, so I didn't really count."

"Did he touch you? Did anybody take anything off?"

Rosie flushed as she remembered their first kiss on the stairway beneath the chandelier. They'd still been dressed then. Even though their mouths and bodies had fit just like always, something had felt wrong to her. She'd kissed him harder, searching for what she'd once thought she'd had with him, but the soul-deep wrongness had persisted.

So why had she ended up naked in his upstairs guest bedroom? If it hadn't been for her hearing that noise in the master bedroom and getting spooked, no telling what might have happened.

"Pierce refused to pay the rent, so I left."

"That's it? You were there an hour. No funny stuff?"

Rosie remembered quarreling with Pierce when she'd heard that sound in the next bedroom. She'd accused him of inviting her over to make Anita jealous. He'd sworn they were alone. Then she'd heard another sound and had grabbed her clothes and had made him go check the rest of the house. Rosie had left too fast to locate her underwear.

Rosie rubbed the back of her neck where the muscles had begun to tighten. Then she drew a deep breath.

"Okay. I get it. There *was* some funny stuff."

"I didn't go to bed with him!"

"Since he's dead, I think you'd better get your story straight before you say something really stupid to Nash. Make an appointment with Joe. Besides being my next-door neighbor, he's an old, old friend of mine."

Translation: a favorite lover.

"You remember, he came to the Christmas block party."

And got soused on the bourbon-laced eggnog and left a bruise the size of an apple on my left butt cheek when he pinched me.

"Just don't talk to the police without him being there. He knows his stuff."

"The police?" Rosie squeaked. "You really think they'll...that Michael will think...that I..."

"I think it's wise to consider worst-case scenario."

Rosie swallowed. No sooner had Yolie said that than the image of her own slender neck on a chopping block sprang up in her mind.

"A high-profile murder like this? The cops have got to pin this on somebody, sweetie-pie. Who better than the girl who tried to mow him down with her

Beamer? Don't you think it's odd that he died on the night you say he wanted you back?"

"Okay, he got me naked." A shiver of remorse traced through Rose Marie. "I got cold feet, though. We had a fight. When I left, I…I couldn't find my bra and panties."

"So, they're at Pierce's?"

They stared at each other. *Or the police have them* was the thought that ran through their minds.

Rosie lay back down on the chaise longue and stared up at bright spots of blue through the trees. "I never thought people we actually know—respectable people—got themselves murdered. Handsome, wealthy plastic surgeons, not even jerks like Pierce, don't get hacked to death by some knife-wielding maniac."

"Too bad for Pierce the murderer didn't read your little rule book."

"This whole thing is making me sick." Rosie shivered. At the same time, the more stories she read about his glamorous ex-wives, including Yolie, the more she began to feel ignored, invisible. It was a feeling she'd experienced growing up poor in East Austin. She hated it.

"I was his fiancée. But do I merit so much as a footnote?"

"Be careful what you wish for, sweetie-pie." Yolie flipped a newspaper page and then sighed in disgust. "Where do these yokels get their information?

'Austin has lost a self-sacrificing missionary….' Self-sacrificing, my ass. Those surgeries he did in Central America on all those kids with cleft palates were all about his precious image."

"You don't know that for sure. I went with him on lots of those trips."

"And you never doubted his motives?"

"He was a doctor with valuable skills. I just assumed—"

"When are you ever going to wake up? Pierce was so aware of appearances," Yolie continued. "When I started gaining the weight, he was on me all the time about it, taunting me about other women, wanting me to do liposuction. All he ever cared about was making money and getting his name on the front page while squiring some stick-thin stacked bimbo around."

Very conscious of her C-cup boobs that Pierce had enhanced, Rosie glared at her.

"Sorry."

"He taunted me because of my low-class background," Rosie said.

"Looks like he finally played his little games on the wrong woman."

"So, who do you think killed him?" Rosie asked.

"Lots of people probably weren't exactly thrilled with him. But to kill a person with a knife, you've got to get up close…and get ugly."

"There was that guy who sued him because he wasn't thrilled with his penile implant."

"Not to mention Pierce had four wives, and God knows how many other women. And that's just his sex life, which wasn't really all that hot, now was it? But who stabs a lousy lay? I mean, why bother?"

Yolie's analysis was making Rosie increasingly uncomfortable.

"And then do you ever wonder why Pierce was so hard to get to know?" Yolie continued. "Remember how he used to have to control every damn conversation? When we went out to dinner, we always had to discuss some bullshit story he'd read in the *New Yorker* instead of real life. Intelligent conversation, he called it. Whatever it was, it was impersonal as hell, and he had to be in control. I was married to him for a lot of years, and I don't think I ever really knew him. Do you ever wonder if there was anything there…beneath his external glamour? It was scary, in a way."

"What are you saying?"

"You don't just get murdered for no reason. What if there was some dark secret in his past? Or a secret vice or addiction? I mean, why was he always as closed-up as a damn clam—if he wasn't hiding something?"

"That's so melodramatic."

"Hey, getting your head nearly chopped off is pretty melodramatic." Yolie stabbed a fingernail at a front-page article. "It says right here he grew up in Beaumont. He never said a damn thing about Beaumont to me. Did he ever talk about his childhood to you?"

Rosie shook her head. But then, she'd never talked about her childhood, either.

"So, he's either a blank disc or there are plenty of secrets on the old hard drive," Yolie said. "He had a quick temper and a sharp tongue and the endearing quality of abusing his women when he was in a certain mood…at least verbally. That we know. Then there's the drinking. Not to mention his mysterious disappearances."

"Are you going to the memorial service?"

"I've got a son by the arrogant bastard and no alibi. Of course I'm going! In situations such as these, appearances are everything."

"Alibi?" Rosie's heart jumped to her throat and began to thump.

"The cops are going to want to know where everybody was if his killer doesn't walk into the police station and hand them the bloody knife. Except for talking to you on my mobile, you and I've got zip for an alibi."

Rosie shivered so hard her teeth chattered. "At least you weren't actually *there!* You've been happily divorced from him for years. That's hardly a motive."

"I hated the son of a bitch. Does that count?"

"I, on the other hand, ran out of his brilliantly lit mansion braless and pantyless on the night he died. Anyone, a neighbor, a jogger, might have seen me. What if he or she misinterpreted what he saw? What if the cops find my bra and panties?"

"Then your underwear is hanging out in plastic Baggies. Call Joe. First thing Monday. "

Feeling too hot, Rosie got up and dived into the pool. She didn't come up until her lungs were burning for air.

If Michael had her underwear in plastic Baggies and he found out about Carmen, which he would if he hung around at all, he'd nail Rosie just to get revenge.

Unless she solved the murder for him.

Six

A former linebacker for the University of Texas A&M, Joe Benson loomed behind his polished mahogany desk like a sleek, dark bear who looked slightly embarrassed to find himself all dressed up in a three-piece power suit. He had hooded black eyes, heavy brows and a strong jaw. His glossy-black hair might have curled if hadn't been clipped so close to his scalp. Not that his hushed office, his attire or his military haircut were enough to dispel Rosie's feeling that he wasn't quite tame. Still, at least he was sober.

"So, how long have you been living with Yolie?" he asked, his curious voice oddly soft for so large a man.

Control. This man was into control. Just like Pierce had been.

"I don't see what that has to do with—"

"Right. It's just that she's such a great woman." His

eyes lit for a second or two at some forbidden memory before he caught himself.

"Yolie told me you two used to date before you married Bridget and adopted Jennifer."

"Did she now?" His smile was quick and a little uneasy. Then his cheeks reddened and the smile vanished.

No way would Rosie repeat what Yolie had said on the matter.

I never could figure out whether he was attracted to me or to my big house and money. He's extremely ambitious, you see, but then that's what makes him good at what he does.

"Well, no hard feelings. Bridget's great, and Yolie's like a sister to me now," Joe said, a little edgily.

Bridget was an ice cream heiress with a large fortune. Joe was her fourth husband. Yolie said Bridget, who seemed all fluff, had had him sign an airtight prenup.

"Yolie mentioned you were in some sort of a jam."

"Well…not yet. Hopefully, not ever."

"If I were you, I'd trust her judgment. What's wrong?"

Without further preamble, Rosie told him about her involvement with Austin's front-page murder victim. She repeated a few of the most damning things she'd said to everybody about her revenge fantasies. Joe's frown deepened when she told him about her bra and panties.

When she finished, he propped his big brown hands

together and leaned forward. "Rule number one. Don't say anything to the police unless I'm there."

"But don't they have the right to question me?"

He held a finger against his lips and shook his head. "You let me worry about doing right by the police, little girl. All you need is rule number one."

Little girl? She was forty. Not that she was about to admit her age.

"But…"

At his dark frown, she fell silent. She hated it when terrified patients and their families kept asking her the same questions over and over again.

"I don't like it that you know Nash, who's in charge. Or that he took the call about your missing granddaughter. You dumped him, you said. Judging from the time frame, he'd already been at the scene. Obviously, he was suspicious. He could be holding a grudge."

"From high school?"

"Did you kill the good doctor?" Joe asked, his eyes boring into her, which gave her a worse feeling than when he'd pinched her.

"Of course not!"

"You just told everybody in this town you wanted to."

"I was joking."

"A lot of people are going to think it's odd that you saw him the same night he was murdered. That's quite a coincidence. Cops don't like coincidences. Neither do juries."

Rosie squirmed as droplets of perspiration tickled her spine. "If I had stabbed him, trust me, I would have aimed a lot lower."

Benson winced. "I wouldn't share that with anybody else. Understand?" After her nod, he sucked in a long breath. "So, is there anything more you think you should tell me before we call it a day?"

Again she remembered being panicked in her Beamer that night, racing past the fancy houses carved into the limestone cliffs and oak trees of Westlake Hills, each fake palazzo more outrageously posh and ridiculously overdone than the last one—mock Tudors with skylights, Tuscan villas constructed out of plywood.

"Any little detail? A car parked out back? A cigarette butt on the drive? Anything?"

She remembered how she'd heard something in the next room when Pierce had been about to make love to her. She'd made him go check it out, so she could run. But why load Benson down with too much information?

"There is something?" he said, seeing through her.

"Not really."

He insisted that they go over everything again. Their meeting went fifteen minutes longer than the designated hour, but he never hurried her. Why would he, at his hourly rate? He simply listened, nodding thoughtfully from time to time, looking increasingly dissatisfied as she repeated her story. Once in a while he jotted a note to himself.

She finished with a question. "Is it okay if I go to his memorial service?"

He sat up straighter and shook his head. "I think you should be as inconspicuous as possible. Do what you normally do. Don't change your habits. Don't act too interested in this case."

"That's going to be hard."

"Go to work as usual. Since you weren't in his life on a regular basis before his death, I wouldn't go to the service. Oh, and watch your mouth from now on. And I'd avoid reading the papers."

How could she act like she wasn't involved, when she was? Pierce had deliberately drawn her into his life again. Why? Had he been afraid? Had he known who was in the next bedroom? Had he known he was in danger? Had he been protecting her? Himself? Or had he really wanted her? Was that why he'd been so angry when she'd accused him of using her in his marriage battles?

When Joe pushed back his chair, she got up silently.

He came around the desk and took her hand. She felt lighter, somehow, after talking to him. It was as if she'd seen a priest and confessed.

Her relief was unwarranted. So far, he'd done nothing but listen. But then the most important emotions in people's lives were often based on illusions, like her messy relationship with Pierce.

She let Joe pat her hand even though she wanted to yank it away. "You tell Yolie I said hello, you hear?

And call me first thing when Detective Nash contacts you."

"You really think he'll—"

"With any luck he's got the murder weapon and the murderer behind bars as we speak."

"But if he doesn't—"

"Sooner or later he'll send a man with a badge to knock on your door. When he does—"

"Rule number one," she replied meekly, even as she wondered if she should wear gold beads to Pierce's memorial service.

No, severe white cuffs against black would have just the right stark touch; as would her two-carat, fake-diamond ring. No way could she appear ringless around all his ex-wives, who had so many carats they could barely lift their hands.

"If only all the rest of my clients were as obedient as you," Joe said.

She smiled, and he grinned as if he was very pleased with himself.

No sooner had Rosie stepped out of the firm's offices than she was rethinking Benson's advice.

Not go? She'd never forgive herself if she didn't go to Pierce's service.

Rosie was shaking her head back and forth as she observed Yolie's reflection.

"Okay, sweetie. You win." Yolie looked glum as she

replaced her red frilly dress in the closet and pulled out a sober black one.

"Good decision," Rosie said. "You did say that, in situations like this, appearances are everything."

Yolie's scowl deepened at being bested with her own words. She looked very cross indeed as she unzipped the more conservative choice and stepped into it.

"Happy? I look like a nun now," she growled as she turned toward Rosie. "A F-A-T nun. I wish you'd be as smart as me and do what Joe told you to do."

"I don't see why I shouldn't go to Pierce's memorial service. I was engaged to him!"

"Not something to brag about, sweetie! And it's just too damn bad for you everybody in this burg knows it."

"And I was there at his house right before—"

"That's the point! Nobody is supposed to suspect that, you obsessed idiot! You need to lie low. Book a session with Nan or maybe catch a movie."

Rosie guessed now wasn't the time to confess she'd just canceled her session with Nan because it conflicted with Pierce's service. And she didn't plan to make any more appointments, either.

Where had therapy gotten her, anyway? She was forty, single, a slumlord, and now possibly a murder suspect. It was time she realized she was a grown-up in the big, bad world, time to come to grips with the fact she had to fly solo.

"I want to know who killed him. I feel…like since I was there, I'm somehow responsible. Maybe I should have looked around downstairs. Maybe I could have prevented—"

"And what if you had? Then you'd be in a cardboard box today, about to be sprinkled on your favorite mountaintop, too."

"You could have a small point," Rosie conceded.

"So, let's look at this from the bright side. You got what you wanted. He's dead. So, forget about him. And quit reading all those newspaper stories."

"I have this feeling I've missed something, and that I should make it right."

"Let it go. Let him go. Use that overdose of compassion and curiosity you were born with on your patients. Folks who stick long noses into hot flames get nose hairs singed."

"Right," Rosie said, looking down at her watch. "But if you don't hurry, we'll be late."

"You're still going? Did you hear anything I said?"

When she straightened and began buttoning the white cuffs of her black dress, Yolie let out a howl. "Lady Long-nose, you bought a new dress! You did!"

Fortunately, Darius and Todd honked from the drive just then, distracting her. Yolie raised the window and hollered down to them to hold their horses, she'd come when she was damn well ready.

"So, you finally convinced them to go," Rosie said.

"Not easy, let me tell you. They're as hardheaded as their father. Would you button my neck?" As she turned her back to Rosie, Yolie began spritzing her golden hair so that it stood on end. "Pierce was hardly the saintly father the papers made him out to be. But how would it look if his sons didn't go?"

She picked up her purse and scooted out the door. "There's nothing like death to turn us into hypocrites, is there? I'll be so glad when this is over and I can quit pretending I'm a grieving ex-wife. Weird role, isn't it?"

Over? Rosie's temples grew hot as a weird sensation of panic swamped her. Feeling hopeless, she trailed Yolie down the stairs.

When would it be over—for her?

Seven

The chapel was a grandiose, high-ceilinged room with tall stained-glass windows on all the walls. A floodlight shone down on the altar and the golden urn that contained Pierce's ashes.

Oh, my God! Was that Mirabella Camrett, her next-door neighbor, in the very front row? Had she even known Pierce?

Oh, no. She was turning around!

Zippy lyrics of a contemporary Christian song seemed to roar in the sanctuary as Rosie ducked behind Todd and Yolie, who were threading their way down the aisle, through the throngs of people and extra chairs that had been crammed at the ends of each pew.

A little more than a year ago Rosie had attended this church with Pierce on the Sundays he hadn't been on call. They were to have been married here. Instead she'd hacked her wedding cake to pieces and had chased him around with fistfuls of icing and a knife.

She'd forgotten all about that until now.

A knife. The memory brought a shudder.

Show your joy to the Lord with dancing.

The crowd was bigger than she'd expected. Maybe it was only natural that the notoriety and mystery surrounding Pierce's death had attracted more than just family and friends. The mourners' mood, although somber, was also edged with that curious excitement that goes along with scandal and murder.

Trying to be discreet, Rosie lowered her lashes. There had to be three thousand people assembled. Their jewels and silk and smooth faces made her feel a little old and dowdy, or at least most definitely past her first youth.

Her stomach went hollow. While a lot of faces were vaguely familiar, there were many more she did not recognize. When she looked closer, she saw lots of Pierce's former patients, his staff and partners, other doctors and nurses and members of the medical community.

Doubtlessly, they recognized her, too. Not that they caught her eye or spoke.

Men in dark suits lined the walls. Just as she was wondering how many were police and how many were funeral directors, she spotted Michael in a black suit that was so rumpled, she wondered if he'd slept in it on a stakeout.

Suave, he was not. His broad back was glued to the wall as if he needed its support. Beneath his dark tan, his face was gray. His eyes were closed, with a look of fatigue rather than spiritual conviction. Indeed, he seemed so battered that despite his tough appearance she felt sorry for him.

Her heart hammered as she imagined him poring over blood and gore. Was Pierce's murder getting to him? Or was it just his life?

Michael was a rougher, less elegant sort than Pierce. Maybe his father's violent death had hardened him. Maybe growing up poor had done it.

Being a cop couldn't be an easy job. Maybe he'd never had soft edges. For as long as she'd known him, he'd had a core of steel. Still, even with his eyes closed and his skin ashen, he oozed testosterone.

Quickly, before he opened his eyes and misconstrued her interest, she tiptoed faster and caught up with Yolie. Why hadn't *she* headed their little parade up this aisle? She would have sat them down long ago so they wouldn't call attention to themselves.

Clearly, Yolie wanted to flaunt her presence at Pierce's funeral, as well as his sons'. Why was it so important to her that everybody see her grieve? Was the killer here, too, driven by his own agenda?

When Yolie saw Kylie Rae Carver, Pierce's second ex-wife, sitting all by herself, she shot her former rival a Texas-size smile and then slid in beside her.

Rosie jerked her by the sash.

Normally, the two ex-wives avoided each other like they would a contagion. When Yolie kept sliding toward Kylie, the black satin ribbons came undone and flowed over the pew.

Kylie, who lived in their neighborhood and walked her poodle in their park, couldn't be more than forty-one. She was razor-wire thin and looked years older than she was. Pierce had always said such unkind things about her, too.

My worst wife, and that's saying something. Drug addict. Alcoholic. Poodle nut. Nymphomaniac. And now a lez.

Whether she was any of those things was anybody's guess. Rosie had always been dying of curiosity to know. Kylie never drank in public. But as Pierce had pointed out, she did have those fleshless legs that alcoholics sometimes have.

Once, Rosie had asked Yolie if there was such a thing as a lesbian nymphomaniac.

Yolie had laughed. "In his wet dreams."

"But Pierce always said Kylie hit on him even after their divorce, and told me that if I was smart, I'd keep my distance from her, too."

"Liar liar, pants on fire. He just didn't want you two talking. The bastard's secretive. Not that she's ever said more than boo about him to me. When forced to see each other, we always stick to safe subjects like our poodles' latest neuroses or bowel habits. The truth is, I'd give anything to talk to her and to Vanessa, especially Vanessa—since I sort of ended up dealing with Darius, who wasn't the easiest kid."

Vanessa had been Pierce's first wife, as well as Darius's mother. The marriage had ended when she'd hanged herself in their newly decorated shower one gorgeous fall morning right after she'd driven Darius to private elementary school. She'd put the trash out, said hi to her neighbor and tidied up the house. Then she'd taken that final shower.

"Not that I really need to talk to Vanessa. The facts speak for themselves. Wife number one kills herself. Kylie drinks and gave up men for good, and me, wife number three, gets fatter than a house. Maybe you never made it down the altar with him, sweetie, but he did a number on you, too. You hyperventilate every time you gain an ounce, and I see the way you're always looking scared when you get around a mirror, like you're afraid to look. And that lifting the chin thing you do lately…not to mention the boob job you let him talk you into. What does that say about him? About us?"

As if Rosie had wanted to analyze *that*.

Kylie smiled coolly at Rosie without speaking, and then stared ahead in the direction of the urn, her tired face going blank again as she studied it. She did, however, resume singing, "Dancing With My Father in the Fields of Grace."

Naturally, Rosie couldn't help noting that Kylie's diamonds were even bigger than Yolie's or that real diamonds sparkled better than her own fake stones. Had Pierce bought every woman he'd ever known serious jewelry but her?

Arranging her plump, bejeweled hands in her lap so that every ostentatious diamond blazed to full effect, Yolie was overcome with sniffles every time she looked at the urn. While everybody else sang, her wet, glazed eyes grew fixed on that object. She sobbed and then dabbed dramatically at her running mascara, diamonds flashing, of course. Kylie's face grew stonier with every sniffle.

Was Yolie for real? For all her usual show of bravado, did she still care about Pierce? Was that why she'd never married again? Why she'd never really had a serious relationship with a man unless you counted the handsome young hunks, like Xavier, who had paraded through her bedroom's revolving doors? Not to mention Vicenzo, whom she'd met in Italy. Or was she faking this torrential flood for the sake of appearances?

Rosie stared at the urn, hoping Yolie's deluge would inspire at least one tiny tear for Pierce.

Dry-eyed, she watched as the preacher stood up and lamented the violent death. Anecdotes about Pierce's life—his adult life—were recited in glowing detail. Friends got up and spoke. Not that their eulogies captured the Pierce Rosie had known.

Was it just her? Or had Pierce concealed his real self from everybody else, too?

Fortunately, the service moved right along. Soon everybody was singing "Amazing Grace" and then saying the Twenty-third Psalm in unison. When the impersonal service was over and people were starting to get up, Rosie suddenly felt compelled to do something, anything, to make Pierce seem real and alive to everybody.

Hardly realizing her intention, she lifted her right hand and made the Hook 'em Horns sign. Shakily, she began singing "The Eyes of Texas," and for the first time was struck by its gruesome lyrics.

Everybody turned and gaped. Mirabella Camrett stared at her as if she'd gone crazy. Then, remembering what a huge University of Texas fan Pierce had been, individuals joined in. Soon the entire congregation, even Mirabella, were flashing the Hook 'em Horns signal as their singing grew louder and louder.

"'The eyes of Texas are upon you/all the livelong day….'"

When the University's most sacred song was over, a shocked hush fell over the chapel. Except for Rosie, who was responsible for the spontaneous outburst, there wasn't a dry eye.

Why couldn't she cry?

Would everybody think it was because she was glad he was dead? Why was she always worrying about what other people thought?

Well-dressed women swept past her, commenting on how lovely the service had been. When Ticia

Morgan passed her, she averted her gaze and quickened her pace. Several of Pierce's staff, who'd worked with Rosie, rushed by without speaking, as well.

"Oh, my God. Yolie…they don't think—"

"Don't make me say I told you so."

An hour later, at Pierce's house, the crowd had thinned to a more manageable number. There were two gatherings after the funeral service—one in the church parlor for his patients and the general medical community, and one at his home for the family.

As the mother of his son and the stepmother who'd raised his other son, Yolie decided she was family—at least for today. Rosie knew she shouldn't tag along, but she felt drawn to the scene of the murder and couldn't stop herself. If the police suspected her, she had to learn all she could.

When Yolie and Rosie entered the grand salon, the first thing she saw were the shoes. Pierce would have had a fit. Everybody was wearing shoes on his spotless carpets, even the widow and her girls.

Anita, who was slim and dark, struck just the right note in black silk and hose and black pumps as she sat sobbing quietly between her sulky teenage daughters on grandiose, pink leather couches beneath Pierce's portrait.

Couches I picked out, Rosie thought, trying not to feel resentful even as she avoided looking up at the painting she'd done of Pierce when they'd first met and she'd been in love.

Mother and daughters had the huge, teased hairdos and heavy makeup of Latin American movie stars. Even though Rosie felt an unpleasant jolt at the sight of her younger, showier replacement and her truly enormous diamond rings, she tugged Yolie's sleeve.

"She looks so sad. Do you think we should go over and say something to her?" Rosie whispered.

"If you had a brain bigger than a peanut, you wouldn't even be here, much less ask a stupid question like that."

"Okay. I get it."

Anita looked up at her, her dark eyes glittering with dislike…and something else.

"No, sweetie, you don't," Yolie said. "That's the problem. She almost looks scared of you."

Feeling worse by the second, Rosie scuttled quickly toward the dining room, where the table was piled obscenely high with platters of food—salmon, deviled eggs, fruit, fried chicken, ham, chips and dips. Even though she'd skipped breakfast, she had no appetite. She wanted one thing—to see the bedrooms upstairs.

Rosie left Yolie and the boys loading their plates, and stealthily headed for the staircase, which she ascended quickly. Trying not to look at the yellow tape that sealed off the master bedroom at the end of the hall, she marched up to the door of Pierce's guest bedroom. This door was also shut, but the knob turned easily. She looked around the hall and, when she saw no one, slipped inside quickly, shutting the door behind her.

Walking briskly toward the bed, she knelt and lifted the dust ruffle so that she could peer under it. Her heart thudded, but all she saw were a few errant dust bunnies; no sexy bits of black lace.

Hopefully, Pierce had found them and hidden them from Anita before his death. Rosie got up and walked around the queen-size bed, kneeling several more times on the wild chance they were still there.

Nothing.

She stood up slowly. Then she raced out into the hall.

She was about to go downstairs again when she turned and stared at the yellow tape. Would it be so terrible if she went inside? She looked around, and when she saw no one, slipped under the yellow police tape forbidding entrance. Careful to make no sound, she went inside and shut the door.

The drapes of the master bedroom were partially drawn. The room was dark. Aware of an antiseptic smell, she shrank against the door. When her eyes grew accustomed to the gloom, she shivered at the sight of dark stains and spatter on the light-colored carpet and ceiling.

Pierce had died here. Even in this taped-off room of death, why couldn't she get that he was really gone?

Other than the bloodstains, the room with its

purple bedcovers was exactly as she remembered when her designer had finished with it a year ago. Glancing furtively over her shoulder to reassure herself she was alone, she went toward the dark spots and stared down at them.

Pierce… At last she felt a warm wetness trickling down her cheeks. He was gone; really gone. She'd seen people die—many people, but not like this. Never like this. And she'd sent him into this room.

She wanted to scream that this couldn't have happened, that this couldn't be his dried blood. He couldn't have been here, so vital one minute, and then just be gone. Not when he'd consumed so much of her heart and soul for so long. Not when he'd begged her to come back.

Death.

People died. She was a nurse. She knew that. But she was feeling mystical and sad, not professional. Everybody she knew, everybody she loved, would die, and who knew when or how?

She couldn't take it in. She felt some huge disconnect with a universe and a God that could let things like this happen just when new possibilities had presented themselves. One minute you were rocking along, and then wham—a rampaging elephant stepped on you. Even vibrant, little Alexis could be gone in a heartbeat.

Rosie turned away from the blood stains, feeling exhausted and jittery.

She wanted to run out, to escape this horror, but, oh, God, she needed to think about this, too.

Cold beads of sweat trickled down her back. Instantly, fear snapped her out of her muddle. She had to get out of here before someone found her.

She was walking rapidly toward the door when the curtains were yanked open. "Looking for something, Ms. Castle?" Michael's hard, all-too-familiar voice called.

She jumped, caught in a brilliant streamer of sunlight.

"An intimate item of apparel? Black lace, I believe? C-cup...? Matching thong panties?"

"Michael!"

When he stepped out of the shadows, she sprang toward the door.

"I—I saw you at the service," she whispered. Her heart pounded so loudly she was sure he could hear it.

"Ditto." His dark face was grim. "There's a theory that killers like to return to the scene of the crime. I wondered who'd get curious and have to come up here."

She notched her chin higher. "I'm not a killer."

"What were you looking for then?"

"Nothing." She dusted her hands together.

"Did you know that Carver's hands were bound in front of him with a black bra? C-cup? You *are* the girl who likes to play bondage games."

"There wasn't any mention of a bra...in the newspapers," she said.

"You got naked here that night! Why?"

Backing toward the door, she shook her head.

"What the hell were you doing here that night?" He moved closer, invading her space, terrifying her so completely she shrank against the door. "You told everybody in town you wanted him dead."

"I—I wasn't serious."

"Like the night you stalked him with your Beamer?"

"I wasn't stalking him that night! He owed me money! I—I told you.... I wanted to talk to him."

"My men have been asking around. You worked on your house the night he died. You got a call, and you left about eleven. We haven't got the phone records yet, but you didn't go home right after you left your house."

"I don't see how my personal life is any of your business."

"I'm investigating the murder of your former lover."

"Fiancé."

"A man you repeatedly threatened to kill. You came here on the night in question."

"I didn't admit—"

"You took off your clothes, and now he's dead. Those are facts. Then there's your personal history. Your father shot..." He stopped, his face haggard.

She, too, felt faint. Long ago, they'd agreed to put the tragedy behind them.

"To some people in the department, to most of my best men, even my partner, it all adds up. They think

I'm here to bring you in. They want this case to go down fast."

She closed her eyes, trying to shut him out.

"You're in deep shit, up to your nose and sinking fast, princess."

She was about to yell that she was innocent, but just in the nick of time, she remembered Joe's orders and clamped a hand over her mouth. "I can't answer any of your questions without my attorney present."

"So, you've got an attorney already?"

"Joe Benson."

He whistled. "You *are* running scared."

"The way you're harassing me, wouldn't you be?"

"I'm not your problem." He didn't smile. "Believe it or not, I want to help you before you screw things up even worse than you already have. What's going on, Rosie? Talk to me. What the hell were you doing here?"

Feeling like a child lost in the dark, she blinked rapidly at the sudden gentling of his tone. Then his predatory gaze pinned her again, and she realized who he was.

"Why do you have a bandage on your finger?"

She balled her hand into a fist and hid it behind her back. "Joe said talking to you wouldn't be smart. You're a cop. Homicide. The city pays you to put people like me in prison."

"I put murderers in prison," he amended. "The last thing I want to do is convict the innocent. I got over that, if you'll remember, in high school."

She remembered. Oh, yes, she remembered it too well. It was why she'd ridden away with him to Mexico.

"Did you kill him?" Michael whispered, his hard, cop tone snapping her back to the present.

"I said I didn't."

"Then I'm your best friend." His voice was quiet, credible.

"If you believed me—maybe."

"Trust me, talk to me. And maybe I will."

She almost succumbed to some idiotic, feminine instinct to do just that, just as the young Rosie had succumbed to him way back when. But then she remembered everything she'd suffered because of him.

Her father had gone to prison for shooting Michael's father. Michael had blamed her and made her young life hell all through middle school. Then, after they'd fallen in love and had run off together, he'd sworn condoms never failed. Who'd wound up pregnant? Who'd paid for that by missing out on art school? Then there was the more recent humiliation of waking up naked with a hangover in Michael's bed after he'd ticketed her for stalking Pierce.

She'd had to pay that ticket, too!

She backed away from him, hoping to diminish the effect of his brilliant, dark eyes on her nervous system. Then, before he could question her further or sweet-talk her into confiding, she bolted.

Eight

Visiting hours.

Late afternoon sunshine blazed through the hospital windows as Rosie got off the elevator and made her way through the psychiatric wing's maze of halls to Hazel's room. Today corridors and waiting rooms were filled with patients in blue gowns walking beside their visitors. Even though she was a nurse, Rosie hated being a visitor herself.

Rosie rushed past a man in a wheelchair, who tried to grab her. Some of the patients looked zonked and were clearly on strong medication. Others appeared perfectly normal.

She hoped Hazel would be more lucid today. Pierce's murder had her very stirred up. Even before Rosie reached her door, she heard her mother's agitated voice.

"Ask anybody. She's still in love with that motorcycle guy, the son of…"

Oh, God, don't let it be Carmen in there with her.

"That's why she killed Dr. Carver. Had it coming though, didn't he?" Hazel chuckled. "I told her to quit talking about killing him and to just do it."

Rosie blinked rapidly. Hopefully, her mother was simply babbling to the blank wall and not to some nurse or orderly.

Then a deep voice from inside the room sent chills through Rosie even before she recognized it.

"Let's see…you were admitted the night of Dr. Carver's murder? Am I right—Hazel? Mrs. Castellano."

"She takes after her father, you know."

"In what way?"

"Has his passion. Bad temper, too. He killed a man, you know. Rosie won't ever go see him. Prison didn't break his heart. She did that. His own daughter is as cold as ice. Do you think she comes here, to see me? She's ashamed of me and the old neighborhood and who she really is. That's why she changed her name to Castle. She always wanted to be rich and famous, anything but what she was. Which is why she set her cap for Carver. He was a rich doctor."

Who needed enemies, when you had a mother?

"So, you were admitted the night you heard about Dr. Carver's murder?"

"It's hard to keep dates straight," Hazel said. "All the drugs they give you in a nuthouse… But I think the story was on television and maybe I started cheering so loudly the neighbors called the cops. Somebody called my granddaughter, and then an ambulance came to haul me away. But it was my daughter, Rosie, who signed the papers to admit me."

Rosie banged the door open. Her gaze shot from her mother to Michael and then back again. "Mom, you don't have to tell this man—every damn thing you know!"

"Well…finally you get around to thinking about me," Hazel said. "Long time, no see. I'm changing my will when I get out."

Guilt swamped Rosie. As always, she felt she should be at her mother's side twenty-six hours a day—even if they drove each other nuts. "Mom, I was here just this morning!"

"I think I'd remember my own daughter if she came to see me."

"I was too here," Rosie whispered to Michael. Why did she feel the need to defend herself to him of all people?

"I believe you," he said quietly.

When Michael shut his notebook and rose from his chair beside Hazel's bed, Rosie leveled her full attention on him. "You believe me. Cut the nice-guy crap!" Her voice strengthened. "You snake! You have no right to crawl in here, asking slimy questions of a mentally ill woman!"

"Watch who you're calling mental!" Hazel shrieked.

"How did you get on this floor, anyway?" Rosie

demanded, turning her shoulder to her mother. "You're supposed to have a pass. You're not family! Where's your pass? Where is it?"

"Just doing my job," he muttered, but he had the decency to redden.

"You bulldozed some cute nurse with that smile and those huge, dark eyes of yours, didn't you?"

"Bulldoze isn't the word I'd pick," he said softly.

The chiseled line of his jaw blurred in a green haze of violent emotion that didn't bear analysis as Rosie imagined his mouth nibbling a pretty *young* nurse's neck while he pleaded for a favor.

"I'll bet the twit was young enough to be your daughter!"

"Probably. But if you'd answered a few simple questions when I asked them, then maybe I wouldn't have had—"

"Don't you dare lay your despicable behavior at my door!"

"Careful. The nurses around here might put you on medication, too. Which might not be such a bad idea." On the surface his voice was light, but she felt the edge underneath. He was investigating a murder.

A murder he suspected her of.

Hazel's eyes brightened with sudden interest as the sparks flew between them. "So, are you that motorcycle guy? Mike Nash's son?"

Michael nodded.

"Think I saw your picture once. It was cut up in

about sixteen pieces in our trash can, but I pasted it back together just to see what all the fuss was about."

Rosie had cut up all his pictures during the sixth week of her pregnancy, when she'd thought her life was over forever and that he'd sailed on with his own life without a care in the world.

"Mother!"

"I always wanted to meet you," Hazel confided shyly, her eyes glued to his face.

"Ditto," he replied, his gaze on Rosie.

"If you're him, I was always sorry," her mother began, "about your dad." She turned to Rosie. "He's got eyes just like—"

Rosie's expression must have been formidable, because Hazel instantly covered her mouth like a naughty child.

"Goodbye, Mr. Nash," Rosie said abruptly, furious at them both now and more than a little terrified. He was closing in, and so was Hazel.

Talk about the past catching up with you at the worst possible moment! Why, oh, why did her mom have to blab about everything under the shining sun?

"Goodbye, Mrs. Castellano. Nice visiting with you," he said. "Did anybody ever tell you you look young enough to be your daughter's sister?"

For that Rosie kicked him in the shin.

"Ouch!"

"Out!"

Despite his limp Michael managed a final, polite

bow in Hazel's direction. Then his fake smile twisted, and his big brown hand closed around Rosie's wrist like a claw. Before she could yell for help, he yanked her out into the hall and backed her against the wall. When Hazel cried out, he waved to her and then closed the door gently.

"I want my lawyer," Rosie said, tugging at his hand.

His fingers ground flesh into bone. "Why? You haven't been charged yet."

"*Yet?*" she squeaked, completely terrorized by that perfectly ordinary word and yet determined to go down fighting.

"Don't kick," he ordered, just as she pulled back her foot.

If only she'd been sensible enough to shut up and stop with the violence, maybe he would have been content with a mere threat and a little rough handling.

As they say in Texas, it's easier to let a wildcat out of the bag than to stuff it back in again.

She was past being sensible, past keeping cats and other vicious creatures in their proper bags.

She slammed her foot down on his big toe, and he yelped in pain and then, much to her delight, hopped twice on the other foot. Everybody in the crowded hall turned to stare at them.

"You can't scare me, you big bully! I have no intention of ever talking to you! Do you hear? I've a good mind to charge you with...with sexual harassment! *Do you hear?*" She jabbed a finger to his nose. "Do you—"

"Do I look deaf?" His dark eyes glittered.

Out of thin air he produced handcuffs and dangled them in front of her. "Castle, you and I are going to take a little ride downtown."

"Downtown?"

He opened one ring of his handcuffs. "If you can be a good girl, I'll let you say goodbye to your mother. I don't like upsetting her. I like *her*."

Stricken mute with fear for a second or two at the sight of that open ring, and at a new fear—that if she resisted him, he might really arrest her—she nodded.

"He's such a nice man. I really like him," Hazel said when Rosie stormed back into the room to snatch her purse off the bed. "He took me for a walk. Such good manners, too. Bought me a Coke. That's more than you ever do. Said he'd check on the cats, too."

"How could you, Mother, when you know you're a borderline diabetic?" She shot Michael a killing glance. Not that it had any effect other than to further annoy him.

"I guess I'm not the only lunatic." Hazel sighed as if in acute dismay. "He says 'yes, ma'am,' and 'no, ma'am.' Why are you always so rude to the nice ones?"

"You coming?" the nice one snarled from the door.

"He's a cop, Mom. Please don't talk to him if he shows up again…not about anything, even the dull color of these walls…unless you want me to wind up in prison for the rest of my life—just like Daddy."

"Prison!" Her mother snorted. "Well, take the

word of someone who's visited one—as you haven't bothered to—it's no worse than this. Everybody's nuts here. When do I get out? I'm sick and tired of crazy people."

"Tomorrow," Rosie said through gritted teeth. "Maybe…"

"Maybe? You're supposed to be a nurse. Call Dr. Moran. Get me out of here—now!"

"I can't. If I don't go downtown with Mr. Nice Guy right now, he will arrest me for real and lock me up and maybe throw away the key."

"Then who'll call Dr. Moran and get me out? Who'll feed Charlie and all his friends?"

"Exactly—Hazel."

"For the last time—don't call me Hazel. Carmen's driving me crazy with it."

A cold metal cuff snapped around Rosie's wrist, causing memories no nice girl with a normal sex life would have. "You're driving me nuts," Michael said, yanking her toward him. "Come on."

"That makes three of us," Rosie whispered.

The next thing she knew, he had the other half of the handcuffs locked around his wrist and was half marching, half hauling her down the hall.

Mouths agape, patients and visitors and a young nurse she knew from the E.R. stared after them.

"You've ruined my reputation forever," Rosie muttered as he dragged her into the elevator.

"I thought I took care of that in high school."

On the ground floor, she covered her face with her purse and walked in sullen silence to his unmarked, blue Crown Victoria, which was parked out front. Once in the car, she rallied and gave him hell all the way to the police station.

Nine

"Shut up!" Michael ordered, finally out of patience. He slammed two diet soda cans onto his gray metal desk beside a thin stack of lined notepaper and a ballpoint pen.

"But I'm not through telling you—"

"What a complete asshole I am."

"Exactly."

A red-faced Officer Keith was laughing at them through the open doorway.

"Brother!" Michael sighed wearily, closing the door. Then he threw back his head and took a long swig from his soda. "If you were smart, you'd quit."

Just as she was about to start in on him again, her cell phone rang. When she grabbed it out of her purse, Harry's number flashed.

"Don't answer it," Michael said.

She hadn't wanted to until he'd ordered her not

to. He must have caught the defiant gleam in her eye because he seized her phone, flipped it open and then shut. Then he shoved it back into her purse and slung her purse on top of his desk, out of her reach.

"You hung up on Harry!"

His savage look made her swallow. Did he have to be so mean? She wished he'd sit down. She'd didn't like the way he towered over her, which was probably why he was doing it. Cops must learn tricks like that in bad-cop classes.

With the door shut, he seemed a whole lot bigger, and the walls seemed to close in on her. Suddenly the room felt so small and stuffy there seemed no way to keep a safe distance from him.

What vital thing had she been about to say before Harry had called?

Oh! The Michael-you're-an-asshole speech... Inspired, she brightened.

"As long as you understand that I will hate you forever for this," she began. "How could you handcuff me at the hospital where I work...? *Where I work?* And bring me here? Parade me in front of your men out there? In front of that Keith guy? How could you let him slap you on the back and make that sly joke about me? Which you laughed at? I'll probably get fired now. You do know that, don't you?"

"You're screeching again." His jaw was steely.

He took another long swig of soda. Then his brows shot together, and he set his can down. Slowly, as if he dreaded what he had to say, he pulled his chair too close to hers and sat.

When she felt the heat of his body and caught the tang of his lemony aftershave, she remembered nights of wild, wanton sex. She scooted her chair back so fast, it clunked into the wall.

"Tiny office. They probably don't pay you much—but then, what do you do besides torture innocent people?"

His frown deepened. "I'm not a rich doctor with a plush office, but I may be your only friend."

"Then I am in big trouble."

"Finally, we agree on something." His mouth thinned. "My granddaddy once had a stubborn mule out on his farm. He used to say that he had to hit it between the eyes with a two-by-four just to get its attention. I'm not sure I ever understood what he meant until I met you."

A thousand emotions surged through her, most of them murderous, but some embarrassingly sexual, maybe because he was so close, which augmented the more violent emotions she felt. Well, maybe not a thousand emotions. But to say she was conflicted on a multitude of levels by being trapped in this airless space with a man she'd gotten naked with on numerous occasions, had done kinky and nonkinky things with—not to mention feeling guilty for having his baby, who was now grown, without ever telling him—was putting it mildly.

For a microsecond, she thought about Carmen and her awful dancing and singing job at that club and her dismal apartment. Rosie thought about how she'd botched raising her, and some rebel part of her wondered if dumping Michael hadn't been a huge mistake, after all. Back then he'd been poor and bossy, and it had all seemed so hopeless. But now... Maybe he wasn't rich, but he'd turned out all right, hadn't he?

"There's no oxygen in this room! I can't breathe! I want to go home!"

"So the hell do I," he said. "Which means the sooner you answer a few questions, the happier we'll both be."

"I told you I couldn't talk without—"

"Your lawyer. Joe? Right." Michael picked up an ancient looking cigarette pack and shook one out. "Feel like a cigarette?"

"What is this? Last rites for the condemned? You know I don't smoke! And if I did, I'd choose something elegant and slim...something with a gold filter and glitzy packaging."

"Look, simmer down. You're not under arrest yet."

"*Yet!* You said *yet*."

"I just have a few questions. And some concerns." Even though his tone was friendlier and more reasonable now that he had her cornered, she had to remember he was the last thing from a friend. He was a cop. Homicide. Not to mention, when he wanted something, he made a bulldozer look gentle.

"Concerns?"

"For your safety, Rosie."

"What are you saying?"

"The crime scene was one of the grisliest I've worked in a while. Lots of slashing. You saw the blood and the spatter. Carver's face was hacked to pieces—deliberately mutilated."

"How do you know it was him?"

"Blood type. Hair samples. DNA. It's him, all right."

She winced, not wanting to go back to that foul-smelling bedroom. Not even in her imagination.

Not that Michael would let her leave it. He slapped a photograph onto his desk. Pierce's pale, startled gray eyes stared out of a mess of blood, pulp and bone with a look of dread and fascination.

It *was* him. But how had the murderer missed the eyes? Gagging, she dropped her head, fighting both tears and nausea.

Pierce…dead, murdered…and she was partly to blame. She clasped her knees and closed her eyes, fighting desperately not to be sick.

"Whoever turned him into so much red Jell-O and bits of teeth and bone is extremely dangerous."

"Am I a suspect?"

He didn't say anything. Slowly she became aware that he was dangling a plastic bag in front of her.

"This bloody knife, the murder weapon…a Kasumi. Yours, I believe, bought in Japan on a trip you two made together…."

Her knife?

"No. No!" She felt light-headed.

"The knife has your prints all over it." He plunked a plastic package that contained what looked to be *her* missing knife onto his desk.

Palms sweating, she stared at it. Horror dawned slowly as she stared from the photograph to the knife. She sprang to her feet, poised to run, but he pushed her gently back into her chair.

"That your knife, princess?"

Beneath his penetrating gaze, she went still, even as her brain raced at the speed of light while her heart thumped like a mad thing.

"Someone is trying to frame me."

His eyes narrowed.

"I didn't kill him. I couldn't do that to anybody."

"But you told everybody—"

"Michael, I can explain…. Two days before the murder somebody broke into our house. We didn't think anything was missing, but the other night, the night you were there…"

"The night of the murder?"

She nodded. "Yolie made me chocolate cake. I couldn't find my knife, but I never thought—"

"We've got some long copper strands of hair the *exact* shade as yours in the deceased's fist. The theory is he pulled them out in a violent struggle for his life."

She had snagged her hair on Pierce's watch when he'd raised his hand during their quarrel. She started to protest, and then stopped even before Michael put a callused finger against her lips.

"No, don't deny they're yours, princess...because I'm pretty sure when we run a match... Besides, there's more. Carver had surveillance cameras outside. We saw you go in. We saw you run out—braless, everything bouncing. We didn't see anybody else."

"I may not have been charged *yet*, but now I'm sure I need a lawyer."

He shrugged. "No, you don't. Not so long as it's just you and me in here."

"Is this room bugged?"

"No."

"I know for a fact cops lie."

"How?"

She scanned the room for hidden bugs and groped under his desk, not that she felt reassured when she found no evidence of them. "I've seen it on TV."

"Everybody lies, princess." He paused. "Of course, you do have the absolute right to remain silent," he assured her in a gentle tone that completely unnerved her.

"I'm not a criminal!"

"Of course not." His voice soothed.

"Somebody's trying to frame me! But then that's probably what all the ax-wielding murderers you interrogate in here say."

He didn't smile.

She stared at the knife for a long time. Then, as

Michael watched, she turned Pierce's photograph facedown.

The lined paper stacked on Michael's desk blurred. She wouldn't cry. She wouldn't give him that satisfaction. But she blinked against the wetness in her eyes.

"Aren't you supposed to read me my rights?"

"Only if I arrest you."

"What are they?"

"Anything you say or write may be used against you in a court of law," he continued, pushing a paper toward her.

She blinked against the hot liquid welling in her eyes.

"You have the right to talk with a lawyer at any time—before any questioning, before answering any questions or during any questions."

His voice and his words had a horrible rote quality.

"How many times have you said all this before?" she whispered in a low, strangled tone.

"This is different...because it's you and me."

"Sure it is."

"I should have had them take me off the case, but I didn't. Our justice system scares the shit out of me sometimes. I want to help you," he whispered. "It's crazy. You probably don't believe me, but I'm crossing a line here. A big one. I hardly believe myself. But then you and me...with our history, our fathers, Mexico— well, everything. You're not just anybody to me."

For a brief instant she remembered how it had

been when they were young. He'd loved her so much, enough to forgive her for being her father's daughter, even.

"But if you trust me," he continued, "I'll do all I can to help you. I swear I'm all you've got. Just about everybody else thinks you did it."

"The other cops?"

He nodded. "Even Keith. Everybody. I know the system, and sometimes it sucks."

His voice was rough and yet soft at the same time. He sweet-talked her like that until she felt rum-dum, repeating that he was on her side again and again. Finally, he either hypnotized her or convinced her.

Barely knowing what she was doing, she initialed the papers he gave her. When she'd signed her name to a document saying he'd explained her rights, she threw his pen at him.

"If you're lying to me…" she whispered.

He caught the pen in midair. "Why did you go to Pierce's that night?"

"He invited me."

"Why?"

"He wanted me back."

"You told everybody in town you wanted to kill him, and he wanted you back?"

"I know it sounds crazy. But then relationships are crazy."

"Yours are, at least." Michael paused. "This your bra and panties?" He dropped a second plastic package containing something black and bloody onto the desk.

He leaned closer. "Did you tie him up with your bra before you fucked him?" His dark eyes shot fire at her.

His question wasn't professional. It was personal.

"You bastard!" A sob caught in her throat. She shook her head wildly. "I didn't sleep with him."

"But you wanted to?" Beneath his tan, his cheeks had reddened. He was angrier than she was, and getting angrier.

"Yes! I mean, no! I mean I don't know! I—I went over there thinking maybe I did...but I was all mixed up...and something felt wrong. And in the end, I just couldn't."

"When he didn't want you, you stabbed him and cut your finger in the process."

"You said you were on my side." She stood up, blinking rapidly.

"Damn it. We pulled *your* knife out of his Adam's apple."

"I didn't put it there! I—I told him to call me...to invite me to lunch. I wanted to slow things down. I did!"

"You went over there, got naked and he rejected you! Is that how it was? Then you got mad?"

"No!"

He sprang to his feet. "He attacked you, and you had to defend yourself? That's how you got cut?"

"No! I'm not a murderer! I'm not like my father!

I'm not!" Tears splashed down her cheeks. She hated Michael for making her cry.

When he grabbed her, she began to pound his chest and struggle frantically. "I was a fool to trust you even for a second. I hate you!"

"Hush," he said.

"A fool!"

"No. You weren't. I had to ask you that."

"I didn't kill him! You have to believe me!"

His arms wrapped her. "I do." His voice rasped huskily. "I swear I do. Too bad nobody else in this damn city does."

Soon she was hugging him back, pressing her body into his. She couldn't forget he was a cop. Not ever again. But it didn't matter. She couldn't help herself.

Fear must be a major turn-on. Suddenly all she wanted to do was hold on to him.

"Why the hell is this happening?" he whispered. "I thought I was smart enough to be done with you."

"Me, too." .

"When you dumped me in Mexico, it hurt for years. I've never felt worse, not even when my father died. Not even when I heard in court during your father's trial that mine was on the take. I hated you for that until I fell in love with you. What happened in Mexico?"

She felt tears burn the backs of her eyes. She felt regret, too, and didn't understand why. But now was not the time to try.

"For me it was just sex," she whispered. "I'm sorry, but you know how wild I was later. You were just the first. I was young, stupid...."

"Shut up. Just shut up," he growled, his tone low and wounded and furious, too.

He cupped her face in his palms and stared into her eyes. "This is insane. You've driven me insane. I almost envy Carver, the poor damn bastard! At least he's out of his misery!"

Then he kissed her.

She knew it was stupid and wrong and a thousand other bad things to open her mouth and let his tongue slide inside; idiotic beyond belief to cling and to sigh when she found him delicious. As always, like a fool, she let her head fall back as his warm mouth moved from her lips to her earlobe to her throat.

She was forty, for heaven's sake. Forty. A reluctant forty. Not a precocious forty, but it was time to grow the hell up anyway. She shouldn't allow this.

He inhaled her. Licked her. Devoured her. And arching her body into his, she loved every minute of it.

Desire pounded through her in a red-hot torrent. Never, not ever with any other man, had she felt like this. Her legs lost their strength, and she sank weakly against him. His hard, warm body felt so good. She wanted him out of his shirt and tie. She wanted to touch his skin with her hands and lips and tongue. She wanted to fling her clothes off and sit on him in his awful office chair, straddling his thighs.

She'd missed him; missed this. What was this *thing* inside her that took over when she was around him too long? With a groan, he picked her up as if she were a rag doll, and then sat down with her on his lap.

"Better," he murmured as he settled her bottom against his legs.

"Much better," she sighed. Half expecting him to rip her clothes off, she made that sound he'd always said reminded him of a kitten's purr.

He folded her closer. Five minutes and many many hot kisses and purrs later, they were both so highly aroused they could barely catch their breaths.

"We've got to stop this nonsense," he finally muttered in between ragged gasps for oxygen.

"As if," she said, her arms clinging to his neck, her mouth nibbling at his bottom lip with both passion and reluctance.

"Not here," he whispered. "Not now. The walls have ears." He put a fingertip to her lips. "Listen."

Even though she kept kissing him, she heard the hum of voices and the buzz of phones and the electronic beepings of office machines from the other side of the door.

"We're not alone," he said. "Cops are everywhere. Keith's right outside guarding the door. I'm supposed to be interrogating you. I'm breaking every rule in the book. They'll fire my ass."

At least one of them still had a functioning body part above the waist.

"I'll be good," she promised, pressing her mouth to his one last time as he disentangled himself and lifted her up, so she could sit in her own chair again. She grabbed her purse off his desk.

While he finger-combed his black wavy hair into some semblance of order, his expression that of a naughty boy who'd been caught with his hand in the cookie jar, she listened to Keith barking orders at someone and to other scary police sounds outside. Drawing a deep breath, she fished in her purse for a compact and brush.

No sooner was her hair brushed and her lipstick on than her common sense returned with a bang.

She groaned. Was she out of her mind?

Always—when Michael was around.

If her near seduction at his hands in the police station, of all places, didn't end with her arrest, she had to get out of here—and away from him—before she got into even more trouble.

When she stood up to go, his tone was semiprofessional again. "I'm afraid I have a lot more questions."

"Somewhere else, then. This room's too small. I— I don't trust myself being this close to you, either— even if *they* are outside."

His grin was a quick flash of straight white teeth. "Finally, you admit it," he said.

"What?"

"That you have the hots for me."

She scowled.

He grinned, and she nearly lost it. Why did he have to have such a beautiful, kissable mouth?

She traced her lips with her tongue, tasting him. He was even more addictive than Yolie's chocolate chip cookies.

"I'll swing by your house in thirty minutes. That'll give me time for a cold shower before we meet again."

"I've got a better idea. Meet me at Barton Springs. Shallow end. Grassy side. Barton's is better than a cold shower anyday."

"Not if you wear a skimpy bikini."

"I'm forty, remember? So I'm not dangerous in a bikini."

"Do me a favor—don't wear one." He grinned. "Our first date was at Barton's," he said, his cop's eyes softening into that bedroom gaze that made her stomach do a flip. "You wore a green bikini tied together by little strings that kept coming undone."

Because he'd kept untying them.

"Funny you can remember that far back," she said.

"I remember everything about those damn little strings," he said. Not that he looked all that happy about it. "You finally tied knots in them. I remember that last night when we danced on the beach in Mexico, the white bikini with the little red hearts all over it, the sex. I remember waking up the next morning and finding you gone...with all my money."

"Fifty whole dollars."

"You never told me why you dumped me."

I was pregnant. And out of my mind with fear.

"Did you ever wonder how I got back to the States with no money?" he asked, looking rather vulnerable. "Did you even care?"

"Quit with the sad eyes! You've always been tough and resourceful. I figured you'd hitchhike or something. Look, all I had money for was a bus ticket. A woman alone in Mexico is in a lot more trouble than a man. I had to do it."

"Why?"

"Does it make you happier to know I starved?" she said.

She'd felt sick to death and scared out of her mind. And sad. So sad. She'd cried and vomited and looked back at the Mexican mountains, thinking of him all the way home.

"Why the hell did you marry a loser like Simon?"

So our baby wouldn't be born a bastard!

In the end *that* had seemed so crushingly important.

"The past doesn't matter now," she said.

"Maybe not to you." His expression was grim, but for once he didn't push.

Carmen was tall like he was, and she had his warm, chocolaty eyes and his thick eyebrows. Only her eyes were usually smoldering with resentment when she looked at Rosie.

Even as a child she'd pushed and fought about everything. Maybe she had her daddy's stubborn determination. Maybe if she ever figured out what she wanted to do with her life, she'd be unstoppable.

Carmen! Common sense returned with a hellacious bang—as it always did after Rosie shot herself in the foot by going nuts over the wrong man.

Carmen. Michael Nash was definitely the wrong man. Not only was he Homicide, he was the very last person she could trust with her heart and her secrets.

No way could she meet him at Barton's!

Ten

Rosie knew how self-destructive it was to meet Michael at Barton's. Naturally, she wound up on big yellow beach towels, lying dangerously too close to him under a century-old, leafy pecan tree swathed in cascading wild grape vines at Austin's favorite swimming hole, anyway.

Okay, so maybe she should have picked a place where everybody, especially him, wasn't half-naked. He still had the honed physique of an athlete. An older guy like him had to work out to keep all those biceps and quadriceps, not to mention his abs, in shape. Obviously, he had been exercising more than a single digit on his right hand flipping his television remote.

Still, how much trouble could a girl—make that a forty-year-old, mature, female person in a bikini— get into with a guy, even a big, hunky guy like Michael at a public pool?

Who was she kidding?

Barton Springs was a long, natural, spring-fed pool with sloping, shady lawns and limestone cliffs. Its emerald-green waters were popular on long summer days. Besides swimming, the younger set seemed to spend a lot of time scoping out each other's tattoos. People lazed on the lawns, and when their blood began to boil they rose languidly from their beach towels and cooled down in the icy—make that 60 degrees Fahrenheit—pool.

"You just had to wear as little as possible," Michael said.

"It's a hot day, and this was the only bathing suit I could find. All my one-pieces must still be in boxes in my garage. I can't remember if I told you my house burned awhile back."

"Well, the less you wear, the better you look," he said, appearing distracted, "which I'm sure you know."

Because she worked at it, just as he did.

Not a breath of air stirred in the pecan branches above her. Because of the heat, the afternoon sky had a milky cast.

Michael brushed the tiny palm tree tattooed above her left breast with a callused fingertip. Her breath caught at his touch, and her gaze flicked to the matching tattoo on his chest.

"Remember when we got these?" Michael asked.

"People should think long and hard about getting tattoos. Unlike a new dress, they're too permanent."

"Hey, palm trees were your big idea. I've taken a lot of ribbing through the years."

"From other women?"

"Upon occasion."

"So, you must strip often?"

He was gazing at her breasts. "Not often enough," he murmured.

Above them cicadas sang. With an effort, she concentrated on the summer bugs instead of him. "I don't think I like where this conversation is heading," she said, scooting a little farther from him.

"Neither the hell do I. I'm supposed to be interrogating you."

His eyes lingered on her body for another second. Then he gritted his teeth and forced himself to look away.

She tried not to let her head swell because he found her so distracting.

"Have you seen your dad lately?" he finally asked, and rather grumpily, as he pulled his little notebook from his backpack.

His question was met with a furious, indrawn breath.

"I think I prefer reminiscing about regretting our tattoos."

His gaze darkened. "Hey, I never said I regretted—" He caught himself. "Have you seen him?" he demanded in a harsher tone.

"If you have to know, why don't you call the

prison?" She plucked a blade of Saint Augustine grass and began to chew it.

"I called." His dark gaze drilled her. "Your father got out of prison two days before your doctor buddy got his pretty face hacked to pieces with your knife."

She winced. *Her father was out?* How had she missed that? There had been a lot of days, of course, when she'd been too busy to read the paper or watch the news. And since she didn't allow conversations about her daddy, nobody, not even Carmen or Hazel, had bothered to inform her.

"Have you seen your father or heard from him?"

"No." She stared at the ground. The man who'd gone to prison was the monster who'd shot a cop and turned her young life upside down. Led by Michael, the victim's son, all the other kids had made her an outcast in middle school. Hazel hadn't understood why Rosie hadn't been able to accept what her father had done, and love him, anyway.

Because maybe she'd had ambitions, and he'd ruined them. She'd wanted to be written about in the papers in a good way. Rosie didn't want to think about the past now, when it was too late to change anything.

She'd loved him well enough before the tragedy. He'd taught her to shoot a gun and play football. Sometimes even now she'd wake up and feel startled to realize she'd dreamed of her father and the things they'd done before the shooting. He'd taken her to parks, to public swimming pools or they'd walked beside Town Lake.

Back then her mother had worked all the time. Her father had loved to show Rosie little turtles that barely filled her palm. They'd fed bread crumbs to fish off a favorite pier.

How they'd both loved the visiting coots that had dived in the lake during the winter months.

"Okay," Michael said. "Doesn't give a damn about her dad."

She was about to correct him and then thought better of it. Still, she wanted to grab his pencil as she watched him scribble that in his notebook.

"Tell me about you and Pierce. Why did he break up with you?"

"He was annoyed I had a granddaughter I was devoted to. You see, he had to be number one. He was a plastic surgeon and into appearances and the fantasy of eternal youth. He thought the twenty-year-old he'd been was the real person, that he should work to preserve *that* guy, and that aging had no place in the modern world. He must've figured I was getting too old, so when he sailed to Guatemala, I guess he was ripe to meet Anita."

"They damn sure didn't last long."

"I'm certain you've questioned her," Rosie said, hoping for unflattering, gossipy and incriminating details.

"So, why do you think she left him?" Michael asked.

"Probably because he tried to control her, and when he couldn't, he got mad and drank and became abusive."

"And you loved this guy."

"Does she have an alibi?"

"Airtight."

Rosie sighed. "Isn't that suspicious?"

"Being the last one to see him alive is suspicious. Fingerprints on the murder weapon are suspicious."

"I didn't kill him," she blurted.

"Well, Anita was at a party at a private club with a hundred people, mostly doctors and their wives. She wore red and made herself very visible."

"I still think it's extremely odd that she has such a good alibi."

"These missionary trips Pierce was so big on— what were they all about?"

"He said many people had done a lot for him and he needed to do something for those who had nothing. You see, people all over the world go without medical services that we, in first world countries like the U.S., take for granted."

"Those your thoughts or his?"

"He said he could dramatically change lives south of our border."

"Don't we have enough poor people here? Why did he have to leave the country?"

"The situation down there just seemed so grave, I guess."

"He made sure he got a lot of press."

"That's what Yolie says."

"So what, exactly, did he do down there?"

"He operated on disfigured kids. Big, ugly moles, cleft palates—"

"Where did he go?"

"Guatemala. Costa Rica. Mexico. Other places in Central America."

"Any place in particular?"

She shook her head.

"Where did he stay?"

"With the other workers in primitive camps. But he knew people down there, and sometimes after we'd finished working in the clinic, we would visit his friends with beautiful mountain and beach homes."

"Did he speak Spanish?"

"Yes. Not like a native. But very well. Why?"

"When a person is murdered, it pays to look at all aspects of his life."

"Even his childhood?"

"Sometimes. He grew up in Beaumont, Texas. Sounds pretty routine. Honor student all the way through school…"

She yawned, pretending she was bored. "So, you've talked to people in Beaumont?"

He jotted something in his notebook.

"What did you write down?"

"I'm supposed to be the detective."

When she reached for the notebook, the muscles

in his arm bunched. Then he grabbed her and pulled her under him.

He was hot and a little heavy, but he felt good. Too good.

"This is a public pool, so keep it G-rated, Nash."

"I warned you not to wear a bikini, but as always, you had to live dangerously." He slid his foot against hers, making sensuous circles against the soles of her feet with his toes. His expression grew serious again. "So, why'd you run from me all those years ago?"

Playing footsie proved highly distracting. So did his abrupt change of subject.

"I thought we were supposed to be working."

He ran his big toe along the arch of her foot. "I'm taking a short break. Why'd you run?"

"If I answer—you'll stop asking."

"If you tell me the truth."

She curled her toes against his and squeezed her eyes shut. "And you really think you can tell the truth from a lie?"

When he rolled back onto his side, she opened her eyes.

"I'm a cop. All I do is sift through lies for nuggets of truth."

"Okay. I was kid. You came on pretty strong. I wasn't ready."

"Why'd you marry Simon?"

"I divorced him, didn't I? Things didn't work with me and him, either."

Michael's long stare began to make her uneasy. So did lying beside him. All of a sudden she was burning up, so she got up and walked to the concrete embankment lining the emerald water. Most people were tiptoeing down a ramp that led into the pool, entering the cold water by inches as they let out little cries and squeals, the process taking some as long as half an hour.

Pierce had told her once that nerves fatigue very quickly once all their circuits were jammed. He'd always jumped into Barton's, and he'd laughed at her when she'd done the inching routine.

Showing off, she walked to the edge of the pool and plunged into the water feetfirst, sinking in an explosion of arctic bubbles. The shock of the cold took her breath away, and she burst to the surface screaming and gasping.

Michael laughed. Then she began swimming fast toward the limestone cliff on the opposite side, away from him. When he didn't jump in, she paddled back to the concrete stairs beneath where he stood, wiggling his toes in the cold water and making grimaces.

"Sissy!" she hollered.

He stuck his entire foot in and then made a face. "You want me to jump in and have a heart attack."

"No, it really is easier if you get in fast and have it over with."

"Then why'd you scream like Comanches had you?" She splashed him.

He let out a war whoop before he leaped, grabbing his knees so that he hit the water in cannonball mode, his huge splash dousing her. When his black head broke the surface, she swam away as fast as she could.

She'd barely made five feet before his strong hand clamped around her ankle and he pulled her to him. Then they were standing up again, his hands gripping her arms now. His chocolate-dark eyes, made more gorgeous by beads of water on his long, silky lashes, devoured her with an intensity that took her breath away.

His fingers brushed lightly down the length of her arms and then slid back up them, causing electrical shivers throughout her body.

Hot skin. Cold water. Man. Woman. Sunshine. Sparkling green leaves against a blue sky. Children's laughter.

When his gaze focused on her mouth, too many feminine nerve endings prickled. Already tasting him, she licked her lips.

Meltdown. Who knew what would have happened next if a little girl with a yellow beach ball hadn't bumped them? Rosie fell back from Michael a little, gasping in shock at the realization that they weren't the only two people in the universe. It took a supreme effort to frame her features into a demure expression appropriate for apologizing to the freckle-faced little girl.

She grabbed the ball and handed it to her. "I'm sorry, sweet—"

Beyond the little girl's wet, red pigtails, Rosie became aware of a young woman on the embankment glaring at Michael. She wore the skimpiest black, crocheted bikini imaginable. If even one itty-bitty string came untied…

Was Michael ogling those strings? Was he?

Rosie went green. All that glowing *young* skin… She would never look that young again. If jealousy wasn't bad enough, recognition dawned.

Carmen!

Her daughter. Correction: *his* daughter, too. She *would* show up practically naked.

"Carmen!"

Carmen turned to her, her expression growing even sulkier as she nudged her sunglasses up the bridge of her nose.

"Damn," Michael said. "Except for her brown eyes, she looks just like you used to back in high school. What a bombshell! Who the hell is she? And what's with the go-to-hell look? Have we done something?"

"We exist." Rosie paused. She didn't like the way he kept staring at Carmen or the way she stared at him. Not that their interest seemed sexual. They were simply curious.

But he was a cop. Which meant he could probably add one plus one and get two…or three…if he were doing sex math.

"We have to go," Rosie blurted.

"Who—"

She was already swimming toward the shallow end.

He caught up with her easily, his strong brown arms slicing the water expertly. "Someone you know?"

"My daughter." She gritted her teeth and swam faster.

"Why didn't you introduce us?"

Rosie heard splashes behind her and turned as he shot Carmen a long, curious glance. Fortunately, her back was to them now as, hips swinging, she strode away.

Michael couldn't seem to stop watching her. "You used to walk like that when you were pissed. What a sexpot. It must be in the genes."

"What?"

"East Austin. You can take the girl out of East Austin but you can't take East Austin out of the girl."

Talk about slamming a fist onto a hot button. But then, he didn't know that Carmen danced half-naked at The Cellar or that Rosie had a guilt complex to end all guilt complexes about it.

"Go to hell. Go straight to hell."

"Only if you come with me." Michael grinned at her. Without missing a beat, he added, "Your place or mine?"

"I'm mad at you," she said.

"You're always hot when you're mad. Remember how mad you were the night I wrote you up for stalking Carver with your Beamer?"

With his mind focused on sex, he'd forgotten

about Carmen. And when he pulled Rosie into his arms and kissed her passionately despite her struggles, she soon realized he intended to make her forget both Carmen and her anger.

And she did. Damn it. She did.

Eleven

Your place or mine?

Oh my God! Was that the oldest line in the book or what? Whatever it was, after Michael had followed that up with a couple of long kisses and by touching her breasts, here she was, her anger gone, underneath his big brown body on his soft leather couch.

Yes, she'd been Bad Daughter, having ignored a call from her sick mother, who was still in the hospital. Michael was kneeling on top of her. His jean-clad legs straddled her waist, and his knees pushed deeply into the cool-against-her-bare-skin cushions.

No sooner had Rosie settled into his cushions than visions of Carmen at the pool started swirling in her head. Not good. Images of Hazel popped up, too. No way would a good daughter choose sex over her mentally ill mother—even if her mom hadn't bothered to tell her about Daddy being out of prison.

When Rosie tried to sit up, his knees tightened around her waist, and he sank deeper into his couch, taking her down with him.

"But my mom—"

"She'll be okay." He paused. "Relax." His voice was hoarse and aroused.

"How can I, with you on top of me?"

"Easy."

"So you have a house and not an apartment," she murmured, to distract him.

"Always the little materialist." She felt his fingertip brush a tendril of hair away from her temple.

"I'm just surprised…about the house, that's all. It's nice."

He kissed her brow. "Did you expect squalor? Bad boy from the east side of town? Motorcycle in the living room with its oily parts all over the sofa?" He was sounding edgier and less aroused by the minute.

His house was in central Austin, which meant it cost a bundle. She sort of liked that, even though she worried about it. Since he was a cop, she wondered how he could afford it. Which, obviously, was none of her business, and wouldn't ever be because she had to end this thing with him—right now, before it got started again.

"Your garage was so neat, and I like your yard," she said, trying to figure out how to shift gears and peddle backward sexually without making him really mad. "But your car is the pits."

His knees tightened around her waist. "The car belongs to the department."

When he undid his zipper, she tried to sit up. "Who mows your lawn and prunes your trees?"

"Do I look like a guy with a lot of servants?" He pulled his jeans down a little, revealing more brown flesh and sworls of black hair.

She felt like sliding her hands down his pants.

"Before I lived with Yolie, my yard was a mess," she said, staring past the tanned male flesh. "And my garage—"

"I don't give a damn about your garage." He took her hand, placed it on his flat belly and then tried to slide it down.

She yanked her arm away even though at that first touch of his hot skin, she'd shivered.

"Well, it's full of all sorts of clutter," she said a little breathlessly.

"Why doesn't your having a messy garage surprise me?" he murmured huskily.

"You have an entire room off the side of your garage with nothing but lots and lots of shiny tools."

"I like to fix things. I'm a guy."

"If I even have a hammer and a screwdriver, I don't have a clue where they are. When things break…"

"You just throw them out in the garage."

"Exactly. Or call Harry."

"Who's Harry?"

"He takes care of my rental houses."

"Hey, you wouldn't need Harry if I hung around your place more often. I'm very talented at lots of good stuff…besides sex."

"Most men make more messes than they clean up." She thought about Carmen and frowned.

Michael's mouth thinned. "What's wrong now?"

Suddenly she felt a little guilty about Carmen. She was beginning to think she'd made a serious mistake never to tell him about his daughter.

Rosie had noticed earlier that Michael's two-bedroom, clapboard house was freshly painted. The roof was sound, too. He took care of what was his. Doubtless, he would have been very responsible about Carmen.

"We can't do this," Rosie said. "I need to call my mother."

"She'll wait." He ripped off her cover-up and then her bikini top. "I can't." He jerked off his shirt and threw it onto the Persian rug.

The red, intricately patterned rug surprised her. It looked a lot like Yolie's Hariz.

"Palm trees," he said. "I feel like kissing palm trees."

The buzz in her arteries turned into a roar. Bad Daughter forgot about his rug and Hazel.

"I have to get out of here," she whispered.

"You should have protested earlier." He was nibbling at her earlobe. "You've really got us going now."

"Us? Don't include me."

The warm, male scent of his body and the erotic

brushing of his lips sent a mad electrical pulse through her.

"You're the main cop on the case and I'm…I'm the prime suspect. Aren't you breaking some law?"

"Shut up. Just shut up," he growled. Then he returned to kissing her, slowly and languidly, and with such lavish expertise she was soon sighing. His lips moved from her ear down her throat, leaving a strip of flaming damp skin in their wake.

"You taste good, good enough to get fired for," he whispered.

She hadn't known she had so many feminine nerves until he set them aflame.

"Michael…" She twirled his dark hair around a fingertip.

"I don't much like listening to lectures I could write myself. I know we shouldn't, princess. Damn it. I know it better than you do." His lips continued their descent across her breast. "But like I said, I feel like kissing little palm trees. And doing all sorts of wild, perverted things with you. Like licking honey out of hidden feminine places."

If only he'd stopped at the palm tree. But of course, he didn't, and all too soon he lost his jeans, and she lost the bottom to her bikini. Within seconds her lips were devouring him in places no nice girl even knew existed. When he finally carried her into his bedroom, her eyes were closed, her heart was pumping and her legs were too limp to support her.

He sat down on his king-size bed with her in his lap, so that she was straddling him. Then he lay back, leaving her on top.

"I like looking up at you." He cupped her breasts. "You look even better than you did in high school."

She remembered Carmen's smooth, ripe flesh. No, Rosie didn't, but she liked him saying it.

Still kneeling, she eased herself onto him. He was huge, and when he slid inside her she felt every long, hot inch of him. Then she leaned forward, oozing down, down, her hair falling softly across his chest. She began moving back and forth, her body dancing with his in the familiar rhythm of longtime lovers.

Not for long, though—because she overheated and caught fire and then exploded like that halogen lamp that had torched her house.

"Talk about a meltdown."

He smiled up at her and smoothed the hair back from her hot, perspiring face.

"I'm drenched," she whispered.

His fingers lightly, lovingly traced the faint stretch marks on her belly. When she recoiled, he gently pulled her closer.

His gaze locked on hers. "I always wanted a baby," he said. "But it never happened."

His hand stilled. "Lucky you. You've got a beautiful daughter and a real cute granddaughter."

Rosie swallowed. When he continued to stare at her and stroke her belly, she felt a connection to him that was deeper than words or promises or passion. Suddenly she wanted to tell him everything.

"I've never been much of a mother. Carmen…she has a lot of problems because of my mistakes. She dropped out of high school when she became pregnant. She dances in a club where the dancers don't wear much."

Rosie tore her eyes from him, shaking a little and quite frightened of the nearly overwhelming instinct she felt to confide all.

"It's okay," he said. "She'll grow up. We did, didn't we?"

"For me, it's still an ongoing process."

He laughed. "Okay. Sorry I got serious. Kiss me again."

"I'd better go."

"You can't stop yet," he murmured dryly. "We've only just begun. I have a long list of favorite perversions…."

"I don't want to hear—" She tried to sit up.

"No more talk."

She didn't protest when he withdrew his hand from her stretch marks and started kissing her again. She wanted him too badly.

When he grabbed the jar of honey, she began to burn even before he poured it on her and began to lick it off. Then his tongue was inside her, and she was reveling in its every eager flick. As she shuddered she felt as if she had every answer to every unsolved equation in her life. And for maybe two whole minutes after her climax, the glow lingered, the way pink light does after sundown.

Only slowly did she come to her senses again.

"Rosie?" Michael pulled her close.

For a second or two she dissolved into his warmth. He felt too good. Way too good. Even if they were both sticky with honey.

"Hazel," she said, pushing him away. "I've got to see about her. I really do!"

She sprang out of bed and ran to shower.

He chased her and flung the door open. When she slammed the shower door and turned on the water, he opened that door, too.

Pulling her into his arms, he said, "I have a very long wish list in my head."

"Of what? No! I don't want to hear!"

"Of all your favorite perversions. And guess what? Today's your lucky day, because I intend to indulge you."

"If only…I'd locked the shower door…."

"I'm going to show you that you don't really mean that."

And he did.

Twelve

Carmen heard the phone ringing in Yolie's pool house and looked up from her algebra text. The damn phone had been driving her crazy all afternoon. The calls had to do with the murder—she was sure of it.

She'd jiggled the door of the pool house, but it was locked. Darius and Todd hadn't been around much since their daddy's death. Xavier had the key.

So where was Yolie's boy toy and his great big motorcycle?

Who cared about *him*, anyway? Maybe he thought he was the hottest thing in tight denim. Well, she knew better. He had a prick and was a prick, just like every other guy she'd ever known. Even so, her heart beat a little faster at the thought of him.

Well, she didn't dare leave the little girls and go inside the house to get the phone. If anything happened to them, it would be one more thing for her mother to hold over her—like, forever.

Babysitting two little brats while she tried to study was the pits. Not that algebra was all *that* hard. Still, who needed it? Why did Jennifer have to be off at some dumb cheerleading meet?

She is your kid! And if her bratty friend weren't here, you'd have to be in that pool playing with her.

Her mother had given her a choice. Carmen could go deal with Hazel's cats and springing Hazel from the loony bin or she could babysit. Like that was a choice!

She'd been to see Hazel earlier in the day and had gotten the surprise of her life. Guess who'd been there? The infamous murderer himself! Pop Castellano.

Not that Pop looked like a killer or acted like one, which just proved that whoever killed Carver could be anybody. Pop's real name was Carlo Castellano. He was small and had a kindly face. He had big blue eyes that lit up when he smiled at her, just like her mother's could. Pop had smiled and told her he liked having a beautiful granddaughter.

She'd liked him saying that. She'd liked it a lot.

"You tell your mama I'd like to see her," he'd said.

"Sure."

As if…

Still, Carmen had felt a little sad, knowing how her mother felt about him.

With his shock of thick white hair, he was kinda cute, she thought, which was strange, since he was so old…almost sixty. And Hazel looked way younger whenever he smiled at her. They couldn't have the hots for each other. No way. They were too old.

Hazel had pulled her aside and said, "Whatever you do, don't tell Pop about that band of yours, the Naked Babies. He might turn up at The Cellar and shoot somebody."

What a family! No wonder she was so messed up! Not that she'd warned her mother about Carlo maybe coming around to see Hazel sometimes. Carmen wasn't *that* dumb.

Wearing only a black thong bikini with the top untied, and *not* thinking about Xavier, *definitely not*, and not listening for that big bike of his, she lay belly-down on a hot-pink towel in the shade beside Yolie's pool, smoking and cheating by looking up all the answers in the back of the book.

The phone stopped ringing just as she finished the test and slammed the book closed.

"Scared to get your hair wet?" Mina yelled at Carmen from the sparkling pool.

"Get lost!"

As a reward for working on her GED all afternoon, which was a secret, by the way, she'd taken out her sketchbook. The last thing she needed was for Alexis and Mina to swim up to the edge and splash her.

"Now you won't look so hot," Alexis teased, playfully tossing handfuls of water.

When a drop landed on her sketchpad, Carmen threw the pad aside and grabbed her bikini top, holding it in place. "You two better leave me alone right now, or I will get in and make you sorry!"

When she stood up and scowled at them as she tied the strings of her top, they began to shriek and giggle. When she ran over to the chrome ladder, they swam away to the shallow end.

Was I ever as young and innocent as Alexis? Or ever half so happy?

Carmen rearranged herself on her towel. Then she stubbed out her cigarette. Was it Alexis or the memory of her mother looking so young and happy with *that* man, that sexy detective, whose picture she'd seen in the paper, that had her so upset?

Her mom was stupid to fool around with him, *the* cop on *the* case, but then she was stupid when it came to men, period. Who but a dope would have messed around with an asshole like Pierce Carver?

Detective Nash had had a palm tree tattoo just like her mother's, with lots of overdone palm fronds just like her mom's. Same place on his chest, as well.

What was up with that?

Matching tattoos were serious. How come her mother had never talked about him, not even once?

Just thinking about Rosie with a man disgusted Carmen. Of course, she knew older people had sex, especially her mom, who was still pretty hot. So why was she, Carmen, so angry about this guy?

All she could figure was that the sight of her mother with Michael Nash had made her acutely conscious of how abandoned she'd felt her whole damn life.

Even now, hours later, the mere sight of Alexis laughing with her bratty, loudmouthed friend at the other end of the pool made Carmen feel even lonelier and more left out than she had at Barton's.

According to her stupid shrink, Nan, feelings like this had caused her to sleep around and get pregnant. She'd actually been dumb enough to think the prick had really loved her. After he'd taken a hike and she'd had the baby, she'd wised up about him and men real fast.

She'd hated getting fat and feeling like even more of an outcast. Her labor had been really really terrible. Scary, too. Everybody had been afraid she'd die, but they'd been more afraid for Alexis.

She remembered how ugly and horrible Alexis had looked right after being born. Her face had been all mashed in and her scalp had been black with blood. The baby had seemed so helpless and totally dependent, too. When she'd curled her tiny hand around Carmen's pinky, Carmen had felt something really scary. The kid must have felt it, too, because she'd held on tight.

Carmen had yanked her hand free. Who had ever been there for her?

The nurse had asked if she'd wanted to breast-feed.

"Who, me? No way! Yuck." She'd pulled the sheet up to her neck and shut her eyes, wanting to die or at least sleep for a month. In the end her mother had taken the baby home.

Just until you adjust…

Motherhood had sneaked up on her, broadsided her.

Because of Alexis, Carmen had dropped out of school. She hadn't been happy about that even though she couldn't care less about dumb old high school.

Carmen had never had many friends at school the way Alexis did. What made some people so lovable and others so…?

She heard a motorcycle roar up the lane. When a lawn mower started up in the distance, she got out her brush and ran it through her hair. When the sound began to fade, she decided it couldn't be Xavier after all, and quit primping. Not that she was interested in *him* even if he was a hottie with a great big bike.

Carmen bit her lips. Her thoughts returned to high school and how she'd hated the legions of schoolmates who'd teased and tormented her, especially the ones who'd taunted her about her nonexistent father.

Someone named Simon. Why had he left her?

Why did she even care?

She didn't! She hated her daddy! She hated him more than she'd ever hated anybody—even her mother, who'd always been too busy to pay attention to her.

Instead of talking to her herself, her mother had taken her to Nan and to countless psychiatrists, who'd prescribed medications.

With a sigh, Carmen picked up her sketchpad and began drawing Alexis floating on that stupid green raft that was designed to look like a gleeful frog. Carmen hadn't told her mother she was going after her GED, or that maybe she wanted to take some classes in junior college. She hadn't told her that maybe she wanted to be an art teacher, either.

Why did Alexis's frog have a smile on its face? Carmen drew a frown on her frog.

Why didn't toy makers ever, just once, paint a frown on a float or a toy? In all her school pictures except one, she'd been frowning.

The phone began to ring again. She didn't even look up.

"Hi, there," said the deep, pleasantly accented voice she'd been hoping she'd hear all during this long, boring afternoon. "You gonna catch that phone?"

Pretending indifference even as her heart fluttered, she turned, lifting herself off the towel just enough so Xavier could catch a peek of her rounded bosoms. Then, as if she remembered she was practically naked, she let out a little cry and pulled her towel up.

His mouth quirked cynically. "*Dios*, you don't know when to quit, do you?"

"What's that supposed to mean?" she said.

The phone stopped ringing.

"I'll bet you think you're just about the hottest babe in town."

"What if?"

He leaned down so that his handsome, bronzed face was mere inches from hers. "Maybe I like a woman who's interesting to talk to."

The girls in the pool had gone as quiet as mice as they paddled closer to get a better view.

"It's not like I'd care what you think," Carmen said, lowering her voice.

"Good," he exclaimed. "That makes us even." He stood up again and then moved a potted plant and picked up a hose. "How come you never smile? You might be really pretty if you did."

"Like Alexis's stupid frog? Is the frog pretty?"

"No, but it's cute."

She slammed her sketchpad facedown. "I don't care what you think. You're just Yolie's stupid yardman."

"Oh, well, if we're going to slot people, then you're a rude, coldhearted *puta*, who uses sex to get attention because she's such a mess she thinks nobody would be with her if she didn't take off her clothes." He toed her algebra book. "Hey, what's this?"

Ohhh! She was stuck on the P-word. The sun seemed to vanish, and the trees and pool became very dark. Alexis's spying blue eyes were huge now.

Carmen's brows whipped together as she grabbed

the textbook and hid it under her towel. "I've seen you come into the club! You watch me just like all the others!"

He laughed.

"Well, you buy drink after drink."

"So, I like to have a beer or two after I get done here."

"You can't take your eyes off me."

"Tits and ass. Every girl's got them, no?"

"And that's it?"

"What do you want it to be? You said I was a stupid yardman, which means you must think you're too good for me."

"You're Yolie's boy toy."

He leaned closer. "How come that bothers you?"

"I couldn't care less."

His slow, quiet smile said he didn't believe her.

She pushed a strand of red hair out of her eyes. "What if I told you that you're wrong about me...in a lot of ways?"

"Am I?" he whispered.

"Interested in finding out?"

"Maybe."

"So, how about you? Do you belong to Yolie?"

"Like you, a lot of people think so. Maybe she likes them thinking it. I clip her hedges. I mow her yard. I clean her pool. I work at Taco Bonito, too."

"And that's all? No other, er...services?"

"I like talking to her a lot. She's smart."

"Smarter than me?"

"She talked me into going to school. First, I studied English. Now I'm trying for my GED."

His eyes began to burn her. "Why do you strip? What other services do you provide where you work?"

"I don't need this shit. Not from you."

"Looking for love in all the wrong places—"

"Love—four letters that mean what? A lot of crap, that's what." She was getting really angry now. "Guys like you, handsome guys—"

"Handsome? Hey, thanks. A compliment. Finally something nice comes out of that pretty mouth."

His cocky smile made her bite her tongue. "Jerks like you think that if you say the big L-word, you can get anything out of a girl."

"Hey, whatever works. I'm a guy, remember. A boy toy."

"Well, it won't work with me, boy toy."

"What will, then?"

"Why don't you come to the club tonight and find out?"

"Do you really want me to?"

She didn't know why, but she did. Not that she could admit it. She smiled, and it wasn't one of those fakey smiles she shot at all the strange men whose tongues hung out when she danced, so they'd tip her. The smile felt real. It felt good. For the first time ever, she almost felt normal. She wasn't mad anymore. Not even at Alexis.

"If you do come, I'd let you buy me a coffee." She couldn't seem to stop smiling at him.

"Do they even sell coffee at The Cellar?" he asked.

"If they don't, maybe we could just talk. Or go somewhere else."

The phone started ringing.

"You gonna answer it this time?"

"The pool house is locked," she said.

He pulled a key out of his pocket and loped toward it.

Her eyes sparkling, Alexis swam up close to her. "Do you like him, Carmen? Are you going to kiss him? 'Cause if you do, Yolie will get real mad."

"What the hell are you staring at? My life is no concern of yours."

Alexis's smile died. Her eyes grew huge and dark with shuttered pain. Then she hung her head and paddled slowly to the other end of the pool. Once down there, she turned her back on Carmen and refused to look at her again.

When the thin little girl's shoulders slumped, a lump formed in Carmen's throat. Knowing she'd made Alexis sad brought back her own pain as a kid. She was about to go check on her when Xavier came toward her with the phone.

"I don't know who it is, but she wants your mother. Says it's urgent. Says she'll speak to you since you're the only one here."

Carmen took the phone. "Carmen Simon speaking."

A crisp, businesslike, feminine voice nearly bit her ear off. "I'd like to ask her a few questions."

"About what, if I may be so bold as to ask?" Carmen deliberately mimicked the woman's superior-sounding tone.

"And you are whom—"

"Her daughter."

"Her relationship with Dr. Carver," the caller replied.

Strangely, for once in her life Carmen actually felt protective of her mother.

"Carver? He deserved what he got. I'm glad he's dead. For your information, my mother has had nothing to do with him for a year! She didn't kill him. She's a nice person. She wouldn't kill anybody! So leave her alone!"

When the woman brought up the Beamer incident, Carmen hung up on her and scowled down the length of the pool at Alexis, who still had her back turned. The kid looked fragile and sad.

Carmen's scowl deepened. Some screwups had long-term consequences. Like getting pregnant and dropping out of high school.

Like Dr. Pierce Carver. He'd never been nice to her mother. Rosie had been blinded by who he was and what he'd had.

And the cop with the palm tree above his left

nipple. How had they known each other? Why hadn't her mother ever mentioned him?

Carmen got up and dived into the pool. Feeling like a fool, she swam toward Alexis. When she reached her, her daughter wouldn't look at her. Before she thought, Carmen said something really stupid.

"I'm sorry, Alexis. I'm not mad at you. It's me. It's all me. It's always been me."

Alexis turned slowly, her face cautious. "I won't splash you anymore. I promise."

When Carmen reached out and stroked Alexis's cheek, the little girl's mouth quivered uncertainly. Maybe she would have smiled at her again if Mina hadn't called to her.

When Alexis swam away, the aqua water looked like a sea of tears.

Thirteen

Their arms crossed over their chests, Rosie and Joe Benson were squared off, facing each other, in the leafiest, darkest and most private corner of Yolie's front yard.

"You went to the bastard's memorial service?" Benson's dark brows slashed together. "Where you then ran into Nash and got so friendly you let him haul you down to police headquarters?"

Rosie groaned. "Not exactly."

"I had a hellacious day in court, lady. I don't need this!"

"Now that you mention it, my day wasn't all that swift, either," Rosie snapped. "The last thing I need is you lecturing me. What was I supposed to do?" Her voice was tense and defensive, she knew. "He took me to the station in handcuffs."

He'd used handcuffs in bed, too.

"Why didn't you call me?" Benson demanded.

"Instinct."

She felt her face turning red as she remembered how submissive and turned-on she'd been when Michael had handcuffed her wrists to the bedposts.

"Damn it to hell! You didn't sign anything, did you?"

Rosie squeezed her eyes shut. "I don't need this."

"Answer me."

When she opened her eyes, Benson's broad face was so dark and his eyes so feral, she was afraid he might start yelling obscenities or maybe even have a heart attack.

"Okay, so he explained my rights and I signed a few documents. He only did it because I told him to."

"You what?" Benson was a truly frightening shade of purple now. "That bastard! I should strangle him. Don't tell me you signed away your rights! Please don't tell me—"

"I don't know. I just signed everything he gave me."

"What? Without your lawyer present?" He really did sound so unnerved, she began to panic. "That slick son of a bitch."

His words made images flip in her overwrought brain, and she saw a sated and triumphant Michael propped against his pillows after they'd done it the third time. He'd been damp with sweat; his black hair had hung across his brow.

"Unlock me," she'd begged.

"When I'm good and ready," he'd whispered,

nipping the edges of her ear with his teeth. "You have to do what I say—"

"He must have had a field day with you," Benson said.

She stared at him, appalled—both by what she'd done and by what Michael had said.

"You are going to pay for a murder you didn't commit unless you start playing it smart. Why'd you hire me if you're not going to do a damn thing I say?"

"From now on, I'm going to."

"Okay. I say don't talk to the press. And don't fucking talk to Nash unless I'm there."

She nodded. She was going to listen to Joe Benson. He was her lawyer. If a girl couldn't trust her lawyer, who could she trust?

Answer: exactly nobody.

Not Michael—that was for sure.

Fourteen

Michael rolled up his shirtsleeves and pushed back from his desk, knowing he should take himself off the case.

He was crossing a helluva line, and he didn't have any illusions about the consequences if he got caught. But he was too scared for her. Scared of the system and scared somebody was trying to frame her. Then there was the sex and the tightness in his body every time he looked at her or held her.

God, she was hot. Hotter than ever. Ten times hotter. Michael couldn't believe how uninhibited she was.

Don't think about the sex, either. Or how good it had been with her even before she'd grabbed his handcuffs and discarded all her inhibitions.

Hell, pal, if you want to get in her pants again, you'd better focus on this shit.

Michael had been going over the evidence and reading all the reports for hours.

It was past midnight, and he was still at his desk, surrounded by stacks of cardboard file boxes overflowing with office reports, lab reports and photographs, all having to do with the Carver case.

The blurry print was beginning to jump off the page. Too many cups of coffee. He'd gotten so frustrated from going over the endless reports, he'd even weakened and taken a couple of drags from a stale cigarette. The cigarette had left a disgusting taste in his mouth.

Lots of the witness statements conflicted. There were Web printouts, telephone bills and various other documents that contained information on Carver and all the people in his life. Hell, for a popular doctor, it seemed that everybody in town had a motive to kill him.

Michael's personal favorite was a report that had to do with a patient disappointed with the result of his penile reconstructive surgery. The guy's dick worked, all right. Boy, did it. It was just way too big to suit him. He'd gotten more than fifty complaints from women in one year alone since his surgery.

More than fifty women in a year—and this ladies' man was complaining? Ronnie Bob Keith had loved it. With a grim smile, Michael mulled over that one for a while. One thing he'd learned—you never could tell who would kill and who wouldn't. Could be the guy with the oversize dick.

When the print began to blur again, he pitched the thick file folder that had to do with Carver's wives and girlfriends. Stifling a yawn, he rolled his shirtsleeves even higher.

All it took was one fact to be wrong and a detective's entire line of thinking could be off base. Something about this case felt off. Whatever it was, was big.

Keith and he had talked to the guys at the crime lab dozens of times. The blood samples and dental records matched Carver's. Carver had had perfect teeth. Not a single cavity. Fifty years old. He'd gone to the dentist twice a year and had flossed regularly. If only the rest of his life had been as orderly.

Michael's office was hot, so he turned on his fan, which caused pages to flutter. Then, leaning back, he picked up a stack of photographs of the surgeon's body, thumbing through them slowly. Next, Michael shuffled through the shots of the various rooms of Pierce's mansion. Last, he glanced at the pictures of the grounds.

Then he flipped through them again, looking for something, for anything he might have missed. Finally he picked the series of aerial photographs taken from the police helicopter. He was tired—and getting nowhere fast.

Damn it. Carver had told everyone he was scared of her. She'd told everyone she wanted him dead.

Everything pointed to *her*. Maybe that was what bothered Michael the most. It was too pat.

Liar. You want her free so you can fuck her brains out for the rest of your natural-born life.

Heat washed him. He felt ashamed for thinking about her in such crude terms, but no sooner did he walk into police headquarters than his mind sank to the sewer. This soul-killing place did something to all the guys. Nothing was sacred. Especially women.

Not even her. Not even after what he'd shared with her a few hours earlier.

She's the best you've ever had in bed. That's all the hell she is.

You wish, you dumb bastard. She's haunted you and you damn well know it.

She'll dump you the day you clear her.

She was pretty and shallow and fast, and she'd never change. As soon as he cleared her, she'd use her talents to nail another rich guy.

The thought hurt. How could she make him feel shit like nobody else, not even his ex, had ever made him feel?

Inner civil war. Rosie had always been able to reduce him to this. Always.

What was it with her daughter? The girl was royally pissed with her. And with him. What the hell had he ever done?

Forget the girl. She doesn't matter. Think murder. Think solution.

One strange thing: the punks he'd interrogated at the scene swore they'd gotten a tip that Carver's garage door would be unlocked. They'd entered the garage just fine, but when they'd touched the car, the alarm had gone off.

Had someone wanted the neighbors to hear and call 911?

When Michael had tried to track down the guy who'd tipped the kids off, he'd gotten nowhere.

Was he too close to the case to think rationally? He ran his hands through his hair. Maybe the department had thrown too many men at this, but when a case got a lot of press, the captain always had to turn the investigation into a five-star cluster-fuck. Now it was way beyond any one man's control. Hopefully, all the legwork would pay off.

Leaning over his desk, Michael looked at the crime scene photos again. The same mutilated bits of pulp and bone that had once been Pierce's face lay on the white carpet at odd angles. His neck was contorted. The bloodied arms were still extended in a reaching motion, his bound fists clenched, most of his fingers nearly severed. The poor bastard had fought for his life.

The gruesome pictures produced nothing in Michael that even remotely resembled an emotion. Was he a cold son of a bitch or what? Even the night of the murder, the sight of the body and the heavy, coppery stench of the victim's blood had barely affected him. Keith and his men had been throwing up and cursing and making crude jokes. Michael had ignored them and snapped on his gloves.

That's the way he was at a scene. He'd always been able to put distance between himself and the murder victim. It wasn't ever a conscious decision.

He relied on his coldness. Such icy detachment was necessary if he was to have any hope of rationally figuring out what the hell had really happened.

Emotions got in the way. That's why he shouldn't even be on this case. He didn't give a damn about Pierce Carver, but he sure as hell cared about Rose Marie Castle.

Everybody in the department except him thought she'd done it. Even Keith thought Michael was wrong. In vain, Michael had cautioned them not to rush to judgment.

"What is it with you?" Keith had yelled. "The bitch bragged to everybody in town she was going to do it—"

The other guys had supported Keith and read him quotes from their interviews.

"—her knife—"

"—she was there, Nash—"

"—what about the incident with the Beamer—"

"—she giving you head—"

Was she ever! While cuffed to his bed.

Damn! That last time he'd never felt so all-powerful. Michael bowed his head and clasped his hands together.

He should take himself off the case. But if he did, a uniform would knock on her door tomorrow, and the handcuffs wouldn't be for fun and games. Maybe she had a nutty streak, but she hadn't done this. Maybe her daddy had put a bullet into *his* daddy, but *she* hadn't done *this*.

Obscenities rolling off his tongue, Michael picked up the pictures again. Then he kicked his chair back, stood up and threw them down. The D.A. had more than enough to make his case.

Michael had to get the hell out of here or go crazy.

He forced himself to sit back down. There had to be a way to rethink this. There had to be.

His cell phone made opera music. Expecting the worst, he flipped it open.

"Hi," Rosie said softly. "It's me."

He hated the way his heart accelerated. "I know."

"We can't see each other again."

He turned Pierce's photos over and stared at them. "Then why are you using your silky bedroom voice, princess?"

"Because I'm sleepy."

"So this is a Dear John call," he whispered, closing his eyes against the pain, and so he wouldn't see Pierce's startled eyes, preferring the image of her coppery hair spilling across a white pillow dappled with sunlight.

"I guess. You know it's the smart move for both of us."

He opened his eyes and was jarred once again by those eyes in the photos. Michael flipped Carver's pictures facedown again.

"What are you doing right now?" she asked, prolonging the call needlessly.

"I'm in the office."

"Oh." She paused, and he felt the tension between them build. "My lawyer stopped by the house and gave me hell for even talking to you," she said. "Says I shouldn't trust you."

"If I were any other cop, I'd agree."

"I'm so confused, not to mention scared."

"Anybody would be."

"I have to do what he says. I don't want to go to jail."

"Rosie, I need to see you. We have to talk."

When she hung up on him, he stood up and stretched.

So—she'd dumped him again. He pitched his phone down on his desk.

Like hell.

He sat down again and worked for another long, frustrating hour and got nowhere.

Why couldn't he ever be blessed with one of those suicide murders the other guys got all the time—where the killer shot his lover and then killed himself? Guys like that were great. Sure, the crime scenes were so gory Keith and the guys lost their lunches and refused to eat pizza with him for a week. But Michael ate them up.

They made a homicide detective's day.

Telling Michael she couldn't see him anymore had shaken Rosie up more than she'd realized. When she went to bed, her mind wouldn't stop. She counted sheep. Then she sang, counting bottles of beer on the wall backward until she was hoarse. When she finally nodded off, she had nightmares.

First, she was cuffed to a bed and Michael was making wild, violent love to her. Suddenly Joe Benson popped up at the foot of it, wearing long black robes and glowering at her. Then a jail door clanged.

When she'd jumped up in a cold sweat, she'd bounded to the bathroom to splash cold water on her face.

In her second nightmare, she'd been in a dark, airless cell. Then the dream twisted, and Pierce was in the cell, too, and she was handcuffed to the bars. He kept saying over and over again, "I don't love you, and I never did." Then he pulled out her knife.

In her next dream she was at Barton Springs wearing nothing. Pierce had one of her hands and Michael the other. Everybody was staring at her while the men played tug-of-war, each pulling on her so hard she felt like she was being torn apart.

Enough already. Exhausted, she arose before dawn and dragged herself from the bed into her bathroom, where she grabbed her old white terry-cloth robe off a hook. Her sleep-mussed hair stuck out in all directions, and there was a bad taste in her mouth. She lowered her head and brushed her teeth.

Since she couldn't sleep, she stumbled down the stairs into Yolie's home office and sat down at the computer. In seconds she was surfing the Internet, skipping the news stories about the murder, reading only Pierce's bios.

There wasn't much about his early beginnings, and what there was conflicted. She found a reference to Beaumont, Texas, but another one to Lake Charles, Louisiana.

She shut off the computer, went to the window and tried to remember everything he'd ever said or done, as she watched the sky brighten above the pecan trees. Lost in thought, she stayed in the office even after she heard Yolie get up and start moving about in the kitchen. Even after she smelled coffee and heard Lula barking to be let out.

Finally, Yolie entered the office, holding two cups of coffee and a newspaper. Although still in her silky red robe, her blond hair was smooth instead of spiky, and she had her makeup on.

They hadn't talked much since the memorial service. Mostly because Yolie had been out of town dealing with a remodeling project at her biggest Taco Bonito restaurant in Victoria.

"You look like something the cat dragged in," Yolie said.

"Couldn't sleep."

Yolie's keys jingled. "I picked up a box of doughnuts this morning. Hopefully, a sugar high will make you feel better."

Why couldn't Yolie learn that doughnuts were

off-limits to forty-year-old-pluses with too many fat cells and slowing metabolisms?

"Don't you dare set the box anywhere near me."

Yolie handed her her coffee first and then the newspaper. "Drink! I bought doughnuts and made the coffee because I wanted you to be fortified *before*... Oh! I nearly forgot. Your guy, Harry, gave me a new key to the warehouse. I'm sending some men over to pick up some tables and chairs."

"Fortified before *what?*"

"Before you check out today's headlines. You're a celebrity, sweetie. Are you sure you won't have a chocolate doughnut?" She pushed the box within grabbing range.

"A celebrity?" Rosie gulped too much hot coffee too fast and yelped when it burned her lips, tongue and throat.

She was strangling when Yolie said, "Front page! Right here!"

Yolie patted her on the back. "Remember how you were upset because all his wives were mentioned in the newspaper and you weren't? Well, this just goes to show you should be careful what you wish for!"

Rosie flipped the paper open. A huge, horrible picture of her filled the first page. She let out a shriek. "My hair!"

"Deep breaths, sweetie."

In the picture her hair was blowing wildly. She was scowling as she ran barefooted from Pierce's house.

"I look so old! What fiend put this in the paper?" Rosie grabbed a doughnut, and ripped off a sweet, gooey chunk and began to gnaw at it.

"If they hadn't blown it up so that it takes up the entire front page, it probably wouldn't be *that* bad," Yolie said.

"But they did blow it up. I look like a crazed ax-murderess. And my hips! Are they really that gigantic?"

"Have another doughnut."

After practically inhaling doughnut number one, she seized number two. "How will I face people? I look way way older than forty! How come I look so mean?"

"You'd just seen Pierce. It gets worse. Read the article. Right here—under the headline Paramour Flees Surgeon's Mansion the Night of Murder."

"Oh, my God! Paramour? I was his fiancée!"

The article began as a rehash of all the other pieces that the paper had run thus far about the murder, until the sadistic journalist brought up Rosie's long-term relationship with Pierce, and her age. They'd interviewed Hazel, who'd said she was glad he was dead, and Carmen, who'd agreed he'd had it coming.

"Oh, my God, did they have to say Daddy was in the mob, too, and that he killed Michael's father? This case is a soap opera."

"No wonder the whole town's hooked on it," Yolie said.

There were various damning quotes from Rosie

about Pierce, each more violent and colorful than the one before.

"I never said half those things!" After gulping down the last of doughnut number two, Rosie reached for a third.

"Maybe you should double up on the folic acid. That's supposed to work wonders for the little gray brain cells. You certainly did say you wanted his head on a platter. And not a week ago, sweetie."

Rosie groaned with her mouth full. Not a pretty sound. "It looks so much worse in big black print! And out of context. I was joking with a friend."

"Well, I for one continue to love the image," Yolie said. "I think it appeals to my religious nature, not to mention my own secret ex-wife fantasies about offing Pierce."

"Michael and that partner of his are going to nail me to the cross."

"I just thought you should see the paper before you go to the hospital and have to face everybody."

"Thanks so much."

"I've got to go."

"Where to this time?"

"Back to Victoria."

"Leave the doughnuts."

Fifteen

How the hell had that damn picture gotten leaked to the newspapers?

Michael sat huddled over the newspaper in his office, glaring at the hideous photo of Rosie, his cup of coffee cold in his hand. He liked the story about Carlo Castellano having shot his father even less. Journalists—they made their living stirring the pot.

Just as he was wondering where the hell to go from here, the door behind him banged open and Captain Steven Foster stepped inside.

Big-boned and tall, Foster filled the tiny office with his forceful presence. Michael snapped to attention and managed a tight smile. His boss's face hardened.

Foster had been a jock in college and had worked his way through school with the help of scholarships, just as Michael had. Like Michael, he'd joined the force and had come up through the ranks. He'd done a stretch in homicide, and had been talented at it.

Still, he'd had a knack for getting himself into trouble and had wound up on the wrong side of several administrations. That he'd gone so far after two very serious political blunders that had involved police corruption at the highest levels was testimony to his iron will and stubborn perseverance. Too bad Foster wasn't one of Michael's fans.

Foster picked up the paper and then set it down. "So, you've seen it. Good. Which brings me to the question everybody in your unit, including your partner and every law-abiding citizen in Austin, is asking—when in the hell are you going to arrest her, Nash?"

"She didn't do it," Michael said, his voice as cold with contempt as the captain's.

"And you know this how?"

"We were kids together." *Lame*. That was the lamest answer he could have given the big man.

"What's this crap about her father shooting your father?"

"Old news. Bottom line—she doesn't have it in her."

"Damn. You knew her? That's it? That is proof positive there's always trouble when a case gets personal."

"I told you. I knew her a long time ago. That's not *that* personal."

Foster picked up the newspaper again. "Her father shot your father. *That's* personal. I'm out on a rotten limb here. You got anything else to give me then, even a tidbit I can feed the sharks before the limb snaps and I'm shark bait?"

"Carver's security cameras are the kind that tape over themselves every thirty minutes. Somebody got to them and stopped them right after she ran out, so she'd be on tape and the real murderer wouldn't be."

"Ever think that maybe this is one of your simple cases—your favorite kind? You know, the perp's so obvious you don't have to think?"

"I don't think so. She's not a danger to the community, and she's not going anywhere. She's got a grandkid and a sick mother. So why pick her up?"

"So my damn phone will stop ringing. I need a report. Today. On my desk before noon! Write me a memo I can take to the mayor or anybody the hell else who calls and stomps all over my ass because of you. People up in Westlake Hills are terrified. The damn memo better be brilliant!"

The door slammed behind Foster.

As he listened to the big man's receding footsteps, Michael buried his head in his hands. A *brilliant* memo? Who'd the captain think he was—fucking Shakespeare?

Still, Foster hadn't taken him off the case or ordered him to arrest her—yet. Michael supposed that decision was support of some kind.

Like hell.

* * *

Oh, my God! If you think nobody knows you're alive, just become the number one suspect in a prominent homicide case!

No sooner had Rosie stepped off the hospital elevator and headed to the nursing station than she realized a morning that had started off badly was about to slide downhill really fast. Everybody, both staff and patients watched her with grim, judgmental expressions as she passed them. Even Beth, her friend, failed to greet her. And Beth owed her. When she finally did speak it was to tell Rosie she was surprised she'd had the nerve to show up.

As the day progressed, she felt increasingly isolated from her former friends and colleagues and life. Suddenly she remembered the completeness she'd felt in Michael's arms, and a rush of desire to call him slammed her.

She grabbed a rubber band out of a dish, pulled it onto her wrist and quickly snapped it. Then she threw herself into her work. At the beginning of her shift, she had three acute one-on-one patients. If that wasn't pressure enough, E.R. called to tell her they had another admit for her.

"I can't. I just can't take anybody else," Rosie told the E.R. nurse.

"Her name's Linda. A bee stung her, and she took a nosedive off some scaffolding while she was painting a house. She fell three stories. Hit her head.

She can't feel anything from the neck down. She needs a miracle…and a really good nurse."

The instant Rosie heard the nature of the woman's injury, her throat began to tighten, and her stomach got queasy. This sort of injury was Rosie's special hot button.

"Look, that's awfully nice of you to have so much faith in me, but, I can't take her. I'll be glad to call intermediate for you."

"All right." The nurse sounded extremely disappointed.

But the intermediate side of the unit was even more tightly staffed than she was, so Rosie ended by calling the E.R. nurse back. "Send her up."

No sooner did she set the phone in its cradle than a reporter called, wanting to talk about Pierce.

Rosie hung up. Since Rosie was acting so glum, none of the staff or patients asked her about Pierce, which was good, because thinking about his murder distracted her and upset her and made her defensive and utterly useless to her patients.

As the hours passed, the urge to call Michael intensified. She should never have let things go so far. Every time she thought of him, she yearned to call him so much she had to pop her wrist several more times.

Finally, Dr. Clayton, who was one of Rosie's favorite neurologists, arrived to examine Linda and to go over the latest reports on her. He had a high forehead, thick black glasses, an intense black gaze, prematurely white, bushy hair, and brows to match, giving him an Albert Einstein look. They'd had a few lukewarm dates once upon a time and were now back to being just friends.

After Clayton was done with the physical exam, he asked Rosie to step out of the room with him.

"So, will she ever have any mobility?" Rosie asked when he looked up from Linda's chart.

"Her injury is at C five-six level, but the cord looks pretty normal. She's fractured four and five vertebrae, but there's no encroachment…."

Rosie's hands began to shake, so she clasped them together. Linda was a lovely looking young blonde who'd confided to her that she was a single mom with three young boys to chase at home.

"Will she be okay?" Rosie asked.

"Okay?" Dr. Clayton drew a long, impatient breath. "Define okay. If she lives, she'll probably be paralyzed from the neck down."

Rosie must have paled because his face softened. "Let's not count her out of the ball game yet. There's always a chance. We'll have to wait until the swelling goes down."

"But she has three little boys."

Clayton drew another one of his long breaths and stared out a window at the hospital parking lot. Lights flashing, an ambulance was roaring up to the E.R.

"I had a patient once…fell off his motorcycle, broke his neck…. It was bad. Worse than this. I didn't think he had a chance in hell. A year later he could walk without a limp." Glancing back at her, Clayton lowered his voice. "Don't ever stop believing in miracles, or you're finished. There's always hope. That's what keeps us going."

The positive sentiment did little to reassure Rosie.

"Doctors...and nurses can't do all that much, can we?" she said.

"Oh, I know why you're so glum. The newspaper!" He said the word so loudly, three heads turned.

She groaned.

"So—how's it going with you?" he asked. "I mean, seriously."

"Fine, I guess."

"Fine?" Clayton raised his bushy eyebrows. "I mean about Carver...getting himself carved...and the cops?"

"The sooner they find who really killed him, the happier I'll be."

"I'd heard talk about you being the one even before the article. Of course, I knew it was all rumors and speculation." He patted her shoulder. "Don't look so depressed. This too shall pass. Tight spots always appear the narrowest right before they open up. Then all hell breaks loose."

He lowered his voice. "When this blows over...do you think maybe we could go out and have a beer? Maybe give it—I'm talking about *us*—another try?"

Us. He was a doctor. And nicer than most. Way nicer than Pierce.

Was he a possible ticket to the glittering train car?

She forced herself to nod and even to smile, but it was strange how little enthusiasm she felt at the thought of dating a nice, respectable doctor. Instead, she was thinking about a hard, dark cop who'd grown up on the wrong side of town. With whom she had a past. Not to mention a shared tattoo, a sex life and a daughter.

"Maybe you should ask for some time off," Clayton said, "until this blows over."

"I'll go crazy if I don't work."

When Dr. Clayton left, Rosie put Beth in charge, and was about to take her break when Margaret Carson, her supervisor, appeared, looking unusually stern. "We need to have a little talk."

But Margaret did all the talking. Five minutes later, Rosie was off the floor on indefinite leave.

Shaken, she checked her voice mail. Her heart lifted when she saw she had three messages from Michael. Then she popped her rubber band and made herself delete them.

The next one was from Harry. Sometimes it seemed that Harry had been working on her burned-out kitchen since the beginning of time.

Harry had sworn on a stack of Bibles—his words, and worrisome since he wasn't religious—to deliver most of her furniture to her house later today, so she'd trustingly arranged for Carmen to take care of Alexis again.

"Dude—" Harry began.

Harry called everybody, man, woman, cat, dog, ant, mouse, enemy, friend, boss, and himself—*Dude*, probably because then he didn't have to challenge his pot-befuddled brain to remember names.

"Dude—like, four o'clock sharp is okay with me, too. Your place," Harry had sworn. "Like me and the guys'll be there. Really! Stack of Bibles!"

She called Harry back and got his machine.

"—your call is, like, superimportant to the Dude. So, like, leave the Dude a message—"

"See you at four," she said, and hung up.

Mirabella Camrett had left another message.

Rosie punched Delete.

The next call was from a guy who wanted to rent one of her vacant houses in East Austin, so she called him back and left Harry's number.

Since Carmen had Alexis, and Rosie was now unemployed, she had plenty of time to stop by Pierce's office and do a little investigating before her date with Harry. Naturally, Michael had forbidden her to do any such thing, his point being that cops were professionals and she wasn't. But after thinking about it, she'd decided that since she'd briefly worked with Pierce's staff, they, especially Karen, the office manager, who was a friend, might open up to her more than they would to homicide detectives.

She was the one in the tight spot! She *had* to find out if anybody at the office had the slightest clue as to who might have really killed Pierce with her favorite paring knife.

Her cell phone rang. When she pulled the phone out of her pocket and read Michael's name in digital blue, her heart beat faster. When she didn't answer, and he left a message, her heart jumped to her throat and thudded even faster. She wanted to hear his voice. She wanted to tell him that the hospital had let her go for a while and that she felt awful about it. Instead, she popped the rubber band on her wrist three more times.

Sixteen

Oh, my God! There were way too many mirrors!

Except for the lights over Pierce's big, bold paintings, his dimly lit, mirrored offices were lavish and starkly modern. The instant Rose Marie stepped through the chrome-and-glass doors, she was so disconcerted by all her reflections, she lifted her chin. Then she caught herself and felt self-conscious. For a long moment she experienced a terrifying sensation of déjà vu. It almost seemed to her that Pierce would step through the door, call her by name and start complaining that she didn't look glamorous enough, before he started barking orders at her.

Her throat went dry. She wasn't glad he was dead, but she was glad that he was no longer part of her life.

The waiting room felt more like a VIP lounge or a salon rather than a medical office. Long-stemmed red roses graced every corner, bloodred blossoms spilling out of tall crystal vases. Zebra rugs were thrown across the floor with careless abandon. All the chairs were chrome and brown leather. The furniture was huge, too, so that a patient, whatever her size, would be comfortable. Terra-cotta tree stumps served as small tables for magazines and coffee cups, adding just the right quirky touch.

Pierce had always been the first to arrive. He'd straightened the magazines, removed skin creams his girls had left out on the counter. Only when he'd been happy with the way everything looked in the salon had he gone to the back and reviewed the photos of that morning's surgery patient.

The patient photos were always so detailed they'd shown every pore. He would mark them up, making with ink the cuts that he would later make with the scalpel. He'd been very meticulous beforehand because a mistake in the operating room was so costly.

Rosie fought an odd sensation of panic that seemed to have something to do with the persistent feeling he was still alive, just around a corner or behind a door.

Why was she afraid of him? He was dead.

She touched a chair and was flooded with more memories. Determined that his outer offices be perfect, he'd hired designer after designer. In the end he'd thrown all the designers out and had stayed up night after night redesigning the offices himself.

"When my patients enter *that*," he would say, pointing at the front entry, "I want them to know they are crossing a threshold into a completely different world, *my world*, where they can become different people, their dream selves. Here they can dream of miracles."

"Miracles? Are you God?"

"All surgeons desire to play God. I want my patients to believe they can change from the inside out. I mean, to totally change. It's more than the knife."

Pierce had had the typical surgeon's personality. Not for him the treatment of slow, chronic diseases. He'd seen everything in black-and-white. To him there'd been no gray. He'd understood about consequences, too. And loose ends.

"Unlike a painter, I can't throw a bad canvas away. I have to live with my mistakes or be sued for them. I have to pay attention to detail…and tie up loose ends. When I make mistakes, I always try to learn from them."

Not that he'd dwelled on his mistakes. He'd been capable of instant, irrevocable decisions—like dumping her for Anita.

In Pierce's time the waiting room would have been jammed. Today, the hushed room contained only two women. Their gazes lowered, they sat as far from each other as possible. Dr. Morgan must work at a much slower pace.

At the reception desk Rosie asked to see Karen, the office manager. Soon she was rushed back to Karen's inner sanctum.

The two old friends hugged for a lengthy interval.

"Did I come at an awful time?"

"No," Karen said. "As you can see, we're not busy. Not like when Dr. Carver was alive. I do have to talk to Dr. Morgan as soon as he finishes conferring with his next patient. But we can steal a few minutes."

Karen ordered green tea, and they sat down, facing each other across Karen's cluttered desk.

The brightly lit office was plain beige, and her furniture was old and functional; the outer salon was merely for show. Karen had a short pixie haircut and looked far more glamorous than her office. She'd had a lot of work, both to her face and her body. Even though she had to be fifty, she appeared years younger. Rosie envied her perfect chin and the way her green silk suit hugged her lithe body.

"You've lost weight, in all the right places," Rosie said.

"Job benefits. Dream diet…liposuction."

They both laughed.

"I didn't kill him," Rosie said rather too abruptly.

Karen reached across her desk and clasped Rosie's hand. "Neither did I."

They both laughed again.

"I never thought you did," Karen said in a more serious vein, letting her hand go. "You got even when you painted him with a dick that looked like a shriveled peanut. Oh, my God, was he mad!"

"You saw it?"

Karen's smile died. "It must be awful. Your picture in the papers, everybody thinking that you... Not me, ever imagining such a ridiculous thing, of course. You're all talk and no do. Not like Pierce... Dr. Dynamite, our whirlwind in bed and out of it. He always stuck to his plans, didn't he?"

"Right." Rosie bit her lip. "Carson gave me an indefinite leave of absence from I.C.U. today. I don't know what I'll do with myself. From the moment Pierce was found dead, I've been in hell."

"I can imagine. Dr. Carver... He was like a force of nature. Especially when it came to his women. Why couldn't he ever be satisfied with anything or anyone? He made poor little Anita utterly miserable, especially after her daughters came up. He completely overpowered her. And now, even in death, he is still stirring things up for you and probably for her, too. Not that it's his fault he got murdered."

"What if it was his fault? I mean, do you have any idea if Pierce was in any kind of trouble?"

The room went quiet. In the expanding silence, Karen's black pupils grew huge.

"I'm asking these questions because I'm afraid the police will just lock me up, throw away the key, and I'll never find out who really killed him."

"Do you have any idea who did it?"

"No. Only that it's somebody vicious who hates me, who's deliberately setting me up. I don't go around making enemies, so none of this makes sense. So, how did he and Dr. Morgan get along?"

Karen's smile grew tense. "On the surface, they had a polite enough professional relationship."

"But?"

"They never seemed genuinely friendly. But then you knew Dr. Carver better than me. Still, beneath all the outward charm, he was the most deeply reserved man I ever met. He was so me, me, me, wasn't he?"

"You mean arrogant?"

"More than arrogant. Most doctors are arrogant."

"Did Dr. Morgan and he argue?"

"Dr. Morgan accused Dr. Carver of stealing some of his patients. But it blew over."

Or did it?

"How long have you worked for him?"

"Fourteen years."

"What about his childhood? Did he ever mention it?"

Karen sipped her tea. "Once, a long time ago. He mentioned sledding. You know I grew up in the north, so I think I said something about snow. Then he said he used to go sledding with his sister or brother. A sister, I think. I remember he stopped himself. He got very upset when I kept pressuring him to tell me more."

Sledding seemed an odd sport for the places he'd mentioned living, even East Texas.

"Pierce had a sister?"

"When I asked him, he became very abrupt. He

said his sibling died young. I said I was sorry, and he said it had been a long time ago. Then he turned his back on me and walked out of the room. I guess some people never get over early losses like that."

"Did he receive any strange calls, especially in the last few months?"

"As a matter of fact…he did. But something else that was even stranger happened…."

"What?"

"Well, you know how doctors are about being on call. I mean, their schedules are made and posted months in advance. Well," Karen continued, "about three weekends ago, Dr. Carver was supposed to take call for the group. Only he vanished. Into thin air. He couldn't be reached all night Friday, and all of Saturday. Anita didn't know where he was, and seemed to be both frantic and furious at him about it when I phoned her. Let me tell you, Dr. Morgan was pretty upset. He had to cancel a golf tournament. He kept calling me right up until the tournament started to find out if I'd heard from Dr. Carver. When Dr. Carver finally phoned in on Sunday, he acted like nothing was wrong. In fact, he said he'd been on call the whole time, talking to the girls at the answering service, taking calls from patients. He said he'd been hunting at a ranch in the hill country, and his cell phone only worked on a high hill. It was very strange."

"I can't imagine him doing such a thing. Pierce didn't even hunt."

"It was most erratic. He wouldn't talk about it on Monday. By Tuesday he was himself again, and he promised to take call for Dr. Morgan any weekend he wanted him to. The incident was brushed over and forgotten."

"You said someone was phoning him."

"Yes, a man, I think. Dr. Carver seemed upset by these calls, and he always took them in his office. When the calls became more frequent, Dr. Carver seemed increasingly agitated about them. Not that he ever said anything, but I noticed he was always tense afterward. Then this man showed up one day. He didn't have an appointment, but he pretended he was a patient."

"But you didn't believe him?"

"No. His voice reminded me too much of the caller's voice. From across the room, he looked a little like Dr. Carver. Yet when he came closer, he didn't at all. They were the same height. Their posture and their gait and the shape of their heads were similar, too. At first, I thought that maybe they might have been related. When I got a better look at him, I saw how different they were. The stranger looked older and wasn't nearly as handsome."

Footsteps sounded outside. Then Dr. Morgan burst through the door with a couple of thick patient charts in his hand.

He started to say something, and then his jaw dropped.

"Rosie! What are you doing here?"

Rosie stiffened.

"Karen, I should think you'd know her presence here is not at all appropriate right now. *Dr. Carver was murdered.*"

"All right. I'm going," Rosie said.

"Wait!" When he jumped in front of the door, she sat back down in her chair. "Karen, would you give us a minute?"

When Karen looked at her, Rosie grinned. "It's okay. I'll scream if he attacks me. Or I'll hunt up my new paring knife."

Dr. Morgan's smile tightened the instant Karen left. "Let's get something straight, Castle. Maybe you used to work here, but this is my office now. I don't want you here upsetting my staff or my patients. It's no secret you wanted Carver dead. Don't think he didn't tell me what a nutcase you are and how terrified he was of you. Well, now he's dead, and I for one find that highly suspicious."

"So much for your detective skills."

"You are nuts. Don't call my wife again."

"As if I ever would."

"I know perfectly well you two have talked."

Rosie didn't think it was a very good time to tell him that Ticia had always been the one who phoned her.

If only she'd just gotten up from her chair like a lady and tiptoed meekly out the door. But visions of her scowling face decorating the bottoms of every birdcage in Austin because some sicko was out to get her had Rosie on edge.

"You know, Morgan, the reason you're probably so anxious to pin the murder on me is because you wanted him dead more than I did. Does he owe you money or something?"

Dr. Morgan turned purple. "Who told you that?"

She smiled sweetly. "I heard he had problems obtaining medical insurance."

"Out! Now! And don't ever come back!"

"As if I'm enjoying myself *so* much—"

"I'll call the police if you don't leave."

All pretense of trying to act like a lady left her. She took a step toward him. "Careful, you're making me mad."

His eyes bulged with alarm.

She tipped her chin up. "Settle down. I'm not in the mood to slice up another doctor today. One more thing—from the looks of your waiting room, I wonder if his practice wasn't carrying yours. Pierce couldn't have been too happy about that. What about you? Were you jealous of him? Jealous enough to—"

Morgan ripped the phone off Karen's desk and punched 911. In no mood to chat with the police, Rosie stormed out.

She was charging full speed ahead across the zebra throw rugs when her toe caught the edge of a zebra tail. The outer door swung open and Anita ran inside so fast that when Rosie tripped, they collided.

Anita recoiled. "*You!* You, the paramour! You kill my husband! Why are you here? In his office?"

"Could we go somewhere?" Rosie asked softly. "Someplace where we could talk? Have some tea?"

Before we hear sirens?

"Talk? Tea? You kill my husband! He always say he very scared of you!"

"Don't be such a hypocrite. You were separated."

"That's a lie. A lover's quarrel. I was back the next day."

"No, you lie. What unpleasant truth are you covering up? He was abusing you, wasn't he, not me. You had a better reason…"

Anita turned white. Then she ran.

Foot in mouth! Stupid! Why had she said that, of all things?

Rosie hesitated for only the briefest second. Then she gave chase.

Seventeen

"Stop, Anita. Please…I just want to talk to you!"

When she kept running, Rosie raced down the hall to catch up with her. Anita was banging her palm against the elevator buttons when she rounded the corner.

"I don't know why the police haven't locked you up," Anita said, her black eyes huge with fear as she backed against the wall.

"Maybe because I didn't kill him."

"I didn't, either," Anita said, but rather too vehemently.

The elevator doors pinged and then opened. Anita looked inside and then looked at Rosie. The doors pinged and then closed again.

Rosie hit the button once more. The doors pinged and opened.

"Look, I'm just trying to find out who did kill him.

Why don't you let me buy you a cup of coffee…or rather, green tea…or whatever you'd like? There's a nice little place downstairs in this very same building, a healthy café."

She didn't mention she'd helped Pierce design and set up the little restaurant not long before he'd dumped her for Anita. She'd even loaned Pierce some of her own money, which he'd never repaid.

"I—I don't think so," Anita said.

"It's not like you'd be driving to some strange place with me. You'd be perfectly safe. We'll be in a public building."

The doors to another elevator opened. This time Rosie reached inside and held them.

"I didn't like you coming to the house…the day of the service," Anita said.

"I don't like a lot of things about this whole thing myself," Rosie said. "Pierce and I *were* engaged."

"You say you want to kill him. He say he very scared of you. Everybody say you kill him."

"You walked out on him, too. Look, maybe we have more in common than we know. Are we going downstairs together or not?" Rosie asked.

Anita ran her hands through her hair and sighed. Slowly, warily, she unpeeled her tall, slim body from the wall. Keeping alert eyes on Rosie, she backed into the elevator.

"I didn't kill him," Rosie repeated as the doors closed and the elevator whished downward.

Rubbing her arms as if she were cold, Anita stared straight ahead. "Why you here? Why you want to talk to me when I know you don't like me."

"Okay, I admit that I might have been unhappy with you about Pierce jilting me the day of the wedding and then marrying you so fast."

Anita frowned and kept staring straight ahead. "You paint picture of him that make everybody laugh. He hate you for that."

"Okay, not a nice thing to do. All I can say is that I was more than a little unhappy. I was getting over him, but he's dead now. So, you and I don't have to be jealous of each other anymore. The problem I have is lots of people think I killed him." Since she wasn't sure how good Anita's English was, she spoke very slowly and loudly. "This is why I want to find out what was going on in his life. So I can figure out who might have wanted him dead."

When the elevator stopped on the first floor, Rosie got out and then waited for Anita before leading her down the hall to the Health Nut.

After Rosie got her green tea with artificial sweetener and a sack of unsalted almonds, and Anita, who was slimmer and younger, her ice cream with chocolate and walnuts, they sat across from each other in a booth by a window. In between spoonfuls of luscious looking chocolate ice cream, Anita rubbed her slender arms.

"Why did you leave Pierce?" Rosie asked.

"I didn't kill him," Anita said.

"Okay, I believe you. Just suppose for now that I didn't do it, either, and you believed me."

Anita stared at her for a long time. Curiously, the idea of Rosie's innocence seemed to alarm her even more. "I—I still couldn't trust you. You chased him with your big car. You crazy."

"Emotional. He owed me rent. He wouldn't take my calls." She paused. "Look, I know how difficult Pierce can be."

"But you hate me! You probably want me to be blamed because I'm just a poor defenseless immigrant without any friends in this country!"

"Like I said, I probably know better than anybody how difficult Pierce could be."

"You want to know why I leave? Okay, I tell you. Pierce, he don't give me any cash except for food. He make me spend my allowance on his food, and when I cook, he throw it in the garbage. Why he do that? Why he don't give me any cash? He rich. Why he don't leave me nothing in his will? Why lawyer say he no have money? He made millions. I have my daughters to educate. He know that. I didn't come to this country to be poor. Nobody comes to America to be poor. I could be poor in Guatemala. He want me to be his maid—not his wife. That not right."

"Why did you marry him, then?"

"Because I think I love him. He was very nice to me before we marry. He buy me car, take me places.

To the movies. He sail his boat. He pay for operation for my daughter. Then we marry and I move here. When my daughters move here, he change."

Was that true? Had she loved him? Or at least convinced herself she had? She had two daughters to raise and educate. Who knew what her situation had been in Guatemala?

Had Anita wanted the good life, or the party in the sparkling train car just as Rosie had? Had Pierce sensed her need and seen a way to use that?

Anita had certainly left her country and her family. She'd brought her daughters here, and had trustingly made herself totally dependent on Pierce.

Pierce liked seeing himself as superior to his women—financially, socially and educationally. Rosie remembered how perfect he'd seemed in the beginning. Then he'd begun putting her down in casual conversation. First, he'd put her talent as an artist down. Then her appearance and family, especially Carmen.

He'd liked being in control. Maybe he'd liked it too much. He'd wanted a woman to be completely his. That was why he'd never wanted them to be attached to anyone else, like their own children or grandchildren.

"Where did you go after you left Pierce?"

"It was just a temporary separation."

"Where did you go?"

Anita lowered her gaze furtively. "To a friend's house."

"Why did you leave him?"

"He insult my daughters. When they fight back, he get furious and say they have to go back to Guatemala to their father. He break their stuff. He drink. I never see that side of him before. I very scared. But my counselor..."

"Your counselor? Who?"

"I mean my friend." Anita glanced down at her watch. "I late. I've got to go."

"Did he get phone calls from people you didn't know? Did he act upset about them?"

Anita, who was still looking at her watch, blinked rapidly. She pushed her half-eaten bowl of ice cream away and put her hands on her slim waist. "My daughters! They get out of school soon. I have to pick them up."

"Wait."

Anita stood up. "They are very scared and mad with me for bringing them to this country. They say they want to live with their father. I tell them no because if they leave me, I'll have nobody here."

"Why don't you go back to Guatemala?"

"This is nice country, but they don't believe it. Now their father is coming because of the murder. He don't like it that I brought them here, but I know better future here. Whoever kill Pierce, she ruin everything."

"Were you there that night? At the house? The night he was murdered?"

Anita's flashing dark eyes darted wildly.

"You were!"

"I came back for my things. They were in the basement! Why I tell you this—" Anita, her eyes huge, got up and ran.

"Wait! You've got to tell me what you saw that night."

Just as Rosie reached the door of the Health Nut, Michael pushed it open. His eyes were shadowed, weary.

When she attempted to run past him, he grabbed her arm.

"What do you think you're doing?" His voice was low and hard.

"Are you here to arrest me?"

"Don't tempt me. I picked up a call from a pretty irate doctor about you."

When Anita vanished at the end of the hall, Rosie stamped her foot and tried to pull loose. He merely tightened his grip.

"She's gone," he said. "Forget her. Okay, so what are you doing over here, anyway?"

"My lawyer says I'm not supposed to be talking to you, so I'm terminating this conversation."

"The hell you are. I've gone out on a long, very rotten limb for you, princess. And I've put a lot of important people on that limb, too."

"Your choice."

"My captain wants me to arrest you."

"Go ahead...or let me go!"

"At least if you were in jail, I'd know where you were. Ever since you got yourself plastered all over the front page, the department has been besieged with phone calls from all sorts of people. And now here you are, out stirring up more of Austin's citizens."

"Have you checked Pierce's phone records?"

"Don't tell me how to do my job."

There was that tone she hated. "Have you? Did you know he received threatening phone calls?"

"I'm probably way better at this than you are, princess."

He was staring at her mouth and then her breasts in a way that distracted the hell out of her, so she crossed her arms.

"Rosie, you've got to quit harassing people."

"I will just as soon as *you* solve Pierce's murder." She glanced down at her watch. "Oh, my God…" She tried to pull free, but his hand clamped harder.

"I've got to be somewhere," she said. "People to meet."

"Who are you going to harass next?"

"I wish. But it's just an appointment with Harry. Don't look so glum. I told you about him. His guys should be at the house with some of my furniture right now. So, much as I'm enjoying this, he'll leave if I don't get over there."

"I'm going with you."

"I've got a better idea—investigate this case, not me."

"Hey, I'm hanging out with the number one suspect."

"I didn't do it. Go chase number two."

"There is no number two."

She stared at him as he slowly loosened his fingers. The second he withdrew his hand and she was free, she dashed down the hall and out to her car. Unfortunately, he loped along beside her.

When she reached her vehicle, which was at the far end of the parking lot so other cars wouldn't ding it, she was panting a little. His smile as well as the fact he wasn't the least bit winded infuriated her. She was in shape, damn it.

"Quit looking so superior."

"By the way, princess, you'll probably think this is good news—I got a nasty phone call from your attorney."

"Good. It's high time he did something to earn his big fat paycheck." Benson hadn't sent her a bill yet, but she was sure he would. "Michael. Listen. Just listen to me for once. I regret the sex."

"Do I have a vote on that subject? Two of us did the tango, you know. I for one enjoyed the hell out of it."

She felt her cheeks heat and her nostrils actually flare. "Lower your voice—please! And *listen*. I take full responsibility for what happened. But—bottom line—I don't want to see you or date you, ever again. Translation—I don't want to sleep with you."

She unlocked her car.

"And I know why you're determined to believe that," he said, holding her door open for her as if he were a gentleman, which, of course, he wasn't. He was merely holding it, so she couldn't drive off.

"Because I remind you of East Austin and who you really are," he said. "You think you're better than me, but you're not. And you prove it—every time I lay a hand on you in the bedroom. You haven't changed. Don't forget, the handcuffs were your bright idea. Do you remember the night you got me to tie you to the palm tree?"

With a grimace, she pushed at his chest and then grabbed the door from him and slammed it so hard the Beamer shook, which made her even madder because slamming doors was no way to treat the Beamer.

At her show of temper, he smiled.

"Go to hell," she whispered. She turned her key with a vengeance.

"If you'll come, too."

She got the engine started and spun gravel, which she hoped hit him somewhere sensitive. She swerved out onto the street, narrowly missing an oncoming truck. When, after honking madly, the driver shot her the finger, she raised her hand and did the same. Then she stepped on the gas.

The only suspect!

She clenched the steering wheel, furious when the other cars and the trees began to blur.

She wiped her eyes and stomped down harder on her accelerator. Michael had better not follow her.

But when she turned the next corner, she caught sight of his unmarked, blue Crown Vic in her rearview mirror.

Despite being so furious, not to mention upset at him, her mouth twitched.

Knowing he was behind her did not please her.

Repeat: did not please her.

Eighteen

Rosie made the corner onto her street on two
wheels, only to let out a yelp of dismay. Her once-
charming, two-story cottage, shaded by two grandiose pecan trees, seemed lost and ashamed of itself
in the dense shade. After months of work, her
house remained barely visible behind the mountains of lumber stacked on the front lawn that she'd
once watered and mowed so painstakingly to
impress her neighbors. Harry's awful orange,
portable potty still dominated the landscape. Did
he not see the need to ever empty his rusted-out
Dumpster, which was overflowing with Sheetrock,
boards and paint cans?

Rosie's bad feeling got worse when she whizzed
past a line of cars parked behind the Dumpster. The
people sitting in those cars—surely they weren't
waiting for her. But the stern, full-figured woman

standing guard beside the awful, pumpkin-colored portable potty definitely was.

Rosie gritted her teeth and waved at Mirabella just as Scooter, her white terrier, lifted a hairless leg and sent a thin dribble onto the orange potty.

No sooner had Rosie swerved into her drive and hopped out of her car, than she found herself crunching across glass and nails and brown grass on her way to the front door. Car doors banged open. Men and women with notebooks and pencils shot after her.

"Ms. Castle—I'm with the *Austin Weekly*—"

"CBS. We'd really like to talk to you about Dr. Carver."

A dozen flashes went off.

Shielding her face, Rosie made it to her front door in record time. Still, Mirabella, who had to drag Scooter, beat her there.

"Ms. Castle. On behalf of the neighborhood association, I'm here to discuss your portable potty, which has been an issue in this community for nearly a year."

"Not the same one. They change it every week."

Mirabella glared. "I know that. I've left dozens of messages, which you never bother to return. This bathroom facility is a public eyesore and a disgrace, not to mention a life-threatening liability."

"Life-threatening? Surely you exaggerate."

"If you'd ever listen to your messages, you'd know that only yesterday Dougie Thompson locked my Henrietta in it for three whole hours."

Reporters were writing in their little notebooks. Henrietta, a bossy, stout, little big-mouth in blond pigtails, was a miniature Mirabella. Needless to say, she wasn't the most popular of the pigtail set, who cruised their bikes up and down the block. She'd made Alexis's life miserable, too.

"I'm sorry. I'll talk to Harry. First thing."

"That giant-size child who supposedly works for you? He backed his truck over my petunia bed yesterday when I was telling him to move the potty."

Fortunately, before Mirabella could list any more of Harry's crimes, Michael's brakes squealed. Since there was nowhere to park his Crown Victoria on the street, he swerved into Rosie's driveway, narrowly missing the Beamer's back bumper.

"Your house has become a blight on the neighborhood. Where did you grow up?"

"East Austin," Michael replied cheerily as he alighted from the Crown Vic. "So did I." He crunched through the glass and hurried past the horde of reporters, who had them surrounded now. Within seconds he loomed over Rosie and Mirabella.

If everybody else in town could get here, where the heck was Harry? Not to mention her furniture?

"You're that cop," Mirabella said. "I saw your picture in the paper."

When Michael nodded, an excited murmur went through the reporters, and they edged closer.

Michael's features hardened, maybe in an attempt to look professional.

"And I saw your picture, too!" Mirabella added, glancing back at Rosie. "I guess I should be grateful you didn't stab him in your house! I wouldn't want property values to plummet."

"I didn't kill anybody!"

"The portable potty is probably almost as bad as a murder," Michael said, with such cheerfulness Rosie felt like smacking him. Instead, she fished her keys out of her purse.

For a split second she almost wished she still lived in East Austin. Over there a usable portable potty that paid professionals replaced on a regular basis would have been deemed an asset.

Rosie had worked hard to buy this house because people who lived in neighborhoods like this were accepted. She drove her Beamer, instead of a Honda like the one she'd bought Carmen, for the same reason.

So, with such a house and car, why didn't she feel like she was partying in Woody's sparkling train car?

When another reporter rushed up and snapped a picture, Rosie began fluffing her hair. Before she could smile, Michael grabbed her key out of her hand, jammed it into the door and opened it. Then he seized her elbow, pushing her forward.

"Are you here to arrest her, Detective Nash?"

"Any day now." He shot the woman the same

lopsided smile that had seduced Rosie twenty-two years ago under those palm fronds.

"Why not now?" the reporter demanded, holding her microphone close to his mouth.

"Jails are expensive, and she's high maintenance. Let's just say I'm saving the taxpayers big bucks. Not to mention headaches. Oh—that's off the record."

He shoved Rose Marie farther inside and slammed the door.

"Jackals," he growled, shooting the bolt. Then he turned and studied her across the mountains of boxes that contained her household goods, which still reeked of smoke. His dark face was stern.

"Did you hear even one word that I said in the parking lot?" she muttered, noting the progress Harry had made painting the inside of her house.

"I heard."

"Since I'm not supposed to be alone with you or talk to you, I'd better call Benson."

Michael moved in closer. "You're full of crap. You know that, don't you? We click."

"We don't click." Breathing faster, she moved around a pile of boxes as if to hide from him.

"Is that a challenge?"

"It's a simple statement of fact."

"Facts?" He leaped around the boxes. "You aren't into facts. I'm into facts. You, princess, are into fantasy. That's one of the things I like about you, but it's what's gotten you into so much trouble. You're always trying to be something you aren't, and to impress people who don't matter and who will never care about you, when all sorts of perfectly nice people like me really do care for you."

"I want you to go. Harry will be here any minute. Look at this place. Surely, even you can see there's a lot to do."

He ran his hand through his hair. "My men want this case to go down. All of them are second-guessing me. Every hour, they show me a new nail to put in your coffin."

"That's really really great news. Thanks for sharing."

He went to the window and stared out at the crowd of reporters in the front yard. "I don't know how much longer I can protect you." His dark eyes were bleak when he turned back to her.

As she looked up from reading a label on a box, she realized how hard this must be for him. "I neither want nor need your protection."

Liar.

"All right. I'll tell my captain you'd rather go to jail."

"I didn't say that."

"What did you say?"

"How much time do I have?"

"A day, maybe two. Hell, who knows? Maybe a week. Maybe more. Maybe everybody will simmer down. Maybe we'll get a break."

"Like what?"

"A juicy copycat murder, committed when you have an alibi."

She went to the window. Mirabella was skulking off toward her own house, dragging Scooter, who was digging his toenails into the sidewalk, behind her. The reporters were back in their vehicles, windows rolled up, air-conditioning on.

"If things are so dire, then why am I moving back into my house?"

"You tell me. Why are you?" His voice was husky. "Maybe so we'll have somewhere private to make out."

"It's over," she whispered.

"That's why you slept with me and were multiorgasmic. Hell, I had to pull your fingernails out of my back."

"Not something I'm proud of. I hadn't had sex in a year!"

"Aha! Since me!"

She played hide-and-seek behind her boxes with him. After a brief chase and scuffle, he caught her and pulled her into his arms.

She knew she should take affront at his cocky attitude, but before she could muster an intelligent argument, his mouth was on hers, savage and hard. She forgot all about struggling because the instant her skin touched his, she felt herself pulled into a vortex of pleasurable sensations she was too weak to resist.

Still, she tried. "I—I told you—you and me—it can't work out."

"Right." With a fingertip, he lifted her chin.

"You'd rather unpack boring boxes than kiss me? Funny, you don't seem the housekeeper type."

His knuckles slid against her temples, skimming her skin and wreaking havoc with her nerves. Her breath sped up. So did her heart.

"Give me one good reason and maybe I'll give up."

"I thought *no* was supposed to be all a girl had to say."

He rubbed his nose against hers. "It would be if I wasn't so sure you felt differently."

Oh, why couldn't she resist laying her cheek against his? Feeling his warmth in every pore of her body, she snuggled closer. His arms tightened around her until they were molded pelvis to pelvis. After that it was only natural to sigh as she inhaled his scent. Then, for the life of her, she couldn't resist putting her arms around him, too, and pressing her body into his.

When she moaned in longing, he kissed her again. This time, he was as awkward as he'd been as a crazy kid under those palms, his kisses hungry, his tongue plunging inside as deeply as it would go.

Abruptly, he let her go, but his hot eyes moved over her. Wanting the same thing he did, she stepped into his embrace again, gasping his name. "Michael. Michael. You make me so crazy. You always have. You always will."

She reached up to unbutton his shirt. She hadn't managed even three buttons before she laughed and started tugging him by the collar down the hallway.

"We don't have much time," she whispered, frantic to have him now.

They were halfway down the hall when a heavy vehicle backfired on the street outside and then jumped the curb and drove up across the lawn. Even before the truck doors slammed open and the men shouted, she knew who it was. Only Harry parked on what was left of the grass.

"Harry," she moaned, at the sound of his heavy boots storming up her sidewalk.

A hard fist banged violently on her front door. Next, her doorknob jiggled. Her doorbell buzzed four or five times. The fist-banging resumed.

"Don't answer it," Michael whispered, his breathing labored.

But she was already pulling away and running a hand through her hair. "Button your shirt. Fast. Harry's got a key."

No sooner had she said that than the bolt slid in the lock.

"Saved by the cavalry," Michael whispered in a low, raw tone.

By the time the door opened, Rosie and Michael were standing on opposite sides of her living room, goofily innocent expressions on their flushed faces as they tried to press the wrinkles out of their clothes. When Harry roared inside, and then stopped, Michael turned his back and stared out at the backyard as if fascinated by a pair of squirrels squabbling over acorns.

"Dudes! Am I interrupting something?"

"No!" Rosie snapped.

"'Cause if I am, we could do this another time."

"This is a great time." She ignored Michael's groan. "But why do you have to always park on the grass?"

Harry's face went blank the way it always did when she tried to have this conversation.

"Is he a cop? *The* cop?" Harry muttered under his breath.

Michael flashed his badge.

"Dude!" Harry held his hands up as if in mock surrender. All-business, he turned back to Rosie. "Like, where do you want your stuff?"

"You can put the beds in the bedrooms. My big bed in the biggest bedroom."

Harry headed outside and shouted to his men. "Dudes—"

"You mean you didn't even have a bed?" Michael's eyes glittered. "What did you have in mind? Something kinky—like standing against the wall with me slamming into you from behind?"

"Go! Now!"

"Your big friend has definitely ruined the mood, and I've got to get back to work," Michael said, his tone glum. "The main thing was, I didn't want you coming over here alone."

"Why?"

"Gut instinct says this whole thing is as much about you as it is about Pierce."

She shivered. Sometimes she hated it when people agreed with her theory.

When he went outside, she wandered through the house, forcing herself to make a checklist of everything that still needed to be done. But her hands shook.

The bedrooms looked good, almost livable after Harry's men set up the beds and her chests of drawers.

"Dude. It's just the kitchen, really," Harry said, joining her there. "That's really all that's left. "We're going to install your granite countertops tomorrow."

Taco, Harry's right-hand man, lifted a slab of granite. "Love the color," he exclaimed.

"Well, I didn't pick it out," she said. "Harry lost my list and chose the wrong color."

"But it's great, and like, it was way cheaper," Harry stated.

"It's...okay."

She was tired of their futile argument, so to avoid more bickering, she went to her back window and watched Michael outside. He strode to the edge of the overgrown lot behind her house, his tall form vanishing into the woods for a while. Just when she was growing anxious, he popped out of the trees and headed toward her shed, disappearing inside for another long spell that made tension build within her again.

What was he looking for? He thought she was in danger. A chill went through her. He was trying to protect her. On some level she liked that, even though his concern terrified her.

She touched her lips, which still burned from his kisses. It was strange the way their paths kept crossing. Sort of nice…but scary, too. Because it meant she might have to change some things.

Suddenly she knew that even if they didn't make it, she had to tell him about Carmen. She had to tell Carmen, too. It was the right thing to do. It was time. Way past time.

Later. With Pierce's murder, the time to confess wasn't right now. While her thoughts and emotions were still in a muddle, Harry joined her.

"Dude, like, we're done moving your furniture."

He saw Michael. "Like, I'm sorry about all the trouble you've been having. Bummer."

"Thanks."

He slapped his forehead. "Dumb and getting dumber."

"What?"

"I nearly forgot." He opened her hand, pulled a tagged key out of his jean pocket and dropped it into her open palm.

"Your new warehouse key. I've been meaning to give it to you."

"New keys again?"

"I told you, remember? I got a call. Somebody saw a light on in your warehouse down on Fifth Street. Said the door was left open, so anybody could've gotten in. I checked it out."

Awhile back, against Pierce's advice, she'd bought

a huge warehouse downtown, not far from the entertainment district, because she'd believed it was a good investment. Plus, with her rental houses, she'd had a need for additional storage space. She used the building to store extra kitchen appliances and remnants of carpet. When her house had burned, she'd moved a lot of her furniture down there as well.

The warehouse had three floors, all with individual locks. There was a cranky freight elevator and a basement. Yolie kept some of her restaurant stuff on the second floor, and Pierce, who'd decided he needed storage space, too, had some medical records on the third. Rosie hadn't planned to charge him rent until he'd jilted her.

When she'd told him he'd have to start paying, he'd laughed. When she'd changed the lock, Pierce still hadn't paid. Only lately had he demanded access. The night he'd died he'd promised to pay the rent. Only he hadn't.

"Harry. I think I should go to the warehouse and do an inventory. As well as check the building."

"I should go with you. That place always creeps me out even when I'm with the guys."

"Tomorrow? Say, maybe two o'clock?"

"I'll be there," he said. "I swear on my mother's grave."

Nineteen

Oh, my God, I can't believe I totally believed Harry would be here. How stupid was that?

Her eye on a group of panhandlers across the street, who watched her open the warehouse door with what seemed to her an excessive amount of interest, Rosie shakily punched in Harry's cell number so fast she left out a digit.

The next three times she tried to reach him, she got a message that said No Service.

This was bad.

Cell phones were too much like Harry. When you needed them, they totally flaked out.

She was pacing back and forth when her fourth try got through, or rather it went to Harry's voice mail.

"—Your call is, like, superimportant to the Dude. So, like, leave a message—"

She dialed him again and got static.

"Come on, Harry! Pick up! Like, you swore!"

"—your call is, like, super—"

She flipped her phone shut.

Of course, her warehouse had to be located on the *wrong* side of Red River Street, this part of Red River being about as far east as most nice people with an extra dollar in their pocket cared to venture unarmed after dark.

Not that it was dark—*yet*. And not that the danger wasn't a wee bit exaggerated. Only with the leering audience across the street, she didn't feel safe hanging out here all by herself.

"Hey, baby—" A tall, lean tough from across the street crooked his finger at her, beckoning her as he might a stray dog.

Rosie whirled and dialed Harry again, only to get a repeat of his idiotic message.

If he ever showed up, he'd better run…because she was going to strangle him.

"Baby!" Her tall suitor was getting more excited by the second. She scanned the shadowy storefronts all with iron bars on the windows. Except for a skinny girl in a skintight miniskirt two blocks away, plying her trade, the street was as empty as a ghost town.

Her admirer started toward her. Rosie stared at him and at the big open door of her warehouse. He was still advancing when she saw a big truck that looked like Harry's speeding toward her.

Finally!

She darted inside the warehouse. Despite the sky-lights and windows and the heat outside, the building was cool and dark. She turned on her flashlight, praying that Harry would pull up any minute.

She flipped on all the light switches, but the ceilings were so high and the bulbs of such low wattage that she had to keep her flashlight on even though she'd left the tall, roll-up door wide-open behind her.

A pungent odor hit her. Urine? Had one of those bums gotten inside?

Boards creaked and groaned as Rosie moved toward the wooden stairs that led up to where Pierce and Yolie stored their things. When she reached the steps, she hesitated. She had a fear of heights as well as of the dark, and the ancient handrail was sagging in places. Deciding to make her inspection a quick one, she clung to the rail as she began her ascent, and soon had more than a splinter or two in her fingers.

The higher she climbed, the darker it became despite the skylights high above her. The air was hotter and closer, and the stairs themselves seemed to grow more rickety as well. Rosie became aware of the musty scents of mold and rat leavings and rotten wood, of decaying cardboard and cloth.

She was coughing when she heard the door roll a little on its track, and then what sounded like careful footsteps below her.

"Harry?"

He didn't answer.

Breathing fast, she stood very still, listening, to the thud of her own heartbeats. Suddenly, the urge to run back down the stairs and out of this place while she waited for Harry was nearly overpowering. Then she remembered the thug and remained frozen for several more minutes.

Why had she been so impulsive? She should never have come in here alone. She should have waited for Harry or driven off in the Beamer. But since she was here, and he was bound to turn up, she might as well accomplish what she'd come to do. She'd just hurry.

When she strained her ears once more, and heard nothing other than the scuttling of roaches or rats, she resumed climbing. First, she unlocked the door to Yolie's section. Quickly, she strolled past commercial stoves, restaurant booths, flooring tiles, stacks of drywall, huge cooking pots, tables, chairs and paint cans. There were footprints in the dust, and she remembered Yolie telling her she'd moved out some tables and chairs.

Satisfied that nothing was wrong here, Rosie locked the door and climbed to the third floor, where Pierce kept his stuff. She unlocked his door. An immense pile of neatly stacked and labeled boxes on shipping crates occupied most of the room. The majority were labeled "Medical Records," but she thumbed through a few just to make sure they were old charts. The dusty boxes didn't appear to have been opened by anyone since they'd been left here.

In the last of the tall rows, two yellowing boxes at the bottom of the pile caught her eye. One was labeled, "Johnson/Denver/Colorado," and the other, "Medical School."

Both cartons sagged from the weight of the medical records on top of them. The Denver box had gotten wet at some point and was bent double, threatening to spill its contents. For no reason at all, Rosie's pulse sped up.

Carefully, she removed the boxes on top of the two that interested her. But just as she was lifting the yellowing, crumbling lid off the Denver box, she heard footsteps downstairs.

"Harry?"

When he didn't answer and all the lights went off, it was all she could do not to scream.

The big door on rollers crashed down. Wings fluttered somewhere above her and then stilled. She flashed her light at the shapes flitting against the ceiling.

"Open that door!" Rosie yelled. Wings flapped again, and she felt something brush her face. Quickly, she sank to her knees behind the boxes. Not that there was any response to her outburst other than more flapping in the rafters.

Bats!

Austin was famous for its bats. Somehow, up close they lost their appeal, but at least now she knew the source of the pungent odor. Somewhere in a wall or ceiling, there had to be a hole.

As the bats settled down again, fear numbed Rosie's brain, and she forgot practical landlady concerns such as holes in walls and roofs, the need for repairs, and the need to take an inventory.

She stared up at a dirty window, which emitted feeble, gray light. Time spun out interminably as she dug in her purse for a possible weapon. Finding nothing of use other than her cell phone she crouched behind the boxes and once more dialed Harry.

His message came on. No sooner had she flipped the phone shut again than she heard a footstep on the stairs.

Her heart skipped a beat. She opened her phone and punched in Michael's number. When more boards creaked on the stairs, her fingers shook so badly she misdialed.

Another noisy step sounded and then another. She barely dared to breathe as the phone began to ring.

"Nash—"

"Michael, I...I—"

"You sound scared! Where are you? Answer me, damn it!"

Fortunately, Harry chose that exact second to return her call.

"Hold on a sec!"

"Goddamn it, don't call me like this and then put me on—"

She punched Answer.

"Hey, I'm sorry I'm running late. Like, I had a flat in your driveway. I picked up a nail or ran over glass, or that neighbor of yours, Mary Bell, or whatever slit my back tire. Like, she *had* to come over and gloat while I was changing the damn thing. She either has the hots for me or she hates me."

"Where are you?"

"Outside the warehouse unlocking the door."

Unlocking the door? Had the intruder left? And locked her inside? "Hurry!" she screamed.

The big door shuddered as it rolled upward, and she heard crashing sounds on the stairs. Bats spun madly around her again. As their wings brushed close to her face, she felt cold. Frozen.

Then a welcoming square of yellow light flooded the lower floor and bright streamers peeked through the floorboards. Harry yelled her name.

"I'm on the third floor. Get up here!" She returned to Michael, who was still on hold. "False alarm," she said meekly. "Sorry I bothered you."

"Where the hell are you?"

"I'm okay."

"Talk to me!"

"I'm truly sorry for bothering you."

"Don't give me that crap, and don't hang up, either!"

"Just for the record, I hate it when you do that," she said.

"Do what?"

"Boss me in *that* tone. You don't own me, you know."

"What tone?" he demanded, in that exact same tone.

The line exploded with static, and she flipped her phone shut. Hopefully, he'd think her cell phone was on the blink or that they'd been cut off.

While Harry fumbled up the stairs, she quickly transferred the records she was interested in to newer boxes.

She told Harry about the panhandler and the noise on the stairs. With Harry leading the way, they turned on all the lights and checked every floor together, but there was no sign of the intruder.

"Looks like he's gone," Harry said.

"You were supposed to be here at two! On the dot! You swore!"

Harry shrugged.

Nagging Harry never did any good. Rosie was suddenly so glad he was here, and the intruder was gone, she didn't care that he'd been late.

"There's some boxes on the third floor. Would you mind carrying them down for me?"

"Sure."

"We'll do the inventory some other day," she said.

When she pointed out the boxes in Pierce's pile, Harry easily hefted them onto his thick shoulder. When they got to the street, the panhandlers were gone.

Twenty

The old neighborhood was going downhill fast. The Rosie who'd wanted to be in the sparkling train car had always been totally mortified to drive up to Hazel's one-story frame house surrounded by decaying buildings.

That Rosie hated the two new massage parlors and the bar in the same block. Today, however, after the warehouse, she found her mother's house a welcome sight.

Thanks to Harry's work and Rosie's money, the house had a new roof as well as a new front sidewalk.

Unfortunately, Hazel had never met a cat she didn't like. Cats of all ages, sizes, colors and sexes lay all over the porch, the chairs, the sidewalk and the ancient trucks in the drive. Harry's, no doubt. He collected old trucks.

Since Rosie was carrying the heavy file boxes and

had to watch out for cats, she couldn't take out her notepad and make her usual list for Harry. But she did make mental notes of things that needed doing.

As always, the yard was overgrown with weeds. Tall, unruly shrubs covered the windows, too. Was that a third rusted pickup in the drive? Oh, my God, it didn't have tires.

Rosie staggered up the sidewalk and banged on the screen door. Cats of all varieties swirled around her legs, mewing.

Hazel unlatched the door. "Looky, Charlie, what the wind blowed in—my long-lost daughter!"

Charlie was Hazel's only house cat. He alone had a proper name, but as was often the case, his superior lot in life had not improved his personality.

He hissed at Rosie from his side of the screen.

"Behave, Charlie," Hazel ordered.

When the door was pushed open, the cat flattened his ears and hissed again.

Hazel looked young and healthy and much too bright eyed. She could snap in and out of sanity in a blink, and today seemed almost well.

Her coppery curls were swept away from her face and secured with barrettes that looked like orange cats. She was perfectly made up, if a little too heavily around the eyes. Hazel had painted black wings with eyeliner at the corner of each eye. Orange cat earrings dangled from her ears. Her oversize black T-shirt had a huge orange cat in the center.

Long ago, right after Daddy was sentenced, Hazel had had a Chinese roommate who loved cats. If one asked Mei Ling why she fed all the stray cats in the neighborhood or bought things like towels or sheets only if they had cats on them, she'd always replied, "Cat cutest animal."

Eventually, Mei Ling had moved on, but Cutest Animal stayed and multiplied. From time to time, Rosie had Harry trap them and haul them to the vet, who neutered and vaccinated them. Harry always dragged his feet about that task.

"Dude, cats have teeth and claws. Like, they don't dig being put in cages, or going for a truck ride, either. They damn sure don't dig the vet snipping their family jewels! Like, the Dude has to ask himself, is he being a friend or foe of the universe?"

Hazel pushed the screen wider.

"What's the story on those three trucks?" Rosie asked.

Her mother squinted into the sun. "So, finally my daughter, she pays me a visit."

"You must be better." Rosie shifted her file boxes and stepped past Charlie, who hissed again.

"You've stayed away so long, even Charlie, who's sharper than a sticker burr, doesn't remember you. Carmen, she comes by more often than you do. Charlie sits on her lap and lets *her* pet him—even if she just calls him Cat and gripes about cat hair."

No use reminding Hazel she'd been here twice already this week, Rosie decided.

"Sorry, Mother. In your next life you get a perfect daughter. In this life you get me. Who knows, maybe I'll get a sweeter mother—one who doesn't lie about me to the newspaper people. Mothers are supposed to be on their daughters' sides!"

"I am! You should have killed Carver years ago after he told you I was crazy and you took after me, which is what I told that bossy reporter lady, who keeps coming over here and telling me he was a saint. I told her your father would have shot him years ago if he hadn't been in prison."

Rosie sighed. "What about the trucks?"

"Harry said not to tell you."

Rosie made another mental note to herself: *Kill Harry.*

"So, have you gutted up and told that cute motor-cycle guy about Carmen?"

"Can we have a nice normal daughter-mommy visit—just once? You mind your business and I mind mine?"

Hazel recoiled a little.

Rosie set a file box on the kitchen table beside all the pill bottles. With a landlady's eye, she glanced approvingly at the fresh paint, the shiny new linoleum, the brand-new granite counters and the gauzy pink curtains Harry had installed.

He had done such a good job, she almost forgave

him for the trucks and for being late at the warehouse. Almost.

"Your daddy loves the way you fixed the place up."

Rosie whirled. It was bad enough her mother hadn't bothered to tell her Daddy was out. Now she was inviting him over.

"Please—tell me you're not letting him come around."

"Beats the hell out of conjugal prison visits."

Granite counters spun. Rosie felt faint all of a sudden.

"He's curious about the murder, and he's been doing some investigating of his own. He says he can get his friends to look into—"

His friends? Who? The mob?

Rosie pressed her fingertips against her temples and told herself to breathe deeply. "No! Do you hear me? No!"

"You look like you're about to spout steam," Hazel said without a trace of motherly sympathy.

"Let's just don't talk for a minute, okay?"

"What if you just talked to your father?"

"Just be quiet."

"I married him, didn't I? I owe him something, don't I? He's your father. Maybe you owe—"

"I'll be the judge of that."

Hazel crossed both arms across the giant orange cat emblazoned on her ample chest. "I can't help it if I get lonely." She clenched her teeth and sat in stubborn silence for a long moment. "He said he's been lonely, too. Don't you ever get lonely?"

Rosie shut her eyes. A maniac had killed Pierce with her knife and was trying to frame her. Maybe he'd been at the warehouse.

She had a lot to think about, a lot, but she was so upset with her mother, she felt as if Hazel had stuck an eggbeater in her head. Who could think, much less talk?

When she didn't answer, Hazel made the most of the opportunity, as usual.

"I keep remembering how he was before he got into trouble. He was all right. He drank some, like most men, but only on the weekends." Her voice softened. "He used to love you more than anything, and you loved him back. He taught you to shoot."

"Of course. He knew guns. He was in the mob."

"He was a bartender. All kinds of people walked into that bar. Maybe some of them were in the mob. So he knew a few mobsters? He was a good husband and father, or at least he tried. When you'd get scared in the night, you'd run into his arms and he'd hold—"

Closing her eyes and swallowing hard, Rosie stumbled blindly to the window over the sink. "I can't stand hearing this."

"Because you've been too hard on him and you feel guilty."

Rosie grabbed the countertop and held on tightly. "He'd hold you until you quit crying and fell asleep again. Then he'd carry you back to bed. Why do you have to be so high and mighty? Why can't you just forgive him? He made a mistake, but he paid for it."

Rosie whirled. "Because…maybe he ruined my life. Maybe I paid for his mistake, too! Maybe I'm still paying for it! Why can't you see that? It wasn't bad enough to be born poor. To be nothing. To have nothing. He had to go out and be a criminal, too. Everybody hated me after he shot Mike Nash."

"Since you've been accused of killing Pierce Carver yourself, I'd think—"

"Stop. The two things are totally different. I did not stab Pierce. Daddy shot Mike Nash. A cop. Maybe a corrupt one, but a cop. Ten people saw him."

"But it was an accident. How many times do I have to tell you—he was firing at Louie, who was about to shoot the cop? Nash jumped away from Louie and into the path of your daddy's bullet. Nash was on the take. He wasn't any better than Carlo or Louie. If you ask me, he was worse. Because he was a cop."

When Hazel paused for a breath, Rosie covered her face with her hands. "I'm glad that all makes perfect sense to you."

"Your father wants to see you. This is killing him, too. He knows too well what you're going through."

"Well, I don't want to see him!" Rosie felt tears on her cheeks and brushed at them wildly. "I don't care about him!"

It was crazy, but she sort of did want to see him.

He would know what it was like to face something like this, to face prison.

"You've always had way too much false pride. You're no better than me or your father. Or that cop you've been keeping your big secret from. Because you didn't think he was good enough? We didn't do so great with Carmen, now did we? You know what I think?"

"No, but you're going to tell me."

"I think Carmen could use a man in her life like him. I think you should tell him. The sooner, the better. I think you're far too hardheaded."

No way was Rosie about to give her extremely irritating mother the satisfaction of telling her that they were in agreement about Carmen and Michael.

"I will not discuss this with you."

"If I saw it the first time I met him, he's damn sure going to see it, being as he's a detective investigating you and all. You'd better tell him pretty quick, or he'll be madder than hell. And how do you think Carmen will react when she finds out? Her temper's probably way worse than his."

Rosie drew a deep breath. Not that it calmed her much. "I—I hear the TV in the other room. Weren't you watching something before I came, and you decided it was more fun to butt into my life?"

"Oh, I get it. You don't want to talk to me now since I mentioned your daddy and your dirty little secret. You want to sit in here and sulk in the kitchen all by yourself...but stay long enough so the neighbors will give you credit for visiting your sick old mother and maybe your long-lost daddy, too."

"Is *he* here? Tell me he isn't here."

"He isn't here. I knew you were coming, so I asked him to go."

"Okay, maybe I would like to sulk for a minute or two in here all by myself."

Hazel paced back and forth for a spell.

"Nash will figure it out, you know," she said.

"Mother! I really would like some alone time."

"Oh, all right. I was just trying to help." She threw her hands up as if in surrender and trundled toward the living room, stopping only to call Charlie.

The cat probably would have trotted after her if she hadn't wanted him to. But being perverse to the core, like everybody else in the Castellano bunch, he ignored all the *kitty, kitty, kitties*. Flattening his ears, he stalked malevolently up to Rosie.

"Go with her. I don't want you," she said.

Charlie's ears went so flat his head looked like a pancake. His eyes slitted, and he swished his tail rapidly around her leg before gliding imperiously past her toward his bowl.

Stupid cat.

Rosie poured herself a glass of cold water and sank down in a chair at the table. She stared at the file boxes for a long time. The last thing she needed was to think about her father, let alone what to do about Carmen and Michael.

When Rosie finally recovered a little, she opened the box containing the files about Denver. The box brimmed with musty newspaper clippings about people she didn't know, people Pierce had never mentioned to her. Not that he'd ever talked about Denver.

In fact, Colorado was the one state he'd totally avoided visiting. Ever! If a medical meeting was held there, he'd always refused to attend it.

The news clippings were organized in chronological order. They had to do with the story of a mansion that had burned to the ground due to unknown causes. Why had he kept them? What exactly was his personal involvement with this event?

Dr. Adam Johnson, the father, had been an internationally renowned doctor and author in the field of cardiology. He and his wife had both died from the fire, the doctor succumbing quickly, while his wife, Phyllis, had lingered for a month due to head injuries from a fall. Their twin college-age sons, Ricky and Tim, had jumped from the flaming house with the mother, but they had both survived.

Later stories pointed to arson, and then to Ricky, as having caused the blaze. Apparently, Tim had always been the perfect twin in every way, but Ricky had become increasingly difficult as he'd matured, and after he'd experimented with drugs. As boys, the brothers had been close, but when they'd grown older, they'd avoided each other.

Rosie got up and went to the window. Who were these people? Why had Pierce saved these clippings about Ricky and Tim? Had they been friends of his? Relatives? Or had their tragic story simply fascinated him?

Confused, she sat back down and thumbed through the clippings again. Eventually, Ricky had been found guilty of setting the fire and had been sent to prison. But the strangest thing about the tale was that Tim had vanished after his twin's trial and imprisonment. But not before he'd collected large sums from his parents' insurance policies.

Where was Tim Johnson? Apparently, some of his parents' friends had been curious enough to hire a private investigator. Every so often the newspapers reprinted the old stories and told of their efforts to locate him.

In every prison interview Ricky swore he was innocent. In prison, he'd quit drugs and had obtained a college degree. He always vowed he didn't know who'd set the blaze that killed his parents. He only knew it wasn't him.

When asked about his brother, Ricky said he wanted to find him more than anything in the world.

When the television went silent in the other room, Rosie tensed.

"Truce?" Hazel whispered in her bright, little-girl's voice as she tiptoed back into the kitchen.

Charlie raced over to his mistress and meowed, as if now he was glad to see her.

"So, do you have time for tea?" Hazel asked as she leaned down and stroked Charlie.

"Tea would be nice," Rosie said, relenting.

Her mom glanced at the clippings. "What've you got there?"

Rosie held up a newspaper picture of the two tall young men.

"Twins?"

"He's Tim Johnson, the good twin, and he's Ricky, the bad twin."

"I guess it'd be easy to get 'em mixed up," Hazel said after studying them.

Rosie pointed to Ricky. "Bad twin. He went to prison for killing their parents." She tapped Tim's picture. "Good twin. He disappeared into thin air."

Hazel read the headline. "But only after he collected the insurance money?"

For some reason Rosie didn't want to reveal that the files had anything to do with Pierce, but her mom pointed at his name on the label and smiled slyly. "This is about Pierce! This has to do with him getting stabbed!"

"I don't know. Michael said we should leave the detective work to him."

"He's a man. Most men need a lot of help from their womenfolk. Not that they'll ever admit it."

Rosie fought a smile. For once, it almost felt good to argue with her mother.

"So, how have you been feeling?" Rosie lifted a

couple of bottles of pills from the table, read the labels and set them back down. "There are an awful lot of pills in these bottles. Are you sure you're taking—"

"I feel great, just great since I got out of the loony bin and quit taking all those damn pills. They turn your brain to mush. The only reason I even keep the pills is because Charlie likes to bat them around the floor while I cook his turkey."

"Great. You're off your meds again. You could have a breakdown anytime…."

"I prefer that to brain mush."

Hazel pitched a bottle onto the floor, and Charlie batted it under the stove.

"Great," Rosie whispered. "Just great."

Twenty-One

It was hot, so hot all Rosie wanted to do was get naked and lie out by the pool. Yolie had left yesterday for Victoria again and wouldn't be back for at least a week.

So, what else was new? Since the murder, Yolie hadn't been around much. Nor had her son or stepson.

Because Rosie believed herself alone in the privacy of Yolie's shady backyard, she wore her skimpiest black bikini and a little nothing of a gauzy cover-up. After all, why wear clothes just to splash water on thirsty roses?

"The contractor chopped the restaurant in two," Yolie had said in the driveway right before she'd gotten into her Cadillac yesterday.

"You're kidding!"

"I wish. He bulldozed my building."

"Without your permission?"

"We talked, but I certainly didn't tell him to chop it in two. Now I've got to go figure out how to fix it."

"Well, good luck." Rosie had hugged her.

"Good luck to you, too, sweetie. I hope by the time I get back, you'll have ended your career as the notorious barefoot murderess. Ever since you got famous, you've been hell to live with. By that I mean you haven't paid nearly enough attention to me."

"Sorry," she moaned. "Just trying to slip my neck out of the noose before the knot tightens."

"Oh, if Xavier comes around or calls, tell him I have my cell on."

Since Xavier had not shown himself lately, Rosie didn't think she'd see much of him. Experience had taught her that the vanishing male routine usually meant a girl was being dumped.

Not about to be the messenger, Rosie had merely waved as Yolie drove off in her white Cadillac.

Michael had been equally elusive, damn his hide! But Rosie *had* told him she didn't want to see him ever again, which technically meant she'd dumped him. But—hello?

She had called him when she'd been scared out of her wits at the warehouse. And what had he done? He'd gotten mean and bossy. So, was it her fault that she'd hung up on him?

Would it have killed him to follow up with a concerned call or visit?

Not wanting to think about her neediness in

certain areas, Rosie sprayed the roses with a vengeance, her mind quickly drifting to the murder.

Indeed, since Pierce had gotten himself stabbed and she wasn't working, it was difficult to think about much else.

She'd taken long walks, with Lula and sometimes Alexis, too, hoping to chance upon Kylie Ray, so she could question her. As if Kylie Ray, of all people, would know or admit she knew anything. So far, Kylie had been as good at the disappearing routine as Xavier and Michael.

In between dealing with Harry, cleaning up her own house and unpacking, Rosie had taken Alexis to the children's museum and to the zoo—twice. They'd even ridden the little train out at Zilker—thank you for that idea, Mr. Homicide. But no matter what she'd appeared to be doing, she'd obsessed about the murder.

Of course, she'd visited Hazel, and she'd dealt with Carmen as best she could. Surprisingly, her daughter had been less hostile to both Alexis and her of late. She'd seemed strangely restless and less satisfied with her dancing and singing career.

Once Rosie had actually caught her on Yolie's computer looking at a local junior college's Web site.

On another occasion, Rosie had discovered her thumbing through some of her own old art books. But when she'd walked into the den, Carmen had slammed the books shut and told her the Naked Babies was developing a new act.

As Rosie splashed Yolie's dwarf palm, the gate in the wall squeaked on its rusty hinges.

"Long time, no see," rasped a deep, husky and very familiar voice.

"Michael!"

Both thrilled and scared, but trying not to act the least bit interested she whirled with the hose in her hand, spraying him accidentally and then laughing. "That'll teach you to be sneaky."

Grinning, he held up his dripping hands. "Hey, don't shoot!"

She licked her lips and swallowed hard. He looked too good in soft, damp jeans and tight white T-shirt. His thick dark hair was wet, and curling where it stuck to his brow and neck. When he smiled, she felt as if her sex drive, which had been all but absent after Pierce jilted her, received a dangerous jolt of red-hot electricity.

"I didn't mean to scare you," he said gently, "your call the other day worried the hell out of me."

So, he had been thinking about her. That was something.

"You ready to tell me what was wrong?" he demanded.

"I'm okay now." Instead of confiding in him, she concentrated on her watering.

"So that's how it's going to be." He paused. "Good

thing it's so hot. Your little shower felt refreshing." His gaze drifted over her body, which was too clearly revealed by her gauzy cover-up and microscopic bikini.

When she sucked in her tummy, he laughed.

"You sounded scared on the phone."

"I've been a little bit jumpy lately," she admitted, feeling self-conscious about her skimpy outfit. "If I'm nervous, it's all your fault."

"My fault?"

"When the newspapers keep hammering that I'm the murderess and you should arrest me, I get scared."

His expression darkened. "Right, blame me."

"And because of you I just got water all over Yolie's clean kitchen window, too."

"Last I heard, water dries."

"But it'll make spots. Yolie doesn't like spots. Xavier will get into trouble."

"Her young lover, who has not been over here lately?"

"How do you know *that?*"

"In my spare time, I do try to play detective."

"By snooping and talking to the neighbors about Yolie and me…and Xavier?"

Michael had the decency to lower his gaze.

"So, what else have you been doing and learning behind my back?"

"You don't really want to know."

"Surely, my reputation isn't all *that* bad."

He was silent.

Picking up on his sudden uneasiness, fresh dread began to build inside her. So, he was here on police business. Not because he cared about her.

"We need you to come downtown again," he admitted in that low, tense tone she hated.

She arched her eyebrows and managed to stare down her nose at him.

"I hate like hell having to be the one to tell you," he said, "but we need to set up an appointment with the lab so they can take hair samples and do some other routine DNA testing."

"Routine?" she shrieked. "Why me? Why are you after only me? When there are other people without alibis. I have made a long list."

He was staring at the pool instead of at her.

"Kylie," she began desperately.

"Their marriage was over a long time ago," he stated promptly.

"Yolie," she said. "Not that I think for one second she did it."

"She was at her ranch," he answered. "The next morning she met another rancher, who was going to cut her hay."

"But that was the *next* day. Not *that* night."

"She has no motive."

"Do we really know the heart of any woman— even our best friends?"

"Well, Pierce's cameras didn't get a shot of her, either."

"Like I said, I don't think she did it. So, all of this is just theoretical. But I'll bet there are lots of ways for a clever person to avoid Pierce's cameras. And—ever since he died, she's been very preoccupied. What if she never got over him but is too proud to admit it?"

"Thank you for the psychological profile. She got a fantastic settlement."

"So?"

"So—she screwed the bastard—royally. *She got even.* She even compounded that by becoming way richer than him by investing *that* money wisely. For your information, Pierce Carver died broke. Worse than broke. In debt. Yolie's rich and has had lots of lovers. In other words, she seems like she's gone on with her life and made a success of it."

"And I haven't?"

"Well, let's just say she didn't go around saying she wanted his head on a platter. Did you or did you not drive to Rockport and cut all the dock lines to his yacht?"

"Except one! And that was a year ago."

"I was hoping the marina guy lied."

"Doesn't anybody in this city have a sense of humor?"

"Not when it comes to murder in its "safe" suburbs."

"Surely you don't think you can always tell who's guilty or innocent by the way they act."

"True. But, like I said—she's not joking about getting revenge."

"There's Dr. Morgan…."

"Stay away from that man. He let me know he did not appreciate your last visit. For your information, he has friends in high places."

"But—"

"Forget about him."

"What about Anita? She left him. What do we really know about her? She leaves her country, her family—everything—to marry a man she hardly knows. Why? Then she leaves him. Then he dies."

"Maybe she married for love. Again, she didn't make *America's Funniest Home Videos* running out of Pierce's mansion having lost her sexy underwear."

"She's a Latina with a fiery temper. She could have snuck off from that party. I talked to a few people who attended it."

"And you think I didn't?"

"Apparently, there were so many people there, she could have driven to the house for an hour and never been missed. I think she was *there*."

"According to the valet guys, her car was in the parking lot all night."

"She could have taken another car."

Michael rolled his eyes.

"Darius and Todd aren't exactly crazy about their dad, either."

"Though he was supposedly the most popular doctor in town, I'm beginning to wonder who really liked the guy. What the hell did *you* see in him, anyway?" Michael pierced her with a look.

"Exactly. Anybody could have killed him. His patients could have been upset about a bad result."

"There is the little matter of *your* favorite paring knife being *the* knife."

"Which was stolen! Which proves to me that somebody is out to get me. What I want to know is who hates me that much?"

"Forget about this stuff." There was a new tension in Michael's voice, and she realized he was as concerned about all this as she was, although he didn't want to talk about the case with her.

"What about Anita's daughters?"

"Why don't you just let me do my job?"

When she grew silent, his eyes roamed her skimpy outfit. "How come you're wearing that? Were you expecting somebody?"

He was almost using *that* tone that she didn't like, only she rather liked it at the moment. Still, when he lowered his eyes and stared at her body in a way that made her blood heat, she knew she had to get rid of him—fast.

"It's hot—in case you hadn't noticed! And if that's all—"

"It isn't all," he whispered, sliding an arm under her cover-up and around her waist and then catching her to him before she had a chance to even think about running. "Not by a long shot. When you phoned me the other day, you scared the shit out of me. You tell me to leave you alone, and then you call sounding terrified. You put me on hold, then you hang up! I went crazy thinking about Pierce getting murdered, thinking about... I've tried not to dwell on why I might care so much if something happens to you. Or about why I feel this insane urge to protect you. You've always been way too much trouble, you know."

When his large hands molded her to his body, she got so flustered she dropped the hose.

"Please tell me cases like this always get solved," she whispered, wanting to be held and to feel safe even though she knew he was the last man who could actually make her safe.

"Some cases like this do get solved."

"So, do innocent people go to jail for committing murder?"

"Not if I can help it," he growled, threading his hands through her hair.

"But cases, even your cases, don't always get solved...no matter how hard you work on them? Sometimes killers get away with their diabolical plots—"

"Hush. Just hush." He was using *that* tone again.

"Do you think there's a chance I'll go to the gas chamber?"

"Lethal injection."

"Well?"

"Hell, no."

"But you can't be one hundred percent positive I won't, though?"

"Okay. Sometimes, some asshole who thinks he's a genius kills. He thinks he's covered every detail, but he misses something…sometimes something little."

"So, he gets caught?" she whispered hopefully. "By a clever detective like you? At least sometimes…and the person everybody thinks is the killer goes free."

"God, I've missed you," he said, pulling her even closer, his heat causing her body to shake.

It was all she could do not to throw her arms around his neck and say, "Me, too."

But she thought of Pierce's murder, and then of Carmen and the big emotional lie that entailed, and Rosie stiffened. "Let me go. Please…"

"I've tried to stay away," Michael muttered grudgingly. "Damn it, I've tried, harder than I've ever tried at anything." His hands trembled. The anguish in his low voice made her chest ache.

Then he wrapped his arms around her back and pressed his lips against her face. He kissed her brow first and then her nose. When he lowered his mouth and kissed her lips, softly at first and then hard and yet lingeringly, too, she stood on the tips of her toes, her whole body responding with an eagerness that overwhelmed them both. Soon he had her sighing and gasping. With a groan, he flattened her against him. His next kiss sent a wave of desire through her, inflaming every cell and nerve ending. Her toes curled into the rough concrete sidewalk. Even before he started on kiss number three, every erotic zone in her body was tingling.

Long shuddering minutes later, when he finally let her go, her mouth still burned. Other parts burned and ached as well. She was trembling, barely able to stand or to catch her breath.

He smiled down at her a little too triumphantly for her liking. "Ask me to stay, Rosie."

His seductive eyes caused visions of handcuffs to dance in her head.

"Yolie's gone," he whispered. "I could tie you up."

The handcuffs went from a tame waltz to a wild tango.

"Alexis is playing up in her room with Jennifer," she said.

He glanced up at the house and sighed so forlornly Rosie almost pitied him.

"Okay," he said. "But someday…soon." He kissed the tip of her nose."

"You have a thing for noses?"

"Only yours."

At his swift, hot look, she blushed and stared down at the gurgling water hose flooding the thick Saint Augustine grass. What would Nan say about a forty-year-old feeling as silly about this man as she had at eighteen?

"If you put me in jail, don't think I'll ever sleep with you again—even if I do get out before I'm really old and wrinkled."

"Why the hell do you think I'm working day and night?"

She swallowed.

"About those DNA tests…"

Rosie's heart began to thump, and her mouth went as dry as dust.

"I'll set them up and call you," he said, using *the tone*.

Her mood bleak, she nodded.

When he left, she found herself standing in the deepening shade of the hot afternoon as the cicadas sang above her.

DNA tests? And when they came back positive, which they would…

What could she possibly do to save herself?

Twenty-Two

Michael was frowning as he raced inside the gallery. Rosie was at the DNA lab being tested, and he had to get back to her as soon as possible. When she'd walked into his office this morning, she'd been so pale and drawn he'd been afraid she'd faint. At the lab, she'd gone whiter. She was scared, so scared she'd barely spoken two words to him, but when she had, she'd blasted him.

"You're building this case against me, aren't you?" she'd accused. "These tests, everything you do is making my situation worse."

"I'm doing my job—trying to find the killer."

"Trying. Well, maybe you should try a little harder, Detective."

"Right. I'm the enemy now."

"You're homicide. You're building a bulletproof case for the D.A. You figure it out. I should have brought Benson along. I should never have trusted you."

"So, call him."

When the glass door of the gallery shut behind him, Michael waved his badge at Ian Sawyer, the owner, who was speaking on the phone. Ian signaled that he'd be off in a minute.

Michael headed toward the boldest painting in the room. As he stood before it, he glanced around the large, square space, taking in the high ceilings, the modern sculpture and the glass wall.

The Howard Clayton Art Gallery was just off Seventh Street near Lamar, a main north-south artery that roared with traffic this time of day. Michael had never been here and would never return unless another homicide case or a blue-blooded date brought him. Modern art wasn't his thing.

He bent closer to the bright splotches of paint on the huge canvas in front of him and read the title: *Metaphysical Nude on a Subway.*

He stepped back from the painting. The central character was a plaster-cast female with a mannequin head. Her right foot was on top of a man's severed penis. A framed travel poster of New York stood beside her, along with a subway map that had been slashed into four pieces with a bloody knife.

Michael smiled grimly. The discordant elements reminded him a little too much of Carver's murder.

"Isn't the Isaac Muldoon wonderful?" Ian set the receiver in its cradle and rushed over.

"Fifty thousand bucks." Michael whistled. "It had better be. Interesting piece."

They shook hands.

"The piece shakes you up a bit, doesn't it?"

"You called me about Pierce Carver's paintings—"

"They're in the back." Ian made a sweeping bow, fluttered his hands toward a door and then dashed to a storeroom.

"Dr. Morgan brought these in this morning." The gallery owner flipped on the light before pulling out the various canvases and stacking them side by side against the wall. "He wanted me to sell them for him."

Michael knelt to examine the paintings more closely. "I saw these hanging in Carver's office the last time I was there."

"Well!" Sawyer snorted. "They're all fakes."

"What?"

"I'm as shocked as you are. I haven't told John yet." He waved his hands helplessly. "Frankly, I'm dreading telling him."

"Did you know Dr. Carver?"

"I met him at some art openings. He impressed me as an extremely well read and cultured man. He was quite knowledgeable about modern art, too."

"Did he come here often?"

"Occasionally. At one time he was a serious collector. There's a little group of people here in Austin, mostly oil and gas heiresses or the wives of dot.com zillionaires, who fly all over the place in their private jets, buying and collecting art both for themselves and the city. Carver was part of that clique. But I haven't heard of him buying anything of quality in some time."

"Why?"

"I don't know. There have been rumors that he was short on cash, which leads me to suspect that he must have sold his originals, perhaps one by one. He probably used a dealer in New York or Santa Fe, so no one around here would suspect—especially not his partner, Dr. Morgan, who from what he said this morning is a joint owner."

"Thank you." Michael was frowning as he straightened up and shook his hand. "You've been most helpful."

Barking wildly at a black poodle in the dog park, Lula tugged fiercely against her chain and pulling Rosie headlong down the trail.

She held on tightly even though her mind was still back at the lab, where Michael had left her to deal with the lab technicians, many of whom had been suspicious, and some openly hostile.

She was beginning to think everybody thought she'd done it. Probably Michael even thought so.

"Mimi! You're hurting her!" Alexis cried. "It's okay for her to run loose now that we're in the dog park!"

Just as Rosie knelt to unfasten the leash, she recognized a tall, wire-thin woman jerking nervously at her own poodle's leash, in an attempt to hurry away. A younger woman was with her.

Kylie!

Finally! A piece of good luck! How many times had Rosie sneaked out to walk Lula, in the hopes of meeting Kylie here?

When she unsnapped the leash, she held on to Lula's collar so the poodle couldn't get away.

Kylie must have seen her, too, because she was yanking her own black poodle back onto the path as she attempted to follow her friend in the opposite direction.

"Wait!" Rosie called after her.

"Let Lula go, Mimi," Alexis cried.

Rosie released the collar and Lula bounded after Kylie and her poodle, catching up with them easily.

Barking happily, tails wagging, the dogs circled each other. Lula jumped up on Kylie's purple velvet jogging suit and left big, dusty paw prints. To Rosie's surprise, Kylie smiled and petted Lula.

The two poodles sniffed and licked noses and then did the same to all the interesting private parts under each other's tails. Their canine curiosity satisfied, Lula trotted off to smell every tree in the vicinity, with Alexis tagging along behind her.

"Alexis! Don't go in the trees! Remember what

I told you about those homeless men who hang out in the park!"

When Kylie turned her back on her, Rosie jogged over, anyway. "I've so wanted to talk to you."

"I have a doctor's appointment in less than an hour."

"I'm sure you've read the papers."

Kylie's face froze.

"I didn't kill him."

"I wouldn't blame you or any woman who did," Kylie said in a low tone, her eyes alight with frightening passion. "Where's Yolie?"

"Victoria."

"And her boys?"

"They haven't been around much."

As if she, too, longed to escape, Kylie stared down the path where her friend had vanished.

"I'd like to ask you a few questions," Rosie said.

The woman glanced at her watch again. "I've already told the police everything."

"Did Pierce have any enemies? I mean—besides me?"

Kylie smiled as she watched Alexis. When Lula raced after a squirrel, Alexis ran after her, screaming in delight. "Kids have so much energy at that age, don't they? You're so lucky to have a granddaughter."

"Don't go far," Rosie called out as dog and child galloped toward the trees.

At least Alexis's bright red T-shirt stood out against the greenery.

"You asked if he had enemies?" Kylie's laughter sounded hollow. "Only any woman who's ever been unfortunate enough to fall in love with him or sleep with him. Seriously, Pierce is not someone I wanted to keep tabs on once I got free of him, so I'd be the last person to name his enemies. But he was one to carry and inspire grudges. Did you know that he called me until the day he died—because he knew I didn't want him to? In fact, he called me the night he died and told me you were coming over."

Again, Rosie remembered what Pierce had said about Kylie always hitting on him.

"How did you meet him?" Rosie asked softly.

"I was down-and-out in a fast-food hamburger joint in Hawaii without so much as a quarter. He smiled. He was handsome and looked rich, so I asked him for any spare change he might have, so I could buy a hamburger. He laughed. Instead of loaning me a few quarters, he took me out to the best restaurant in town. Then, he took me shopping."

Rosie had been almost as vulnerable as Kylie when she'd met him.

"He was so nice at first," Kylie said. "I think I fell in love that very first day."

Like me, Rosie thought, remembering the wonderful, too-good-to-be-true feeling that she'd clung to through all the bad times.

"We got married pretty fast, too. But when I became pregnant just as fast, he wanted me to have an abortion. When I wouldn't, and I began to show, he said he hated my body. He said I looked fat. I think I've been anorexic ever since."

"Oh, no."

"He couldn't stand that I'd crossed him by not having an abortion. Slowly, I began to realize how into control he was. He'd been charming as long as I'd done exactly what he'd told me to. But when I got pregnant, he thought I'd defied him. From then on, he acted like he hated me."

Kylie's thin face became even more tight and drawn, and Rosie didn't know what to say.

"When I caught him cheating on me, he said it was my fault because I looked grotesque. He started drinking more and became increasingly critical. He wanted me to dote on him, only him. When I mentioned the baby, he would become cold and mean. I actually became afraid of him. He said he hoped I would die giving birth. I lost weight even though the baby grew huge, weighing almost eleven pounds."

"How awful for you."

At the edge of the trees, Alexis was throwing sticks into the woods for Lula to chase. Rosie felt the need to call to her again, but she didn't want to interrupt Kylie.

"The doctor told me I would have to have a cesarean. Pierce and I had a fight when I was supposed to go to the hospital. I got very upset. I don't really remember what happened, or what caused me to fall. I don't really think Pierce pushed me, but I don't know. I was taken to the hospital unconscious in an ambulance. They couldn't get me onto the table fast enough, and I lost the baby."

"I'm so sorry."

Kylie watched Alexis for a while, and Rosie touched her arm. When Kylie finally resumed her story, her voice was lost and sad. "I was very depressed. Pierce didn't come to the hospital until I was ready to go home, and he was bitterly angry."

Kylie swallowed, as if the memories were still painful. "Our marriage was over…but we lived together another dreadful year. I guess I hoped things would get better, since I wasn't pregnant. But I couldn't forgive him, and he couldn't forgive me. So, things went from bad to worse, until they got so bad I finally left him."

"Did he ever talk about his childhood?"

"Once. I think he mentioned a brother, although he said I made the brother up later. And maybe he said something about Beaumont. Or was it Montana?"

"Not Colorado?" Rosie whispered.

Kylie shook her head. "I don't think so. He hated Colorado. Usually he said he was an only child. And really, he seemed like he was born an adult—a god. You know, he could act like he was so grand and be so arrogant he did seem to have sprung from mythical origins. Sometimes, he didn't seem quite human or really real. And sometimes, since the divorce, I've wondered if I ever knew him at all."

"Did you ever meet Anita?"

"I met her at a doctors' wives' function. What amazed me was that when we got to talking, she told me all her problems. I mean, she hardly knew me. It was months ago. They were practically newlyweds. Well, she went on and on about how difficult he was being about money and her girls, and I thought, *I'm the only one who knows what she's going through. No wonder she's so mixed up.* I was scared for her and told her to leave him."

"Why?"

"He hit her, and he threatened her girls when he drank. He said he wished they'd die. He threatened he'd do something bad to them if they didn't go back to Guatemala. Her daughters were terrified of him."

"Did he hit you?"

"Like I told you, I fell, or so he told me, the night I lost the baby. I think he really must have hated me after I got pregnant. He hadn't wanted Darius, you know, and he'd given Vanessa hell for having him. I think that was why she killed herself. If he couldn't control you, he had to get rid of you. I know his patients loved him, and I guess he was good to them. Maybe he really loved them, too, or maybe he was just in a position to be in control, so he felt comfortable. But I…I think there was a coldness in his core. I think his charm was false…at least with me. I remember the way he could snap and become someone totally different in a heartbeat. Since Pierce, I've never been able to be with a man again. He broke something in me. Sometimes I think I'll never get over him."

She hits on me. Every time I see her.

Michael said everybody lied. Where was the truth?

"I—I've got to go," Kylie said.

"I'd better get Alexis, too." Both Rosie and Kylie turned toward where they'd last seen the child.

"Where's your little girl?"

Suddenly the juniper that edged the trail looked dark and forbidding. Where was Alexis? Rosie's heart jumped into her throat as she remembered the homeless men who often slept under the bridges and trees of this park.

"Sorry! I've got to find her!" Rosie knew she was probably overreacting, but the DNA testing, plus all that had happened to her lately, had her upset.

"Alexis! Lula!" She put her fingers to her lips and whistled for the dog. Not that the overbred, overweight poodle usually came when called.

"They were just over there," Kylie said, pointing to the thick wooded area on the hill above the path.

Rosie ran wildly up the slope toward the trees. Mindless of the branches scratching her skin and clothes, she plunged into the woods. Instantly, the dense juniper closed around her, walling her inside a dark, secret grove.

"Lula! Alexis!"

Up ahead she heard wild barking. Then, as Rosie scrambled breathlessly over the limestone rocks, she saw a tall man running through the trees.

The path was steep. She was panting hard before she was a third of the way up the hill.

Her lungs burned as she passed a small tent in the trees. Pots and pans and beer cans littered the ground. Jeans and shirts hung on branches.

"Alexis!" She screamed her name over and over. "Lula!"

Branches thrashed up ahead, and Lula leaped out of the greenery and bounded down the hill. Rosie saw a splotch of red. Then Alexis screamed, "Mimi!" and raced after the big dog.

Rosie grabbed her and fell to her knees, hugging her.

"The nice man that lives in the tent, he drew me a picture. Of a beach. With a palm tree."

Alexis held the picture up for Rosie, who was still panting, to see. "He said palm trees were your favorite. He said he wanted me to give you this picture for a present."

The drawing was crude, but the palm tree on the beach looked a lot like her tattoo.

Rosie froze, her hands gripping Alexis.

"Stop, Mimi! You're squeezing me too hard!"

Rosie caught Lula and snapped the leash back onto the poodle's collar. Taking Alexis firmly by the hand, she led the dog and child back down the hill, and was surprised to find Kylie waiting for her on the path.

"Is everything all right?"

"I'm not sure. There was a man up there, living in a tent. He gave Alexis a picture. Of a palm tree on a beach. He said it was my favorite."

"And is it?"

"Sort of."

Their alarmed gazes met.

"Maybe you should call the police."

"When you're the number one suspect in a murder case, you don't just dial up the cops."

"If I can help—"

"Thanks."

As Kylie walked away, Rosie tried not to think about how close she'd come to losing Alexis.

Never had she felt so threatened or so alone.

Twenty-Three

"Damn it. I don't have time for this, Nash."

Dr. John Morgan managed to stand so utterly still at the door of his office in his blue scrub suit, he appeared not to breathe. Even so, he looked ready to sprint down the hall at the first opportunity. "Sorry." He chopped out the word. "I have surgery in less than ten minutes."

Although Michael was leaning back in Morgan's leather swivel chair, he felt every bit as tense and impatient as the doctor. With good reason. The evidence was mounting, Rosie was avoiding the hell out of him again, and he was getting nowhere fast with Morgan.

Michael stared up at the gaping white spaces where Carver's bold paintings had hung. "Your office seems naked."

John tapped the chart in his arm with his pen. "I

have a reconstruction to do, following a basal cell carcinoma removal by another surgeon. As we speak, the anesthetic is wearing off my patient."

"Those paintings you took to Sawyer yesterday—"

"Look, I'm not happy that he notified you people first. And I'm hardly thrilled to discover my paintings are fakes. But right now, I really—"

"In Sawyer's defense, apparently, he's something of a mystery novel buff. Says he's become a Carver murder junkie. Says he wanted to help the baffled police."

"By incriminating me?"

"No. But I do have to ask—where were you the night Pierce died?"

Morgan pressed his lips together so tightly they disappeared. "I told you, and my wife told you, repeatedly—*at home*. In our bed." He rubbed his eyebrow. "I had a headache that evening, so we went to bed early."

"Right." Michael flipped his notebook shut and stood up. "Your partner had women trouble. He set himself up to look rich and cultured, but he was embezzling from your medical practice. He owed a lot of other people money, money I don't think he ever had the slightest intention of repaying. He had a lucrative practice. Why do you think he was so desperate for cash?"

"I haven't the slightest idea."

"What do you think he planned to do about this situation ultimately…had his life not been cut short?"

"He did not confide in me, either about his troubles or his solutions. I will say that, even at his best, Pierce Carver was not the easiest of men to deal with. He could be arrogant beyond belief."

Yet Rosie had loved him. She'd become engaged to him. She'd gotten naked for him the night he'd died.

It galled Michael that she would probably never consider a serious relationship with a lowly cop like himself—even if she loved him.

"But I didn't kill Pierce," Morgan said. "Not that I would blame Rose Marie Castle if she did—even if she isn't my favorite person, either. He had a way of just turning you off, of shutting down whenever you crossed him on the slightest thing. Somehow he made you think twice about really trying to tell him anything."

"Was he a little scary?"

"Maybe scary's a bit strong. But if she did kill Carver, she did the medical community a huge favor. Guys like him give all doctors a bad name."

"But his patients all thought he was a god."

"I could tell you some stories…."

"I'd love to hear them."

"Talk to Karen. Ask her for the number of his malpractice insurance company."

Michael nodded, and the doctor raced down the hall. Alone in Morgan's lavish office, Michael felt torn as he pulled out his cell phone and tried to call Rosie. She didn't answer. So what else was new?

Michael wanted to solve the case and clear her.

He wanted her to be safe and happy. He didn't like her looking scared and hunted, as she had at the lab this morning. He wanted her all for himself.

Rosie wanted a man like Morgan, a doctor. She wanted ritzy vacations and cars and a fake Tuscan villa in Westlake Hills.

Michael punched in her number again. When he got her voice mail, he clenched his fist. Why couldn't she answer her damn phone? He wanted to find out how she was after her ordeal at the lab, to console her if she was down. He wanted to share his day with her. He wanted to have an intellectual and emotional relationship with her, as well as a sexual one. He wanted to be friends as well as lovers. How crazy was that?

A branch scratched Rosie's living room window, and she jumped. If she'd been nervous at the DNA lab, she'd become a whole lot jumpier after Alexis had wandered off in the park.

Unnerved, Rosie stopped unwrapping the little crystal bird, which reeked of smoke, and held her breath, waiting, listening. Her gaze swept the bits of cardboard and wadded newspapers, plus the stacks of dishes and knickknacks on her carpet. She'd been unpacking boxes for hours, and the living room was a worse mess than before she'd started.

As she knelt down to pick up a stray piece of cardboard, her deck outside creaked. Heart racing, she whirled just as a shadow darted across the makeshift curtain she'd hung over her window. When she chucked the piece of cardboard into her garbage can, another board shifted outside.

She'd been so enthusiastic when the Realtor had told her the house was close to the greenbelt. How she'd loved the way wildlife had wandered into her yard on summer afternoons when she'd first bought the property. Now, when it was dark, the house felt too isolated.

If only Michael would find Pierce's killer. Maybe then she could go back to all her familiar neuroses, such as obsessing about old flames and her chin.

When Scooter began barking next door, Rosie instinctively turned off the light. Nothing else happened, so when her heartbeat began to slow down, she sneaked over to the window and lifted the sheet. Mirabella stood in her bright kitchen window, stroking Scooter as he barked.

Down the hall Rosie heard Alexis singing. She was supposed to be unpacking her bears and toys and putting them into her toy box or onto her bookshelves. If she was singing to her teddy bears, she was definitely playing instead of unpacking.

Not that Rosie could fault her. Hadn't she taken a long break to go through all of Pierce's clippings about the Johnson twins again?

Suddenly, there was a crash in the little girl's bedroom, and her singing stopped abruptly.

"Mimi! Mimi!"

Rosie flew down the shadowy hall. Clutching her blue blanket, Alexis was running toward her so fast they almost collided. Climbing Rosie's jeans, a wide-eyed Alexis pointed back toward her room.

"There's a man at my window! The man from the park! Only his eyes are big and scary in the dark! I don't like him anymore. He's a bad witch!"

When Rosie headed toward the bedroom, Alexis sprang free and began to tug at her hand. "No, Mimi!"

Rosie kept going, but Alexis broke free and refused to follow her.

"What happened to the sheet I had over your window?"

The child shrank against a wall. "Black Bear was cold."

"So you pulled it down?"

"On the bed." Alexis's voice was nearly inaudible.

Her heart thudding, Rosie crept into the room. Sure enough, Black Bear lay on Alexis's four-poster bed, tightly swaddled in the sheet.

"I'm scared, Mimi!"

"It's probably just our big imaginations playing tricks on us, honey."

Alexis did have a huge imagination, especially at night when she was sleepy. She'd likely looked up at the window and realized it was dark outside, and had gotten scared. She'd probably remembered the man in the forest and imagined him there.

Still… Rosie could hardly take their safety for granted.

She went back to Alexis and wrapped her in her arms. "It's okay. I'm here," she whispered shakily, clutching her even tighter.

"What if the monster with the big scary eyes comes in and gets us?"

"He won't!"

"But what's he doing out there?"

"I—I don't think anybody's really out there. But to make sure, we're going to call Michael…no, Harry."

Ever since the lab, Rosie had felt like avoiding Michael. Seeing him at the station and then at the DNA testing center had reminded her concretely that he was Homicide.

He'd been phoning her all day. She thought, *He's the one, all right. He's the one building an airtight case against me.*

Alexis squeezed her eyes shut and held on to Rosie. "Will Harry come scare the bad man away?"

"Yes."

She carried Alexis into the living room and called Harry. For once, he answered his phone.

"Like, it's the Dude…." His words sounded fuzzy even though he spoke very slowly and very carefully. Rock music thudded in the background.

"Like, it's your boss, Harry!"

"Hey, man. No need to shout. I've got ears."

Holding the phone, Rosie carried Alexis from

room to room, twisting knobs and latches of every outside door and every window to make sure they were locked, turning on the floodlights, peering through curtains to see if there was a crazed killer skulking behind a stray patio chair.

"Harry…can you come to my house?!"

"Now?" He sounded really annoyed.

"Now!"

"Like, I'm…partyin' here with the guys…. This is kinda sacred time for me."

"I know. I'm sorry. But, Harry…I'm all alone except for Alexis, and I'm—"

"Like, what's wrong?"

She hated the way his voice seemed to float away.

"Like, just get over here!" she whispered, truly frantic. "I think somebody's outside. And bring your gun!"

"The Glock?"

She'd told Harry she hated guns. A few months ago, when he'd proudly showed her his brand-new Glock 17, she'd hurt his feelings when she'd refused even to look at it, and had lectured him that handguns killed people.

"Bring it!"

"Like, you're scaring me. Should I load it?"

"Load the hell out of it!"

Harry must have put his hand over the phone, because the next thing she heard were some scrambling sounds, as well as muffled curses on his end.

The loud music stopped abruptly. She heard more cursing and doors slamming. Then Harry came back on the line.

"Like, Dude, like we were thinking maybe you should call the police."

"Harry, that's the last thing a woman in my position can do."

"What about your cop friend, that Michael guy—"

"Harry!"

"Like, okay! I get it!"

"Finally!"

When Harry skidded into her driveway, Mirabella's porch lights snapped on. Holding his gun, which he'd bragged was made of lightweight polymer, and wearing only cutoff jeans and a T-shirt, he ran up to her door and banged on it with his fist. When she opened it, she caught a sweet, exotic whiff of something that was probably illegal.

Briefly, she told him what had happened, and he checked the grounds. Mirabella, holding Scooter, watched from her kitchen window.

Harry finally came back inside. "There's some footprints in the mud."

Footprints. "That does it. I can't stay here tonight."

"Like, they could be my guys'."

"I don't care."

"Like, I don't blame you. I'm feelin' kinda creeped out by your neighbor, too. Every time I use the portable potty, I wonder, does she have X-ray eyes? I saw this movie once, and all these guys had X-ray eyes."

"Harry!"

Together they locked the house up and reset the alarm. Together they packed her Beamer, but when she tried to start it, the engine wouldn't turn over.

They had to take everything out and put it all in Harry's truck. Promising he'd take care of the Beamer in the morning, Harry drove them to Yolie's. It was strange, but the whole time she'd been throwing things into her car, Rosie had had the uncanny feeling that somebody besides Mirabella and Scooter had been watching.

At Yolie's, Harry unloaded his truck and carried the suitcases upstairs. Since Rosie didn't know where to put Pierce's file boxes, she left them inside by the front door.

Harry stayed at Yolie's for more than an hour. Rosie made him check under every bed and inside every cupboard six or seven times. Then together, they locked every door and window, too, and then double-checked them several more times.

As he was leaving, Harry handed her the Glock. "I'd feel better if you took it to bed with you."

Even as she said, "I don't think so," she was checking the various safeties.

"Why didn't you replace this inferior plastic sight?" she whispered. Then, with expert ease, she removed and reinserted the 17-round magazine.

"Wow, like, you know what you're doing!"

"My father—" She broke off, not wanting to tell Harry that all good little mobsters' daughters probably knew about guns.

When he finally left, promising again to repair her car first thing, she went upstairs, where she hid Harry's Glock and a large flashlight in the top drawer of her nightstand. Even with the gun in the drawer, or maybe because it was there, it took her awhile to find the courage to turn off the lights, and even longer to fall asleep. Immediately, she had a nightmare and woke up clutching her throat.

In her dreams she'd been laid out on a steel table in the DNA lab as if she were a sacrificial victim. Dressed in doctor whites, Pierce had crept up to her and pricked her throat with a scalpel. Then he'd said in a very cold tone, "The killer's out there. You're next, Rosie."

Sitting bolt upright in bed and yet feeling groggily disoriented, she replayed the dream in her mind several times. Except for the line of light beneath her bathroom door, it was pitch-dark—no moon, no stars, no night-light.

She stumbled out of bed, intending to go to the bathroom for a glass of water and to wash her hands and face. Then she stopped dead in the middle of the room.

Oh, my God! She hadn't left her bathroom light on.

"N-no! N-no…" Staring at the sliver of light, she cupped her hands over her mouth and inched back to the table. Stealthily, she opened the drawer and pulled out the Glock. Then she backed toward her door. Turning lights on, she flew down the hall to Alexis's room, only to gasp with relief when she found her grandchild peacefully asleep with her blue blanket.

Quickly, Rosie went into Alexis's bathroom and washed her hands and her neck. That done, she tiptoed over to the bed and tucked the covers around the sleeping child. She fingered her red curls and then kissed her brow before saying a silent prayer of thanks. A few minutes later, when she'd recovered a little from the initial shock, she went back to her bedroom and grabbed the heavy flashlight. Then she went downstairs.

Carrying the gun and the light, she rechecked all the doors and windows and the alarm. The alarm was still set; all the windows and doors were locked. But as she was rechecking the front door, a scrap of cardboard caught her attention.

Oh my God! Pierce's boxes! They'd been by the front door.

They were gone.

Her heart started pounding all over again. Her legs turned to jelly, and she had to lean against the wall to remain upright.

Michael. She had to call Michael. Even if he was Homicide, even if he was building the case that would put her in prison, he was the only person in the whole world who could ever make her feel safe again.

When she called his cell phone, it was his turn to play hard to get.

"Michael," she whispered into her phone as she re-mounted the stairs with growing alarm, "I'm sorry I didn't answer your calls. But I need you. I need you so much. Somebody got into Yolie's house while I was sleeping. Please...please call me. Please. I'm scared."

When she hung up, she stared at her phone, begging it to ring, counting the long minutes when it didn't.

When a board creaked downstairs, her legs turned to spaghetti and she called him again.

Twenty-Four

Michael pulled out a picture of Pierce and then signaled the waitress. He was exhausted. All day long, ever since his quarrel with Rosie at the lab, he'd driven himself to uncover one shred of evidence that might be a step toward exonerating her. So here he was, drinking at The Cellar. It was way past his bedtime, and he had to be up early tomorrow.

Maybe he was getting old. Or maybe the sulky young redhead in the black velvet G-string, undulating on the golden revolving stage while she belted out songs, looked too much like Rosie. Whatever. The entire scene—her dancing, the men ogling her—bothered the unholy hell out of him.

Michael had his back to Carmen now, because every time he caught a glimpse of a nipple or gyrating buttock, his gut knotted or he tasted acid.

Fortunately, his pretty brunette waitress appeared. "Need another one?"

His mug was half-full, but he said, "Yeah," just so he could talk to her. He handed her a snapshot of Pierce. "You ever seen this guy?"

Her brown eyes studied him. "You a cop?"

He flashed his badge. "Don't tell anybody."

She stared at the picture and then at him again. "Maybe. I'm kinda new."

"Well, think about it. Show it to some of your friends, and get back to me." He slipped her a folded twenty. "Keep the change."

She smiled before heading to the back.

Michael took a long pull from his mug. The Cellar was full to overflowing, which wasn't surprising. The place had a reputation. So did the all-female band. With a daughter like Carmen, Rosie damn sure had her hands full.

Tonight a huge sign outside advertised the Naked Babies. The club's parking lot was jammed, and the club itself was packed wall to wall with men. Soft-faced, excited businessmen sat bunched together, smoking and drinking and laughing, around small round tables near Carmen's revolving stage. The shy guys stood in clumps at the bar beside Michael.

Lots of the men wore expensive suits, but there were a few hound-faced guys with cowboy hats and jeans and big belt buckles. This was Texas, after all.

Michael had had Rosie on his mind all day. He

hadn't liked the way she'd been so hopeless and scared and angry this morning. Since she hadn't taken any of his calls, he'd been tempted to drop by and see how she was doing. But he'd come to The Cellar instead, because Pierce had frequented the establishment. Maybe somebody here could put a different spin on things.

Michael turned around just as the door behind Carmen opened. A tall, dark, muscular young man in a white T-shirt and baggy, ripped jeans, who looked familiar, swaggered inside. She smiled at him and began to sing only to him. He grinned and walked straight up to the stage, where he grabbed a bar stool and sat right underneath her.

It was Xavier, Yolie's lover. No wonder the kid hadn't been watering Yolie's favorite potted roses lately. He definitely had the hots for Carmen.

When the kid never took his eyes off her, Michael's gut cramped so viciously his hand clamped around his beer mug. He felt an insane urge to punch the kid's lights out.

He released the glass and pushed it away. What the hell was wrong with him? Maybe she was a talented singer, but she was the next thing to a stripper. Xavier slept with older women, who took care of him. They'd make a perfect couple.

Fortunately, Michael's waitress returned with his beer and Pierce's photograph before he had a chance to make a real ass out of himself.

"This is Dr. Carver, the guy who got stabbed. I asked some people in the back like you told me to."

The music stopped. The lights around the golden stage went out.

"And?"

"He came here after work sometimes. Not too often. But he was a regular. They said he always seemed pretty tense."

"Was he alone?"

"Usually. But once or twice, right before he died, he met a man here. They were the same height, only the guy was a rougher sort. I don't think Dr. Carver liked him much, either. They always argued."

Michael pulled out a picture of John Morgan.

The waitress studied it a minute. Then she shook her head. "I've never seen him. At least, I don't think so. But I can ask around."

"Thanks." No sooner had she left than Carmen suddenly appeared, wearing little else other than a silky black robe.

"You leaving?" she asked coyly.

Michael glanced across the room. His expression surly, Xavier was watching her every move. Michael's, too.

"Enjoying the show?" she whispered, her gaze flicking to Xavier again before she tilted her red head inquisitively toward Michael.

The kid's face grew stormy.

Michael didn't like the teasing glint in her eyes one bit. "I came here on business."

"Because of Dr. Pierce Carver, I'll bet." Her lashes fluttered as she stared at him.

"How come he came here?"

"How would I know?" she said, dropping her little act and pursing her mouth with displeasure. "I never asked. He wasn't exactly on my Most Favorite People list, you know."

"You have such a list?"

She surprised him with a tight little smile. "My mother didn't kill him."

"Then who did?"

"How should I know? But I can tell you one thing. She was stupid about him. She wanted him back more than she wanted him dead. If he was alive right now, all he'd have to do was wag his little finger, and she'd come running."

That statement felt like a fist in Michael's solar plexus.

Damn. The girl's nearness unnerved him, too. She seemed familiar, like somebody he'd known and forgotten, and yet should remember always.

"I'd let you buy me a drink if you wanted to," she said, lowering her lashes again.

He signaled his waitress. When she came over, he ordered her a beer.

"So, you're a cop?"

"And you're Rosie's daughter."

"Carmen Simon." She held out her hand.

"Michael Nash." He took it. "Glad to meet you. So, how'd you get into this line of work?"

She frowned. "I dropped out of high school, and I had to go to work. I always liked singing. So here I am."

"You enjoy it?"

"The pay is good. That's about all I can say." She bit her lips and set her beer down. "So, how'd you know my mother?"

"We were kids together."

"Back in the olden days?"

"I wouldn't use that term with her."

Carmen laughed. "You don't know me then. That's what I do best."

"What?"

"Get under her skin." She took a sip of beer. "Did you know my father?"

"Not all that well."

"We never hear from him."

When her chocolate-dark eyes flashed with pain, he couldn't very well tell her Simon had always been a prick. What the hell had Rosie seen in him?

"He never even pays child support. It's like he doesn't care…. My mother says she's glad he's out of our lives."

"But you blame her?"

"Sometimes." Then Carmen shook her head. "Mostly, I hate him!"

Mostly? The desperation in her dark eyes was

getting to Michael, and for the life of him, he couldn't figure out why. She was Rosie's rebellious daughter, who was a little too old to still be rebellious. Rosie's problem. Not his.

"You think it's something she did? That that's why Simon doesn't come around?"

Carmen clenched the neck of her beer bottle, but she didn't lift it to her lips. "It's more like I want to think it's something she did."

"So you blame yourself?"

She backed away from him, her dark eyes shooting sparks now. "You're mixing me up! I was a baby when he left. How could it be my fault? It's her fault he's gone! Not mine! I bet he wasn't rich enough. He probably married somebody else. He's probably got lots of kids he loves…. Maybe another daughter."

She shot Michael a final, burning glance.

"What the hell did I do?"

"You got me thinking about him!" She waved to Xavier, who dashed over. Giving Michael a dirty look, he slid a protective arm around her. Then he led her away as if she were *his* property.

From the opposite side of the room, she turned and stared at Michel, her eyes dark and smoldering.

She was looking at him just like his mother used to when he'd been a kid and he'd done something to make her angry.

Her eyes scared the shit out of him. Suddenly, he

was back in Mexico waking up under a hot sun with
a headache and stomachache and the worst sunburn
of his life. He'd rolled over to put his arms around
Rosie. Only all he'd found was a tangle of sandy
sheets. And a note.

She'd left him a damn note saying it had been fun.
Fun!

He'd hated that word ever since. The surf had
crashed outside as he'd stumbled about the cheap
motel room, and the palm fronds Rosie had loved
had been rattling up a storm. But everything had
lost its magic because she had taken her clothes and
all their cash.

For at least a full minute, he'd stared in numb dis-
belief at the empty drawer where he'd kept his dwin-
dling wad of college money.

He'd hitched rides to the border and then back to
Austin. On the way, he'd been beaten up by a gang
of thugs in Monterrey. And all these years he'd
wondered why the hell Rosie had run.

Those eyes.

Michael squinted from pain in his chest as a soul-
shattering realization slammed him broadside.

Suddenly, he knew that a big piece of the puzzle
had to do with Carmen's eyes.

His mother had had beautiful, chocolate-dark
eyes. Everybody had always said he had his mother's
eyes. Carmen had them, too.

Why hadn't he seen the resemblance sooner?

Rosie had been pregnant. Not that she'd ever bothered to inform him. No, she'd married Simon. Probably because he'd been a better catch back then.

Damn her. Then she'd messed up their kid big time.

All these years he'd wanted to know why she'd left him. He'd thought he could put her behind him if he knew.

Wrong. He was more entangled with the capricious, lying witch than ever. And not in a good way.

His daughter worked in a shit hole like this.

He thought about how taken he'd been with Alexis. She'd been so damn cute and lively. He'd been stunned by his feelings for her. Suddenly, he was furious at Rosie, and furious at himself for being so blind. Hardly thinking, he shoved himself away from the bar so violently he crashed into a table. A customer shot out of his chair with raised fists, but Michael raced toward the front door before a fight had time to erupt.

But when he stepped out into the parking lot, Xavier's motorcycle shot out into the stream of headlights, with Carmen, who was practically naked holding on to him.

Oh, my God! She'd never been so scared.

The clock on the dresser in Yolie's huge, dark house ticked loudly as Rosie lay rigidly curled beside Alexis beneath the covers, clenching her cell phone in one hand. She had Harry's Glock in the half-open drawer of the nightstand. The bedroom door was locked. If the handle so much as rattled, she'd point the gun at the doorway.

Still, Rosie was afraid of every sound, even of her own heartbeats. She remembered waking up in the night and feeling like this when she'd been a little girl. Only back then, she'd had her father to run to. He'd always held her until she'd stopped shaking and had fallen asleep in his arms.

Tonight she wanted Michael. She wanted him so much. She didn't care that he was busily collecting evidence to use against her. Desperate to talk to him, she punched his number into her cell phone again.

"Nash."

"Oh, my God! Michael, you've got to come over—"

"Go to hell," he said. "Go straight to hell."

"Michael, please, I'm so scared. Somebody got into Yolie's house tonight. He turned on the bathroom light. I'm all alone with Alexis. He—"

Michael hung up on her.

Twenty-Five

Michael had sounded so cold and horrible, as if he hated her. She had the hall light on and the door open.

Despite Harry's gun beside her, her nerves kept her so wide awake she jumped at every creaking board and at every rush of sound from the air-conditioner.

The instant she heard a car pull slowly into Yolie's cul-de-sac, Rosie sat up. When the engine was turned off, she stole out of Alexis's bed. Seizing Harry's gun, she tiptoed to the front window in the hall. Lifting the lace curtain, she saw the battered Crown Vic with its tall antenna sprouting out of the trunk. Heaving a sigh of relief, she let the curtain fall back against the glass.

Then she raced back to her bedroom and plucked her silk robe off the foot of her bed. She took the clip out of the gun, put the weapon in the drawer and the clip on a high shelf out of Alexis's reach. Then Rosie flew down the stairs.

When Michael just sat out in his car, she remembered how furious he'd been on the phone.

When more long minutes passed, she turned off the alarm, switched the porch light on and threw open the door. When he still didn't budge, she grew increasingly uneasy. Finally, she walked outside and stood beneath the porch light.

Even though she couldn't see him, she knew he could see her. Just knowing he was watching her made her breath slam harshly.

She began to grow afraid of him a little, and her fear angered her. She blamed him for it, because he hadn't come sooner, and because he just sat there. Finally, rage propelled her down the steps and made her run down the shadowy sidewalk. When his car door opened, she stopped.

"Well, finally," she said.

Slowly, he uncoiled his long body. Then, with a carelessly clumsy gesture, he pitched a bottle he'd been holding into his back seat. When glass shattered, he cursed so vividly her stomach knotted. When he took a lurching step toward her, he tripped on her curb and nearly fell.

She forgot her anger and ran toward him, concerned only for him. He pushed himself to his feet again. "What's wrong?"

He weaved unsteadily. When she reached him, he seized her roughly by the shoulders. She caught the stench of alcohol right before he began to shake her.

His black eyes glittered. His angry mouth was a thin slash.

"What's wrong? Are you going to arrest me? Is that it? I don't care, if that's it—as long as you're all right!"

"You lying bitch!" His voice was harsh and cold. Then he began to laugh, and the deep rumble made her angry again.

"Stop it! You're drunk!"

"Very!" He smiled nastily. "And I intend to get even drunker!"

"Go home!" She tried to wrench free of his grasp.

"You said you were scared! So I came running…like some stupid lapdog! What are you scared of, Rosie? Tell me. No doubt I'll risk my stupid neck to save yours."

His grip tightened, and he half pushed, half dragged her back down the sidewalk toward Yolie's house. Once they were inside, he slammed the door and locked it.

"You said you were scared." His tone was louder and more belligerent now. "What the hell scared you?"

"Quiet. Alexis is upstairs asleep." Funny, now that he was here, her fear was gone.

His mouth curled. "*Your* precious granddaughter."

"Yes."

He laughed again, and then he threw her from him, causing her to stumble against the wall.

"*Our* granddaughter, damn you!"

Her hand went involuntarily to her mouth.

When he strode deliberately toward the shelf in the living room where she'd set out all her family pictures, including those of Carmen and Alexis, Rosie gasped.

"I saw these when I was here that first night...when Alexis disappeared. I didn't want to look at them and think about Simon and you and the daughter you conceived by him, because I've always had a *thing* for you." Michael laughed again, as if he thought himself a fool.

When he tried to pick up the picture of Carmen as a little girl in a swing, his hands shook so badly, he dropped it. The frame smashed on the floor. Glass exploded, and Rosie cried out.

He knelt and brushed the shards aside, careless of the damage to his fingers, but careful of the photograph. He wiped droplets of blood on his jeans. Then he lifted the picture from the shattered frame as if it was very precious. Slowly, he traced the features of the smiling little girl, who'd laughingly screamed at Hazel to swing her higher and higher just as Rosie had snapped the picture.

When he looked up at her, the bleak pain in his eyes made Rosie's throat tighten around a giant lump. She forgot her own terrors and felt only compassion for him.

"I'm sorry," she whispered. "So sorry. I was going to tell you."

"When?"

She couldn't speak.

"She has my eyes," he said in a low, broken tone. "And all these years I didn't know."

Guilt washed Rosie.

"So, why didn't you tell me?" His voice was hoarse now, raw. His expression was nakedly vulnerable.

Rosie swallowed. "I think I've been wanting to tell you…for a long time now. I just didn't know how."

"You think you've been wanting to tell me!" He set the photograph very carefully on the shelf. Then he whirled on her. "Don't fucking lie to me ever again!"

"I don't know what to say if you won't believe what I say."

He slammed a fist against the wall and then went white from the pain. "The truth, for once in your damn life! You didn't tell me! You married Simon! Why the hell did you do that? She's got his name! She thinks her father doesn't give a damn about her. She hurts every day because of that."

"I don't know why I did any of it. I was so messed up. Maybe I didn't want to mess your life up, too."

"I don't believe you. You were always looking out for yourself. You wanted the easy life. You thought Simon would be easy. Easier than me. You thought he was better than me. Didn't you? *Didn't you?*"

"Simon was a mistake."

"What was he like in bed?"

"I don't remember."

"Better than me? Is that why you married him?"

"Stop it!"

"When did you tell him Carmen wasn't his? After you married him? Or before? Did you trick him, too?"

"Before."

"And he married you anyway?"

"I was so mixed up."

"Like Carmen is now?"

"Worse, I think."

"Earlier, I went to that place where she dances. I went there for you, because I still gave a shit about you. I was trying to dig up dirt on Pierce, trying to dig up anything that might help you. Do you know how I felt watching her? Sick to my stomach… I've never felt like that before. How could you let her work there?"

"There's no stopping Carmen…."

"Just like there was no stopping you?" He drew in a breath. "Maybe I could have stopped her. Did you ever think of that?"

"Yes. Many times."

"But, you never told me?"

"I'm not proud of what I did."

"So, she has a kid. How the hell did that happen?"

"I don't know. She got pregnant in high school and ended up dropping out. I blamed myself."

"You damn sure should."

He strode back to the shelf and picked up Alexis's pictures. He studied them one by one for a long time before he carefully replaced them.

"Cute kid. *Our* granddaughter." He bit out the words. "She looks like you, too. Only she's darker...like me."

"Carmen resents Alexis."

"As you, no doubt, resented her."

"I was just so busy trying to get a nursing degree and then working."

He sucked in a harsh breath. "She told me she resents the hell out of you."

"Yes. I know."

"With good reason, I imagine. You thought I wasn't good enough. What a laugh. But that's why you didn't tell me, isn't it? I've never been good enough for you."

"That's not true. At least not now."

"That's only because you're using me to get out of this jam you're in."

"No!"

"Yes! I'm the East Austin bad boy who stole your virginity and knocked you up, who ruined your chances for the big score. And I always will be. But I've got news for you—you're the bad girl who screwed up my life royally."

"I love you."

"I told you not to ever lie to me again."

"I'm not lying. I love you."

"Shut up."

"I won't blame you if you hate me for Carmen. I was a total fool...worse than a fool."

"I'm an idiot—to have ever given a damn about someone as shallow and conniving and as vicious as you." His eyes were black chips of ice. His face was carved granite. "I'm through. The next time you see me, it will be the day I knock on your door with a warrant."

"Michael, please…"

When he turned to go, she ran into the foyer after him. She had to make him believe her. She had to. And she had to make him stay.

Acting on blind instinct, she threw herself into his arms and began kissing him even though his face and body, and his lips, felt as if they were made of stone.

"Leave me the hell alone," he growled.

When she clung to him, lifting her chin, meeting his gaze with a proud defiance that more than matched his fury, he hesitated as if struggling with powerful inner demons.

His gaze fixated on her mouth. Her lips parted.

Long seconds passed. Then he was winding his arms around her, tentatively at first.

"I love you," she said, kissing his lips. "You have to believe me. I love you. I'll change. I'll do anything—"

"Shut up," he snarled, but he kissed her back. "It's too late."

"Anything. I'll do anything."

"Anything?" The glittering anger in his dark eyes terrified her. When he crushed her against him so tightly she could barely breathe, she fought to pull away. But his mouth came down on hers with a savagery that blotted out all her attempts to beg for his mercy. His mouth hurt and so did his hands and hard body, but she forgot her fear. She loved him too much, and she was sorry, so sorry for what she'd done.

He kissed her with a fierceness that went beyond passion and fury. Soon, he was shaking even more than she was. When she opened her mouth, his tongue pushed inside to mate with hers, hotly, wetly. Knowing a wild thrill such as she'd never felt before, she clung to him ever more tightly.

I love you. I love you, she thought as she was swept up by desire and love for him, even though his sole intent was to punish. She didn't care if he tasted like beer or even if he was angry. It was just too wonderful to be in his arms. Pulse racing, she moved sensually against him.

With his mouth still fused with hers, he swung her up into his arms and mounted the staircase. Despite the fact that he'd seemed so inebriated earlier, he took the stairs with surprising ease. But when he reached the top, he released her. He stared down at her, his breathing heavy from passion.

She seized his big brown hand and placed it above her wildly beating heart. He cupped her breast, touched her nipple. When she gasped, he lifted his hand to her mouth. She slid her tongue between each of his fingers. Finally, she took both his hands in hers and ran with him down the hall to her bedroom.

Inside, she locked her door. Then she tore at the

buttons of his long-sleeved white shirt, yanking it off, leaving his wide chest and flat stomach bare. When she ran her hands over whorls of dark hair, sculpted muscle and sinew, it was his turn to gasp. But he stood still and let her unbuckle his belt. She laughed when she whipped it out of his jean loops and flung it across the room. Next, she unfastened his pants and pulled them down. When she peeled his boxer shorts to his ankles, it came as no surprise to her that he was fully aroused.

With a soft sigh of surrender, she circled his penis with her hand and began to stroke him. Groaning, he leaned back against the wall as if he didn't have the strength to stand unaided or even to take a single step toward the bed.

When she knelt slowly, his hands moved into her hair. She brought her lips to the tip of his manhood and then hesitated. Boldly, he cradled the base of her skull, and like a conquering warrior, guided her mouth to his sex.

Anything, she had said.

Everything.

Twenty-Six

Her lips and flicking tongue teased him mercilessly, and as her bright, silken head moved back and forth in the dark, Michael tried to force himself to focus on how much he hated her. He had good, sound, logical reasons for hating her.

Rose Marie Castle-Castellano was a liar just like her no-good father had been. Michael had thought she was different, but she'd lied about everything. She couldn't even admit to her real last name.

Castellano. She'd had mob blood in her veins.

She was probably lying now with her seductive lips and body as she cupped his balls and made love to him with her talented tongue.

How many other men had she had besides him? Who had she preferred to all the rest? Pierce?

Michael's questions jolted him. This was wrong,

and he was a fool to hold still for more of her seductive trickery.

But she'd always been like a drug. Never had anything felt so good as the near-miraculous sensations of her warm lips gliding up and down the length of his hot shaft. Every flick of her molten tongue, especially those against the sensitive tip when she made those clever little circles, sent fire and chills all through him. Excitement—pure thrilling, visceral excitement—held him in her thrall.

If he didn't put a stop to this, she would have him totally at her mercy. But, of course, he wasn't able to put a stop to anything that was so infinitely pleasurable.

When she took all of him into her mouth and sucked hard, his fingers dug into her scalp and he exploded.

Every muscle limp, he sagged back against the wall, breathing hard. He wouldn't do it with her again; he wouldn't so much as touch her. As soon as this present crisis shuddered through him, he'd pull on his jeans and shirt, wherever the hell they were, and leave.

But even as he swore to himself he wouldn't, he sank to his knees beside her and lifted her chin. For a long moment he stared into her luminous blue eyes, which were wide with passion and vulnerability, and pain. Suddenly the thought of hurting a single hair of her head was abhorrent to him.

He had to tell her he was going, but the ache in his throat was so powerful, he couldn't talk. He was as surprised as she was when he tilted her head back and kissed her, long and deeply and with a tenderness that tore him to pieces.

What the hell was the matter with him? When he stood up, he wasn't near ready to let her go, so he took her hands and pulled her up with him.

Gathering her into his arms as if she were infinitely precious to him, he carried her to the bed, where he could no more resist cuddling her close and holding her and stroking her beneath the warmth of her sheets and blankets than he could resist drawing the next breath.

When he'd recovered sexually and was fully aroused again, which was amazingly soon, since her satin limbs were tangled with his, he wanted more.

So much more.

Without a word, he stripped the gown off her. Leaning down, he began to kiss the plump fullness of her breasts. When he nibbled at her nipples and along the little palm tree tattoo, she let out a moan of pure contentment. Soon, her nipples peaked into hard little rocks of pink flesh beneath his lips.

She was so beautiful. So damn beautiful with her skin gleaming like smooth, living ivory. His gaze traveled down her flushed breasts to the mound of red curls between her thighs. Then his eyes swept the length of her, taking in every inch of her creamy flanks and calves, all the way to her polished toenails.

She had slim, shapely feet. How could feet be so elegant? But they were. Hell, how could he get hard just looking at her toes?

"Hold me," she whispered, sliding a toe against his calf. "Just hold me."

As if he could stop with holding her. When he pulled her close, she shivered as their lower bodies touched, and the tip of his penis rested against her moist sex.

He reached for a condom and unwrapped it, cutting the foil with his teeth.

"Put it on," he said, handing it to her.

"Not without another taste of you," she murmured.

Lowering her lips, she brushed the length of his erection with her tongue. Then she slid the condom on with a single, deft stroke.

She knew her way around the block, but he was too far gone to care. Everything about her was too perfect. He grabbed her and positioned her underneath him. He wanted these pleasant sexual feelings to last, but he wanted it fast and hard, too.

He expelled a breath and then plunged inside her, consumed with the need to possess her, to make her his.

As always, she felt tight and buttery warm. Wanting these sensations to last, he forced himself to move with excruciating slowness. She grew wetter and hotter, and after only a few strokes, he knew he was about to lose all control.

He was still fighting to pull back from the edge when she stroked his cheek with the back of her hand, her caress infinitely loving. Her mouth met his, and her kiss was so deep and carnal and so utterly possessive and yet tender, too, that he felt completely hers. Crying out her name, he exploded.

The instant he came, she did, too, weeping as she followed him over the glorious precipice. She continued to sob softly afterward, just like she had as a girl that first time under the palm trees. She kissed his brow tenderly as if she, too, were overcome by more than passion.

Damn her. Damn her tears, and yet they gratified deep, all-consuming needs inside him that he did not want to acknowledge. Again, he folded her into his arms, holding her until her sobs died down. Only then did he gather up his clothes from the four corners where she'd flung them.

As he pulled on his shirt and jeans, he was aware of her glowing eyes watching him in the dark. Then she got out of bed and scampered shyly to the bathroom. He heard water. When she returned she was wearing a terry robe. Her face and hair were damp and gleaming, and she looked like an angel.

"I love you," she whispered.

He went still, hating her for that awed tone that made him feel things she had no right to make him feel. He held up a single finger, warning her.

"I do," she said, again in that broken voice that cut him to ribbons.

"Hush. I think you're old enough to know that what happened had nothing to do with love."

When he strode out of her bedroom toward the

stairs, she followed right behind him. He wondered what her next trick would be.

"Michael, if you go, I'll be scared again."

Right. She'd been scared. Reason why he'd come in the first place. He was a cop. How could he have forgotten that?

"Why the hell were you scared?"

When she told him about the man in the park and the sounds in her backyard and the light being on and the file boxes disappearing, he frowned. Then he and she rechecked all the doors and windows and the alarm.

"I'll check outside, too," he said, "and I'll stay out in my car."

"You could stay in here."

"No."

"But, when you leave…"

"If you hear anything, call me."

Her big blue eyes were so wide with fear and hurt, he hated himself for being so determined to escape her. Fortunately, being in the living room where they'd fought grounded him and made him remember about Carmen, so he went to the bookcase and picked up two pictures, of Alexis and Carmen.

"Can I have these?"

Rosie's face went even whiter. When she nodded, he strode past her out the door.

Carmen couldn't believe that she was at a café on Lamar with Xavier, feeling like a college girl on a date instead of an exotic dancer.

"It's late," she murmured, smiling. Was her smile as stupid and innocent as Alexis's frog's?

His gaze was deep and dark and warm. Boy, did he ooze Latin charm.

"I shouldn't be drinking coffee at this hour," she said.

Xavier continued to stare into her eyes as he sipped from his mug.

"If you don't like it here, we could go somewhere and study," he said. "Make the most of our coffee buzz."

Study? She'd forgotten about him being a student.

"I'm not in the mood."

"Neither am I," he admitted. "So what were you talking with that older guy for?"

"Jealous?"

"Were you trying to make me jealous?"

"Maybe."

"That's a dirty trick."

"I'm full of them."

She set her coffee mug down and took a deep breath. For some reason, she didn't want to talk about Nash. He made her feel uncomfortable, and she didn't know why.

"So, you're getting your GED, too?"

"I don't want to be a yardman forever," he replied.

"Or a boy toy?" Suddenly she was angry about Yolie. Not that Xavier's life was any of Carmen's business.

When she picked up her spoon and stirred her coffee much too loudly, just so she'd have something to do, he seized her wrist, stilling her hand.

Her spoon dropped, splashing hot coffee.

"That's over."

"Why?"

"You know why. Because of you."

"Oh, right. I'm so special?"

"If you want to hate yourself, I can't stop you."
He shrugged.

"Does Yolie know?"

"I'm not going to talk about her, either."

"Why?"

"Because I'm here with you. This is about us. Just
us." Slowly, he leaned across the table and kissed her
gently on the mouth.

His kiss made her heart flutter and caused her lips
to feel warm. She was surprised when he didn't
deepen his kiss and push for more. She sort of ached
for him to do that, she who didn't like sex. But
instead, he sat back down and lifted his coffee mug
in a mock salute to her.

She sipped from her mug, and tried to act suave.
Whatever. Acting suave was the last thing from
easy, since his dumb kiss had changed everything,
at least for her.

A new electricity charged the air. A strange ex-
pectancy filled her.

I've got the hots for him, she thought. *That's all. Just
a bad case of the hots.*

"That older guy in the bar. He looks like you a
little bit. He an uncle or something?"

"No!" She felt vaguely shocked. "He's a cop. Homicide. He's trying to find Dr. Carver's murderer. I think he's interested in my mother, though. They used to date when they were young."

Xavier's hand brushed hers. "Why are you so mad all the time?"

"As if you really care."

"As if? I do." He nodded.

If he was for real, he was the first guy who'd ever seemed genuinely interested in who she was. Probably she should blow him off, but for some reason she didn't.

"Why I am mad? If I knew, maybe I could stop. Maybe it has to do with my mother. She…wasn't ever around when I was young. And when she was, I was always in my room with my television and my computer and my sketchpad. Do you think she ever knocked on the door? Do you think she cared if I drew?"

"You lived in the same house, didn't you?"

"Yeah, but…"

"So, she was around."

"That doesn't count."

"Hey, I could tell you a thing or two about mothers who aren't around."

He stopped.

"What?"

He hesitated. "I come from Nicaragua. Life was tough on the farm. Sometimes if a crop failed or the market was bad, we went hungry. I resented the hard brutal farm work. I was planning to run away. Then one night a bunch of thugs showed up. They had guns. We had machetes."

"And?"

"I hid in a storage bin. They did things…to my parents and sisters." His handsome face darkened. His eyes smoldered.

He was so hot looking when he was angry.

"How horrible," Carmen whispered.

"My mother died that night. So did my father. I hid, but I cracked the hatch and watched. They took my sisters with them. I was ten, but I knew I was a coward. I should have tried to save them, but I was too afraid. *Cobarde.*" He spat the word. "That's what I am."

"No…" Much to her surprise, her hand had closed around his, and she was holding him tightly.

"After that I was very angry. I hate that country. I knew I would leave there. I do not want to take a wife and make her work so hard as we worked…or to watch her die. So I walk north, always north. Sometimes I work four or six months or more. Sometimes *La Migra,* they catch me and send me back to Nicaragua, but *siempre* I just start walking north again. *Siempre* I know one thing. One day I be American like you. That's why I study English."

"Like we have it so great."

"You do."

"I was being sarcastic."

"Anybody up here is lucky. Even a yardman like me.

I love this country. At night, you can walk the streets, and nobody bothers you. No police. You can be anything you want to be—if you're willing to work."

She thought about that. "So, how did you get your green card?"

"I had friends who knew Yolie. She knew an immigration lawyer."

"Did she make you sleep with her?"

"No. I liked her."

"But she's old and fat. How could you?"

"I liked her…a lot. She looks good. Healthy. I still like her. She is my friend. Nobody ever better friend. I want to keep my job at Taco Bonito. But I don't want to sleep with her now, so I won't."

"Nobody came in the night and did anything to us, but I blamed my mother for all my miseries."

"You've got to stop that."

"There's no way you could understand what it's like to be me." Carmen lashed out, feeling frustrated because he didn't understand and wasn't trying to.

"After a certain age, you're grown-up. You're all grown-up, Carmen."

"As if anything's that simple."

"You're on your own, really. You're responsible for the rest of your life. Not your mother. If you're going to hate anybody for screwing your life up, you'd better start with yourself."

"Okay! Okay! I get it!"

Suddenly, she didn't want to talk to him anymore.

Talking was stupid. Maybe guys had it right. Maybe dealing with bodies was easier than dealing with minds. He was cute and so hot.

He probably didn't want to talk, either. On an impulse, she leaned across the table and kissed him. Only not like he'd kissed her. She put her tongue in his mouth and sucked hard.

"What are you doing?" he said, his breathing instantly coming rougher and faster.

"You know. Do you want to go somewhere?"

"I live with five guys. It's not a nice place. Where do you live?" he said.

She shook her head. "Apartment. Roommates. Maybe we could use Yolie's pool house."

"Okay."

When they got to the narrow, wooded lane that led to Yolie's, Xavier cut the engine. They got off and pushed the bike the rest of the way, so they wouldn't wake all the neighbors up.

"There's a light on in the pool house. And that's Darius's car," Xavier said. "So I guess we can't—"

"But, look, the big house is dark. Rosie told me that Yolie's in Victoria." Carmen pulled out her house key. "I think Rosie is over at her house, unpacking."

"You call your mother Rosie?"

"To make her mad. What of it?"

Carmen opened the door and turned off the alarm. Once inside, she began to kiss him. Still kissing him, she led him into the den. "You'd better have a condom because I'm not on the pill," she said.

"What?"

"You thought a girl like me—"

"Don't put words in my mouth."

"I haven't done it with anybody since Alexis was born."

"*Porqué no?*"

"Bad experience."

"You don't like sex?"

"Not much," she admitted.

"That could change."

"I don't think so."

He pulled a condom out of his pocket and put it on a table. "We don't have to do it, you know. Only if you want to."

"Kiss me. I like kissing."

He took her in his arms, and his kisses were gentle and tender, like the first one at the café.

She'd thought he'd be all macho and tough, but he wasn't. He'd even told her he was a coward. She'd liked him way better for admitting that. She really thought she might like him a lot. Imagine that.

She lay down on the couch, and he sat beside her. He was smiling, and so was she. Still, there was a haunted look in his black eyes.

She identified with what he'd suffered. Maybe misery did love company. She was very happy with him, which was probably stupid, since he was from

Nicaragua and all. He'd probably never want to talk to her again if they did it. Probably, he'd even think she was a whore.

"Hold me," she said, her voice barely above a whisper.

Twenty-Seven

Yolie's big, white house loomed out of the dark trees.
Home. Well, finally.

It had been a long day and an even longer night.
Yolie was tired of strange beds. Even so, as she stared
up at her house, the hairs on the back of her neck
stood on end.

When she reached for her garage-door opener, it
wasn't there. The hairs arced higher. Then she remembered she'd stashed it in her trunk because it had
kept falling onto the floorboards. Still, she shivered
as she cut the engine.

Why this strange feeling that she was being
watched?

Yolie took a deep breath. She'd worked with her
contractor in Victoria until 8:00 p.m. Then Ralph,
her CEO, had had to call with a fresh crisis about
Lucy, one of her top local managers. Ralph had

accused her of stealing, and Lucy had called to defend herself, and had made countercharges of her own.

Why couldn't Ralph ever, just once, handle anything? Yolie needed a strong man in his position.

Talk about the straw breaking the camel's back. The two phone calls had pushed her over the edge.

She felt betrayed, tired, overwhelmed. She was getting too old for all the emergencies that came from owning her little empire.

Yolie was sick of what the murder and the press coverage were doing to Rosie, too. As if her house fire hadn't been devastating enough. Rosie loved her job at the hospital, and to lose that, too…

Yolie got out of her Cadillac and stretched. Her back was killing her. She punched her remote and popped her trunk. She was rolling her suitcase to the back door when something gleamed in the moonlight.

Her brows knitted when she saw Xavier's big bike among the trees. What was he doing here at this hour?

Waiting for her, maybe? Had Ralph called him?

Yolie smiled. Ralph must have told him about Lucy, and he'd come over to console her.

How sweet. Hopefully, he was waiting for her in her bed.

It was only when she found the back door slightly ajar that those little hairs on the back of her neck began to flair in alarm again. Once more, she felt she was being watched. Immediately, she stopped pulling the noisy suitcase and dug out her cell phone. She slipped off her shoes, too.

All was quiet in the kitchen, but she heard heavy breathing and soft rap music in her den. Her head pounding, she punched 911. Her fingertip remained poised over the send/call button.

The lights were out in the den, but her stereo *was* playing rap ever so softly.

Rap at this hour could mean only one thing.

She didn't call out to Xavier, but when she stepped into the den, her eyes zeroed in on the couch.

Maybe it was dark, but she could still see Xavier on top of Rosie. Not that Yolie could make out all that much of Rosie other than her long, pale legs and her tangled coppery curls spilling over the pink satin cushions.

Feeling sick to her stomach, Yolie cupped a hand over her mouth and backed toward the kitchen. As she did so, she watched the muscles of Xavier's lean, powerful shoulders and his cute brown butt flex and relax.

He looked ridiculous, vulnerable, but hot, too.

God, she'd missed him.

Rosie was moaning softly and whispering, "Faster...faster!"

Treacherous, lying bitch!

My couch! I can't believe the bitch is doing it on my pink chenille couch! She knows I shelled out eight thousand bucks for that couch! She knows I loved it! Loved it!

Yolie was fixating on the couch because her temples throbbed so insanely she was afraid she might burst some important vessel. She felt numb, but she was shaking, too. Thank God she wasn't one of those scaredy-cat women who carried a gun in her purse. She would have shot them both for sure.

Finally, she had the gumption to tiptoe backward until she reached the kitchen door. Grabbing her shoes and tugging them on, she ran outside, where she sucked in huge mouthfuls of warm, humid air.

The moon was very bright and the lane quiet. Cicadas made music in the soft night breeze, which held the hint of rain.

Part of her wanted to go back and throw things at them and yell obscenities. Instead, she went to her car, popped a blood-pressure pill just in case, and then stumbled past her suitcase and headed toward the park. Keeping to the path that led alongside a grove of pecan trees, she walked until she came to an empty bench.

She was tired. Only when she sat down did she realize that her lungs were burning and her heart was beating so hard she was still afraid it might explode. Staring up through the trees at the moon, she fought to catch her breath.

No wonder Xavier had been avoiding the house. No wonder Rosie had been so evasive about where he might be. Bitch! How long had this been going on? Months, probably.

For the first time ever, Yolie thought of cutting back her workload and joining a spa.

Fun question: why was she killing herself with work?

Un-fun answer: to buy chenille couches for her ex-favorite girlfriend to screw her lover on behind her back.

Bile rose in her throat. The trees and moon blurred sickeningly. Gradually, ever so gradually, her furious heart slowed. Still, she'd never felt so old and tired or so utterly drained.

She'd loved that skinny, neurotic bitch.

Suddenly, Yolie heard a motorcycle engine near her house. Was Xavier leaving? That was fast. A quickie?

Well—no time like the present. She wanted Rosie out of her house—now! And out of her life—forever!

"Oh, God! What now?" Rosie sat up in bed. Was that laughter and rap music she heard downstairs?

She'd been sleeping lightly after her confrontation with Michael and the mind-boggling sex. Had he come back?

But rap? What was going on?

Without turning on the light, she rummaged in her drawer for Harry's gun. Only her hands began to shake as soon as she felt cold polymer, and she nearly dropped it. She let out a little cry.

Below her the music stopped. Then she heard frantic scuffling sounds.

She found the clip and jammed it inside. Hurriedly, she pulled her robe on and slipped down the hall to the landing.

All appeared quiet in the den, but when she descended and touched the stereo, it was still warm.

She was turning on the light when she heard a motorcycle roar away. She ran to the kitchen just as Yolie slammed through the door.

"Xavier?"

"No, sweetie-pie, it's me," Yolie said in a strange, dead tone as she flung her rolling suitcase aside, so hard it crashed on the kitchen floor.

Thrilled, relieved, Rosie slid the Glock into the pocket of her robe. "I'm so glad you're home…."

"I'll bet." Yolie flipped on another light. Her ashen face and anguished eyes made Rosie freeze.

Fear rushed at her and she didn't know why. "What? What is it?"

When Yolie didn't answer, an unnerving silence mushroomed in the dark house.

"Bitch! Get your skinny ass and all your crap and Alexis out of my house!"

"What?"

"Now!" When Rosie stood there mutely, Yolie stormed past her up the stairs. "Are you deaf? If you don't know how to move your skinny cheating ass out, I damn sure do!"

"Skinny cheating ass?"

Rosie heard crashing sounds upstairs. Then Yolie appeared on the landing, and a bundle of clothes, a suitcase, a travel alarm clock flew down to the first floor.

The alarm clock shattered, and Alexis woke up and began to cry.

"Get out, both of you!" Yolie yelled down at Rosie when Alexis appeared in the hall with her blue blanket, "before I turn somebody into taco meat!"

Michael felt like hell. Even though he was furious at Rosie about Carmen, and for using sex to manipulate him last night, he didn't want to be here so soon again—not even to arrest her.

Despite his dark glasses, his temples pounded. The morning sun felt way too harsh as he jabbed at Yolie's doorbell. The potent combination of booze, sex and rage, not to mention inner civil war, had him feeling as if he were about to explode.

The captain had pulled strings—lots of them. The DNA results on the hairs Pierce's bloody hand had been clutching had been rushed through. The hairs had been plucked out Rosie's shining mane, all right, just as Michael had suspected.

The captain had stormed into his office with the results. "What the hell are you waiting for? All the evidence points to her. *All!* So much for your hunches! I call this conclusive as hell."

Michael had had a hard time talking him into allowing her to turn herself in with Benson by her side, instead of sending a couple of uniforms out to pick her up. So here he was in person at her door, ready to explain her options.

Behind the door in question he heard an angry shout, followed by running footsteps. Then Yolie stood before him in a pool of yellow sunlight with her hair wrapped in a wet towel, scowling.

"*Well! Finally!* But if you're here to arrest her, you're too damn late. *She's gone.* I have only one question—what the hell have you been waiting for? The bitch is dangerous. She deserves to fry."

"Where I can find her?"

"Try Xavier Hernandez's bed. He's my former pool boy. I just caught her doing the two-timing bastard! On my pink chenille couch!"

Yolie slammed the door in Michael's face.

Thunder rumbled outside. As Yolie popped another blood pressure pill, she could hear the wind, too. She hoped all that howling in the eaves meant they'd get some rain for a change. Like all of Texas, which was under a statewide burn ban, the grass on her ranch was as brown and dry as tinder. She was having to buy feed.

She watched the storm blast the oak trees. After the way her day had started, she was in the mood for a storm. She didn't care if it blew down every tree in Texas.

It was midafternoon, but the sky was dark. This had been a long day. After she'd dealt with Lucy and

Ralph, she'd played catch-up in her office. She'd ordered Ralph to fire Xavier. When he'd asked why, she'd said, "Because I said so."

She was almost done matching invoices to the bids on her Victoria properties and wondering which project to tackle next, when she heard her secretary's raised voice outside.

Sweet, mild-tempered Cory never shouted.

A man's deep, faintly accented voice rose above Cory's.

Xavier.

Yolie threw her pencil down. That Nicaraguan bastard had his nerve.

"She distinctly told me you were not to be admitted, Mr. Hernandez. She said you don't work here anymore."

Yolie heard the heavy tread of Xavier's boots and Cory's scurrying high heels. Without so much as a knock, Xavier pushed his way inside.

His black, long-lashed eyes clashed with Yolie's. When he refused to look away, she flinched at the audacity of his steely gaze.

She was furious, too, but mostly at herself, that she could find him as handsome and captivatingly attractive as ever, despite everything the horny bastard had done.

She'd gone without too long. Sexual deprivation. The cheating rat had been neglecting her. Other than Vicenzo, when she'd vacationed in Italy, Xavier had been it. Hell, she should have diversified her sexual portfolio.

His gaze burned her. His face, so thoroughly masculine, was all sharp, angular planes. He looked young, desperate, but very determined.

"If you're smart, you'll go before you make me madder," she said icily.

"Not until I say what I have to say. Ralph, he call and fire me. I tell him nobody fire me but you."

Yolie fought a smile. She admired determination, even his, especially now, when he didn't stand a chance in hell.

"I'm sorry, Ms. Carver," Cory said from the door, her tone flustered and apologetic. "I told him you didn't want to see him. I'll call security...."

Xavier's eyes never left Yolie's face. For a kid, he had guts. Xavier was smart, too. She needed smart employees. She'd always intended to keep him around after their affair was over. Too bad he'd ruined all that.

"No. It's okay, Cory. I can take it from here."

When she'd left, Xavier tilted his arrogant chin defensively.

"Sit the hell down," Yolie ordered.

He pressed his gorgeous lips together. For a second or two she thought he would defy her.

He was too tall. The last thing she wanted was him towering over her while they had it out. She needed every advantage she could get.

Watching her, he sat down slowly.

"You've got your nerve—coming here," she said.

"I see your Cadillac in the driveway this morning," he said.

She arched her brows.

"I look for you, but I don't find you. I owe you an explanation," he said. He lowered his eyes as if…as if he felt contrite.

Damn him, he was handsome. Tough, but sensitive and sweet, too. No wonder Rosie…

Damn Rosie to hell.

"I should have talked to you first…told you about her. I should never have brought Carmen to your house like that. I'm sorry."

Carmen?

"Carmen?" Yolie almost screamed the name. Intense relief flooded her. She was so stunned, she could only stare at him stupidly as she sank back into her leather chair.

"I saw you two last night…on my pink couch," she whispered.

He looked away as if mortally ashamed. "I was afraid of that. It just happened, Carmen and me. I didn't mean for it to. I'd been hanging out at The Cellar for a while. She's pretty. And pretty mixed up. Not like you. You're very wise."

"But she's pretty. I guess it didn't hurt that she runs around naked all the time."

"But it wasn't just that. She seemed so sad. Like I said, it just happened."

"I understand," Yolie said, and she did.

Men were all the same. They wanted one thing.

Above all things, Yolie was practical. She'd expected this. She just hadn't known the details. Suddenly, all her anger toward him was gone.

Xavier didn't want her anymore. And she didn't care. Not that much, anyway. She was not one to obsess about her lovers, as Rosie had done about Pierce.

Yolie's affair with Xavier had lasted longer than her affairs usually did. All she cared about was that Rosie hadn't betrayed her.

"I feel awful," he said.

"How do you think I feel?"

Let him suffer. Because of him she'd been awful to Rosie. As if Rosie didn't have enough problems.

When her silence brought tension, he got up and moved around her desk.

"I want you to leave," she said.

Like most of the guys she bedded, he wasn't obedient. Passive types did not turn her on. So he kept on coming, assuming rights he no longer had. When he reached her, he put the back of his hand on her cheek.

She jerked her head back. "If Ralph hadn't fired you already, I should fire you for that. I would anybody else." But when he stroked her again, she felt comforted by both his touch and the profound regret in his dark eyes.

"I fired Lucy," she said, to impress him that she could.

"She stole money. She been stealing money a long time."

"And what you did is so different?"

"I should have been honest with you before—not after. But I'm being honest with you now," he said. "That was first time with me and Carmen. You do much for me. I can't forget that. The sex was good between us, but the friendship was even better."

"I can't believe I'm standing here like a sap letting you stroke my cheek and talk nonsense after you screwed my best friend's daughter on my couch. My favorite couch."

"Sap?"

"Get a dictionary. I'm not your English teacher anymore, kid."

"I want us to stay friends. I want to go on working for you. I want you to tell Ralph I'm not fired."

"Maybe you want too much."

Much to her surprise, she didn't fight him when he folded her into his arms. "I will work hard for you," he said. "Harder than Ralph. Harder than anybody." She felt his lips fleetingly nuzzle her hair before he let her go.

"I want you as a friend, too," she heard someone with her voice say. "You were too young for me, anyway."

He smiled. "You are great woman. You need a real man. Someday you find him, I think."

"Okay. I'll call Ralph. I'm not going to fire you today, after all," she whispered. "Maybe tomorrow."

"But then maybe not." He smiled again, and she saw the wild relief in his eyes. "I hope not."

He lifted her hand and brought it to his lips in a gallant gesture.

Why hadn't she seen it before? She'd been drawn to him because they were alike in so many ways. He was brilliant, industrious, energetic and very ambitious. He'd started at the bottom just like she had, after Pierce had dumped her. Only his situation was worse.

Did she want to kill herself working forever? She needed a young man with ambition, and not just for sex.

"You're an incredible woman. I admire you more than anybody I have ever known."

"Enough of your flattery. Just go…for now. I'll be fine…in a few days. Really, I'll be fine."

And she would be as soon as she apologized to Rosie. She was going to have to crawl to her friend on bended knees.

Rosie!

That cop had shown up at her door! Yolie had deliberately avoided watching or listening or even reading the news all day because she'd wanted to put Rosie out of her mind.

Yolie ran across the room and flipped on her office television set just in time.

A beautiful skinny-assed anchorwoman beamed at her.

"A source has revealed that Castle's arrest may be

imminent. After a short break, we'll bring you the latest on this rapidly developing story."

Yolie let out a howl of outrage.

Twenty-Eight

Yolie was right. The captain was right. Michael knew he should be throwing the book at Rosie. So what the hell was he doing here—still hoping to save her?

The women's shelter, a yellow, two-story stucco mansion hidden beneath tall pecan trees, was located on a quiet, out-of-the way street in central Austin. To protect the victims, no sign identified the building's true purpose.

Michael leaned forward across the small, round table that separated him from Mrs. McClarney, the shelter's director. Not that he really saw her. No, his mind was filled with visions of Rosie writhing beneath Xavier's lusty young body on plump, pink, chenille-covered cushions.

"So, you say Anita Carver ran away from the shelter last night?" His deep voice betrayed none of his fury.

Enraged, he'd been racing toward Rosie's, when on

the vaguest of hunches, he'd made a U-turn and ended up here to tie up a loose thread.

Mrs. McClarney took a deep breath and let it out slowly. Her gaze was intense and eager behind her thick glasses. She'd called him this morning, probably because she saw herself as a star witness in a front-page police investigation.

"Our next-door neighbor saw Anita leave…last night around two in the morning," she whispered, attempting to suppress her excitement.

He wrote that down. Then he glanced out the window at the gray, rainy day that too perfectly matched his dark mood. The captain had ordered him to see to the arrest of Rosie Castle—*ordered him*.

"My, but you look tired," Mrs. McClarney said. "You're sure you wouldn't like for me to brew that pot of tea?"

"I'm fine."

"Well…where was I?"

"Anita Carver's disappearance."

"We didn't miss her until breakfast. I didn't think to call you until I saw that news bulletin this morning about how you're about to arrest the killer."

"The suspect," he growled.

"The sooner that woman is locked up, the safer we'll all feel, especially Mrs. Carver!"

"Refresh my memory. How long did Anita live here?"

"She came here with her girls for the first time six

weeks ago. We don't encourage our ladies to converse with their abusers, but she must have. Dr. Carver acted very remorseful, so, after a couple of weeks, she and the girls moved back with him. But nothing changed, and they came back in the middle of the night. Meanwhile, her first husband, in Guatemala, was receiving frantic phone calls from the girls, who were scared and wanted to go home."

"I hadn't heard about the girls' calling their father."

"When Dr. Carver was killed, Anita left the shelter again. We all thought that would be the last we'd see of her."

"Wasn't it?"

"No. She sent her girls back to Guatemala to live with their father, but she's been staying here at the shelter ever since she ran into that awful Castle woman at Dr. Morgan's office."

"What?"

"The Castle woman clearly scared her. We kept telling her that Dr. Carver was dead, that he couldn't hurt her anymore. But she's terrified of that woman. What's strange is that Anita hasn't been nearly as forthcoming in her therapy sessions since his death as she was before."

"Do you think she could have returned to Guatemala to join her girls?"

"Maybe, but she was very firm about never wanting to go back there. She was scared of her first husband, too, you see. He was furious at her for marrying Carver and putting his daughters in danger. She used to laugh and say that she had two husbands who wanted to kill her."

"Laugh?"

"That was her way of dealing with her helplessness. Anita wants to be taken care of. She's not the type to stand on her own two feet. She wants what she calls 'the beautiful life with a strong man.' If you would just arrest that Castle woman, maybe…"

"Right," Michael mumbled.

He shook her hand and then strode rapidly out the door and down the sidewalk through the driving rain to his Crown Vic. Photographs of Carmen and Alexis lay on the passenger seat. Feeling too frustrated for words, he turned the pictures facedown. Then, gunning the engine, he flipped on his windshield wipers and roared out of the parking lot.

He had to arrest Rosie. He'd used everything in his arsenal in the hopes he'd get a lucky break, but he hadn't.

He'd failed her. All the evidence he'd discovered from the knife, the hairs, the video, the fingerprints, to her underwear—all of it pointed to her.

She was going down. Period.

Rosie's stomach knotted when a beautiful anchorwoman beamed at her from her kitchen TV.

"A source has revealed that Castle's arrest may be

imminent. After a short break, we'll bring you the latest on this rapidly developing story."

With a trembling hand, Rosie lowered the volume and returned to her mother and Carmen in her den.

Her arrest was imminent? Alexis was home sick. What would happen to her if Rosie got hauled off to jail?

Still, it was strange how even today her life had the semblance of normalcy, with disaster looming over her as darkly as the low clouds outside threatening rain. Here she was, standing in the comfort of her own den flanked by Carmen and Hazel. Harry was outside hammering away because, after he'd repaired the Beamer, she'd given him a checklist of things to do to complete the work on her house.

As if she actually had a future here.

Michael had sworn the DNA results would take forever. He must have lied.

Why else could the talking heads on all the local news channels be so sure that the Austin PD had damning new evidence that would put her behind bars?

Because things were so bad and she couldn't stand being alone, especially after her scare yesterday, Rosie had called Hazel and Carmen and Harry and begged them to come over to work on her house.

As if she really cared about getting her house in order. She just couldn't stand the thought of being alone after last night.

As always, Hazel had on too much lipstick and eyeliner. Her red slacks and T-shirt were too tight and her dangly, black-cat earrings too gaudy. But Carmen was dressed modestly for a change. Not that Rosie cared what either of them wore. She just wanted them with her.

When a bolt of lightning streaked the rapidly darkening sky, followed by a violent rumble of thunder that shook the house, Rosie glanced out at Harry.

"So, what do you think about Mr. Rabbit up there?" Carmen said, her voice falsely cheery. Rosie's stomach wound tighter. If Carmen was being nice to her, she was definitely doomed.

Rosie tried to concentrate on the Wedgwood bunny Hazel had just placed in the center of her bookshelf. Years ago the mother of one of Rosie's young patients who'd died of cancer had given her the bunny.

Out of the blue, Rosie thought about Linda, the painter who'd been stung by a bee and fallen, the young mother who might never walk again. She needed to call Beth and find out about her.

"Mr. Rabbit deserves a place of honor," Hazel said.

Rosie shook her head. "I can't even see him."

Carmen squinted at Mr. Rabbit. She was about to put in her two cents' worth, but Harry began to hammer with renewed vengeance.

"Who can think with that racket?" Hazel said querulously.

Dragging her blue blanket behind her, Alexis

walked into the den. Her head was drooping and her shoulders were slumped. "Can I stay in here with you and watch *Sesame Street?*" she asked in a low, pitiful tone.

The poor little darling had huge, dark rings under her listless blue eyes. She was brightly flushed, a sure sign of fever. To make matters worse, she began to cough.

"You're only home because you're sick. You have to stay in bed until we can get you to the doctor," Rosie began. "But since you're up, you'd probably better get dressed. Put on something nice. I just talked to the doctor, and he said he'd work you in. We need to leave pretty soon."

"No! I want to watch Big Bird with you all!"

"And why can't she watch him?" Carmen asked, taking Alexis's side for once.

To Rosie's utter amazement, her daughter even knelt. Putting her arm around Alexis, Carmen asked her if she'd like some orange juice. When Alexis snuggled closer and nodded shyly, she picked her up and carried her into the kitchen.

"I could take her to the doctor in a minute…if that would help," Carmen said, when Rosie and Hazel followed them. Her thoughtfulness stunned Rosie.

"It *would* help," she admitted slowly, as she looked out at the dark clouds.

She glanced at Carmen and Alexis. Again, she was struck by how modestly her daughter was dressed—in jeans and a T-shirt that weren't the least bit tight. And what was with the no-makeup routine?

Carmen had left off the heavy eyeliner and lip gloss. No big hair, either. Her bright curls were pulled back into a ponytail, giving her a clean-cut, girlish look.

Unfortunately, Carmen caught her staring. "What? What are you looking at?"

The full force of her chocolate-dark eyes hit Rosie like a blow. Why did she have to look so painfully like Michael today, of all days, when he'd probably turn up to arrest her?

"Nothing," she said, but her heart lurched guiltily.

Being with Carmen when she was being nice and supportive at such a terrible time felt good. Rosie wanted her real life. She wished she were a nurse again, just a nurse, and a grandmother, and a mother, and a daughter—even if she was inadequate in all those roles. Maybe she wouldn't even mind being forty.

Most of all, she wanted Michael. But it was too late—she'd been blind to what was really important far too long.

When raindrops began to pelt the windows, Harry raced past them into the kitchen. First, he poured himself a glass of water, and then he opened her fridge. Without asking, he grabbed the remote and turned the television set up a little louder.

"How come he gets to watch TV—" Alexis began when she heard the television.

"He's a man," Hazel said, causing Alexis to howl.

The abrasive tone of the anchorwoman filled the kitchen and spilled into the den. "This just came in. The APD has conclusive DNA results in the Carver case."

Everybody ran into the kitchen. Rosie turned up the volume. The visual was of an unsmiling Michael striding purposefully through the rain toward his Crown Vic, with half a dozen reporters shouting after him, "Are you going to arrest Ms. Castle?"

Her heart stopped.

"No comment," Nash said.

"We've learned that an arrest may be imminent. Stay tuned, and we'll bring you the latest on this headline story."

Fear built inside Rosie. Quickly, she flipped channels, stopping on Martha Stewart's show. A smiling Martha was explaining how to get red candle wax off a white tablecloth.

"Like, are you going to switch back to the news?" Harry asked.

Rosie found a strange comfort in watching Martha, an ex-con—one she admired, thank you very much— iron paper towels on top of the tablecloth with brisk, sure motions, as if she were solving life's great problems.

"Martha went to prison, and she's doing okay," Rosie said.

"I've got something to tell you, Mother, before we leave for the doctor." Carmen's voice was low and shyly confidential.

When Rosie turned to give Carmen her full attention, Alexis slunk over to the television and switched to a cartoon channel.

"I gave the Naked Babies two weeks to find another singer," Carmen said.

The cartoons were blaring, and a flushed, mischievous Alexis clutched the remote defiantly to her chest. Instead of arguing, Rosie, who wanted to hear Carmen, simply yanked the television plug out of the wall.

"I want to watch cartoons!" Alexis cried, throwing down the now useless remote and clasping her blanket.

"Television rots your brain, young lady. Besides, you need to get dressed." Rosie watched Alexis march out of the kitchen and then turned back to Carmen. "So, you're quitting the Naked Babies?"

"I've already heard this." Hazel plugged the television cord back into the wall and flipped channels until she landed on the news.

Carmen smiled at Rosie. "I'm getting my GED. I—I've been saving money, too. I think I might want to go to college. Maybe study art. Maybe be a teacher or something."

"Why, Carmen…that's wonderful! I can help you…if you need money, or a place to stay…."

But could she, if she was in prison? She'd never been there for Carmen. Never. Maybe now she never would be.

"TV isn't so bad," Harry said.

He could be slow when it came to keeping up with

conversations. He seized the remote with one hand while he slathered peanut butter on a thick slice of bread with the other, and turned up the volume.

"Like last night on this forensic show, there was this case about identical twins," he shouted over the TV. "Did you know twins have the same DNA? Not the same fingerprints, though, just the same DNA?"

"Everybody knows that," Rosie said absently. She wasn't focused on Harry or the TV. She was pleased that Carmen was finally thinking about her future. How and when should she tell her about Michael?

If the talking heads were right, she was running out of time.

When Alexis ran back into the kitchen, she was flushed an even deeper shade of red and coughing, and yet grinning from ear to ear as if she was very pleased with herself and her costume.

"Looks like somebody's all dressed up to go to the doctor," Carmen said gently.

"I told you to put on something nice," Rosie said.

"I did, Mimi."

In spite of her own dire predicament, Rosie smiled.

Alexis's favorite pink T-shirt with the rhinestone blue horse on it was on wrong-side out as well as backward. Her ripped jeans stopped six inches above her ankles, a sure sign they were last year's pair. Her athletic shoes were on the wrong feet, and their grimy shoelaces trailed behind her.

Like any female who knew she was beautifully attired, Alexis beamed.

"Come here and I'll tie your shoelaces," Carmen said. "Then we'll go to the doctor and get you all well."

"I don't want a shot! Mimi, I don't want a shot!"

"Carmen, be sure the doctor calls me on my cell after he checks her. My main phone line still hasn't been reconnected."

"No shot, Mimi!"

Twenty-Nine

No good deed goes unpunished.

Rain drummed on the windshield, and the wipers slashed viciously back and forth. Carmen's hands tightened on the steering wheel as Alexis coughed. The hacking sounds were so long and drawn out, Carmen clenched her teeth and glared at the thousands of red taillights in front of her.

Her cell phone was between her legs, so that if Xavier called, she could catch it. But had he called? What a sap she was for even thinking he would. Doubt was eating away at the sexual and emotional afterglow that had lingered for hours like a magical shield after he'd made love to her.

So much for not liking sex. All they'd had was an aborted quickie, but being with Xavier had been great.

Alexis's coughs were so loud they pierced Carmen's eardrums. What was with this awful storm?

Xavier? Who was she kidding? He'd gotten what he wanted. He'd bought her a lousy cup of coffee and she'd opened her legs. He was probably bragging to all his roommates about how easy she'd been.

The rain was coming down in sheets now. Alexis wouldn't stop coughing. The phone refused to ring, and the freeway was jammed. Suddenly, the violent weather, the stalled traffic and her sick daughter were a metaphor for her going-nowhere life.

Maybe Xavier was just busy. He'd said he had a big test. He worked for Yolie, too. He'd gotten scared when he'd seen her Cadillac in the drive. What if he got fired because of Carmen?

She felt that if she didn't know the answer to her questions about Xavier and last night soon, she'd explode.

Alexis began to gag. Gritting her teeth, Carmen whirled on her. "Stop it, damn it! I can't hear myself think!"

"Why are you always so mean to me?" Alexis rasped, her voice weak and choked.

"You're such a little wimp."

"Because you're so mean." Alexis began to cry, which made her hack all the harder. Her face was red, and she nearly bent double as she clutched her blue blanket, coughing even louder. "I—I want Mimi! Call Mimi!"

Carmen felt as if she couldn't take one more second of being trapped like this. When the traffic began to move, she shot off the freeway onto the feeder.

"This isn't how Mimi goes."

"Just stop."

Spinning gravel, Carmen headed into a convenience store parking lot and slammed on the brakes. Another pair of headlights followed her. It was a black Jeep.

When Carmen parked as close as she could to the store's front door, Alexis crossed her arms over her chest with a shudder as the Jeep parked in front of the Dumpster.

"This isn't the doctor's office!" she said.

"I'm getting you some stupid cough drops. So stay put while I go inside to buy them."

Hating herself for the way she'd been acting, not to mention feeling, Carmen stormed through the downpour into the store, getting soaked in the process.

She rushed from aisle to aisle until she finally found a box of cherry-flavored cough drops. What was wrong with her? Why did she always get so mad?

Funny, how Alexis being sick had her scared to death. Not that she wanted to admit it. Alexis wasn't going to die or anything. This wasn't Nicaragua. Little kids didn't die in America.

But her coughing was really really bad. What if she had some horrible, like, global flu or something?

Three people were ahead of Carmen in the checkout line. Naturally, the blond lady at the front didn't have the right change to buy her lottery ticket.

When she bought one, she scratched her ticket and won another one. So the process started over.

"People, hurry up," Carmen grumbled.

Instead of hurrying, the lady turned to scowl at her for maybe five whole minutes. Then she had to make a big deal about having to start over counting her pennies.

Carmen was frantic by the time it was her turn. Of course, her cell phone had to ring, and when she saw it was Xavier, of course she had to answer.

"Hi, there," he said in that deep, husky voice he'd used last night.

"Hi there, back," she whispered.

She handed the cashier a ten-dollar bill, picked up her change and then rushed out the glass doors. Her head was bent low over her cell to shield it from the rain, so she didn't really notice the black Jeep burning rubber as it hurtled away from her Honda.

Later, she would beat herself up for that.

"Did I catch you at a bad time?" Xavier was saying.

"No. It's a great time. Great time."

"I missed you," he said.

She hated the way her chest got all tight.

"Missed you a lot. I nearly get fired. Then I go to the library and try to study," he said, "but all I could do was stare at the trees blowing in the rain and wonder what you're doing."

"Alexis is sick, and I'm taking her…"

Carmen punched her automatic door opener. When it didn't work, she looked up and saw Alexis's door hanging wide-open. The brat had left the interior lights on, and rain was pouring into the car.

"Damn it, Alexis! Why can't you ever, just once, do what I tell you?" she shouted.

But when she ran to slam the door and scream at her, Carmen saw a curious bit of mud-spattered blue on the wet, black asphalt.

"Alexis's blue blanket," she whispered, her own voice choked with fear. "Alexis!" she screamed as the rain hit her full in the face. "Alexis!"

The passenger seat was empty.

Carmen flipped her phone shut and ran back into the store yelling Alexis's name, asking everyone, anyone, if they'd seen a five-year-old little girl.

Nobody had.

Too late, Carmen remembered the awful black Jeep parked by the Dumpster, the one that had sped away when she'd come out of the store.

She was shaking as she dialed 911. When the operator came on, Carmen could barely speak.

"Please… Help me, please…. My daughter…she's been kidnapped!"

Rain slashed Michael's hood and windshield. It was only midafternoon, but the sky was a dark, dangerous green. All the streetlights were on.

There'd been a bad accident half a mile up ahead, so Michael was stalled on I-35, on the inside northbound lane in the middle of Town Lake Bridge. He'd radioed and gotten all the details.

If he was feeling pressured and impatient about admitting to Rosie he'd failed, and that she had to turn herself in, he went insane after he caught the Amber Alert and heard Alexis's name.

Alexis had been kidnapped. Taken out of Carmen's car. They'd been on their way to a doctor. Black Jeep. No ID on the license plate. Nobody could reach Rosie.

His heart began to slam against his ribs. A steel vise crushed his lungs so hard he could barely breathe.

He'd wished for the Carver case to break wide-open. Hell, maybe it had. What if the same sick pervert who'd sliced up Pierce Carver had Alexis?

Michael remembered Carver's startled dead eyes. Suddenly, he was sweating bullets. He had to get the hell off this bridge.

When he jammed a fist on his horn, everybody else began honking, too. He reached up and snapped on the overhead light. Then he rubbed condensation off his windshield. Hell, all he saw was rain and a wall of cars.

An eighteen-wheeler had skidded on the slick freeway up ahead. Its trailer had flipped, causing a massive multicar pileup, and bringing traffic to a standstill. All the exit ramps were blocked.

He should radio Keith and get him to send someone to deal with Rosie.

The hell with it! Alexis was all that mattered. He would run up to the scene of the accident, flash his badge and borrow some civilian's car.

Michael opened his door and got out. In seconds, he was soaked to the skin.

Please, he thought as he began to run. *Please.*

Thirty

Rosie flipped her cell phone open and punched in Carmen's number even though the infuriating little blue window said No Service.

She snapped her phone shut and resisted the urge to jump up and down or scream. She couldn't stand worrying about her girls and not being able to reach them.

When she looked out the window, the sky was blacker than ever, the rain gushing in torrents. No wonder there was no service.

Why did I send them out in this?

Rosie sank down on the couch beside Hazel, who was kneeling over a cardboard box. Rosie bit her lower lip. Why hadn't she driven Alexis herself? Why hadn't she gotten her regular phone reconnected?

The whys in her life were making her insane. Why

was any of this happening to her? Why had Pierce had to go and get himself killed on the night he'd asked her to come back to him? Why hadn't she listened to Nan and stood firm on the no-man thing?

Rosie snatched her purse off the coffee table and then set it down. It felt heavy because Harry's gun was zipped inside a compartment.

Feeling restless, she flipped her cell phone open again. Once again it said No Service.

Her heart racing, she glanced at Hazel, who'd opened the box and was quietly unwrapping the knickknacks inside and placing them on the coffee table. In a fury, Rosie tossed the useless phone onto the couch only to have the damn thing ring.

"It's ringing!" she shouted to Hazel. "It's actually ringing!"

"Well, untie your panties, and answer it."

The ID window read Unknown Caller.

"Hello…"

She heard muffled sniffles. Then she made out strangled weeping and coughing.

"Hello?"

More choked sobs and coughing were the only response, until a digitally garbled voice screamed, "Mimi! Mimi!"

"Alexis?"

"The man with the scary eyes…in the park…"

Rosie's stomach clenched. Violent explosions of static broke up the distorted, childish voice. "He took me out of Carmen's car…when she went in for cough drops. I'm wet and cold, Mimi! I want my Binkie. I want Black Bear!"

"Alexis?"

"Mimi!"

"Alexis, honey, it's okay…."

A deep, cold voice cut her off. It was also digitally masked and impossible to recognize.

"You heard the brat, bitch. If you want her back, meet me downtown at your warehouse."

"What?"

"Now!" Eerie, sadistic bursts of laugher were all she could make out after that.

"Don't hurt her," she pleaded. "She's sick. She needs to go to a doctor."

"Come alone. Or I'll kill her."

"Who—"

"We're going to finish this, you and I."

"Finish what? Who is this?"

"You just wouldn't quit, would you?"

"Please—"

"I killed Pierce. Do you think I'd stop at a kid?"

The line went dead.

"Who was that?" Hazel's brows were pulled together, making deep, anxious furrows above her thin nose. "Is…is Alexis okay?"

Rosie's fingers curled instinctively around the phone. Then she whirled and glanced out to the backyard, which looked like a dark lake now.

Just as she was thinking the rain was getting worse, headlights arced across her front shade.

"Michael...."

Rosie ran to the window as an unmarked car with two men in it pulled up.

She whipped around. "Hazel! I need you to stay here. And take your time answering the door. It's probably the police...here to arrest me. I'm going out the back way."

"What?"

"For once don't argue...just do what I say...."

Rosie grabbed her purse, which was bulky because of Harry's Glock. When she got to her garage, she didn't raise the door until Hazel let the two tall men inside.

Only when she was speeding down her flooded street did she dial Michael's number.

It rang, but went immediately to voice mail.

"Michael! Somebody just called and said he's got Alexis! He put her on, and she's terrified! I'm afraid he's going to kill her! He told me to meet him at my warehouse downtown, alone." As she was giving him the address, her damn phone quit. The little blue window read Low Battery.

She called him back. Through bursts of static she sobbed, "Michael, he said no cops. Or she dies."

Her cell phone went dead as she raced down Lamar toward town.

* * *

The deserted street in front of her warehouse looked like a river when she finally pulled up. Slowly, she withdrew her key and gazed at the yawning blackness beyond the open warehouse door.

Scarcely feeling the wind-driven rain that blasted her face and plastered her hair to her skull, she got out and rushed through the ankle-deep water.

As she ran, scattered, hysterical thoughts bombarded her.

Michael—she should have told him the truth about Carmen a long time ago. Carmen—she'd been a lousy mother to her in so many ways. She should have told her, too.

Alexis—if she got Alexis out alive, she'd read to her every night. She'd take her out on that little train at Zilker every weekend, too.

Funny how brief forty years suddenly seemed. Rosie wasn't old. She'd barely begun to live. And she wanted to live so badly now. Even the thought of going to prison didn't seem so awful compared to death.

When she reached the dark doorway, her mouth went dry. She stuck one hand inside her purse, unzipped the compartment and wrapped her fingers around Harry's gun. She found the trigger and brought it back a little, reminding herself that to fire a Glock handgun, she had to pull the trigger fully to the rear.

Then, squaring her shoulders, she slipped slowly

through the big doorway, one deliberate step after the other. The stench of guano hit her, but she kept walking.

During that awful eternity, memories flashed in microseconds. Her daddy was crushing her against his chest when she'd been a scared little girl crying in the dark.

She remembered his warm, callused hand steadying hers as she'd held his big gun and taken aim at a soda can floating in a hill-country creek. Next, she was lying on a beach towel looking up at Michael as a palm tree rustled above his dark head and a mariachi band played in a distant hotel bar.

She heard footsteps somewhere deep in the warehouse. High above her, wings rustled, and she remembered the bats. Eerie, familiar laughter rumbled out of the darkness, echoing in the far corners, so that it seemed to come from all around her.

Then the warehouse door slammed shut, and a low-wattage bulb came on.

Lean and tall, a man who was somehow horribly familiar stared at her from the shadows with unmasked hatred.

"You!" she whispered.

He laughed.

For no reason at all, she was thinking about those eyes in the photograph in Michael's office, those gray eyes that had been so gruesomely intact, so horrified and so recognizable. The killer had not hacked madly or blindly, but with deadly, clever precision.

"Pierce?"

"Hello, Rosie."

How could he look so normal, not crazy at all? How could he be standing there, so alive, so tall and handsome? Not that he looked exactly like himself.

No, he was changed. He wore glasses, and his hair was darker and thicker and longer. His fine-boned nose had been broken and flattened, deliberately. His jaw had been softened, too. Instead of one of his designer suits, he wore jeans and a scruffy, long-sleeved shirt.

But his eyes were the same. Not that they looked startled like the dead man's eyes. No, Pierce's eyes were as sharp and as coldly dangerous as silver ice shards.

In one hand he held an automatic. In the other a Kasumi paring knife exactly like the one she'd supposedly murdered him with.

Eyes glittering, he pointed the gun at her heart and took deadly aim.

He was going to kill her.

Thirty-One

"Where's Alexis?" Rosie whispered, trying not to stare down the barrel of his black automatic.

"Shut up about *her*." His voice had a cold, unearthly quality. He took a step closer.

Somehow, she had to keep him talking. "Where is she? What did you do to her?"

"That brat! She's all you ever cared about!"

Her finger tightened on the trigger of Harry's automatic. "All right," she began calmly. "We'll talk about something else. So, you were the one who framed me? You set me up. Why?"

His gun jerked to her purse and then back to her heart. He took a deep breath, as if to reassure himself that he was in control. "Put the purse down—slowly."

If she raised the bag by so much as an inch, he'd shoot. Then what would happen to Alexis? Rosie swallowed and dropped the purse at her feet.

"Kick it to me."

When she did, he knelt and pulled out the Glock. "Nice. I thought you didn't *like* guns." Laughing now, he slid it into the back of his waistband. "I brought some rope. I seemed to remember you like being tied up."

"No…"

"I know all the things that you *like*."

He dropped the Kasumi knife to the ground. "Give me your hand." When she held it out, he tied her wrist swiftly to an exposed pipe that ran along the brick wall. He grabbed her other wrist and secured it the same way, stretching her arms, so that she felt pulled apart helplessly.

"There. You *like* that, I bet." He grinned. "I won't tie your feet," he said, "for obvious reasons, because then we can't have as much fun. And we're going to have fun. Because for once I'll be in total control of you, *bitch!* It's what you always wanted. Your fantasy come true! You'll *like* it!"

She wanted to scream at him, but that wouldn't be smart. So when he placed the gun barrel against her cheek and caressed her skin with it, she bit her lips until she tasted her own blood.

"You want to know why I set you up?" The gun moved along the tip of her nose as gently as a lover's fingertip.

She gasped.

"I could move my finger a quarter of an inch and blow your face away. Just like that," he whispered.

"But I'd rather cut you. It's slower. And I can leave your pretty blue eyes for your cop lover to pour over. Maybe he'll get off one last time."

"You...you were going to tell me why you set me up."

"Let's just say I was a man with too many problems."

"But you had it all."

"The sins of a past life were catching up with me."

He traced the damp fabric over her breasts with the gun. Then he laughed as if he were suddenly enjoying himself.

This gave her an idea. Pierce loved to be flattered. It made him expansive. Somehow, although she felt sick with fear at what he intended, she had to force herself to do that. Maybe Michael would listen to her message and somehow make it in time to save Alexis.

Oh, my God! A past life?

Denver? The Johnsons?

"Why, are you Tim? Tim Johnson?"

"Close."

"Ricky?"

"Bad, bad old Richard." He moved the gun barrel up her neck and then through her wet hair. "Richard, the bad twin," he said. "That's what they used to call me."

Her wrists were beginning to burn where the rope pulled at her flesh, and her arms were starting to ache from being stretched.

"But I thought... I thought Ricky went to prison."

He leaned down and picked up the knife, turning it over so that the blade flashed in the faint light.

"Too bad you found those file boxes. Ricky set the fire. *Richard*. Daddy used to call me *Richard* when he was angry. I couldn't do anything right. I meant for Tim to die, too. I drugged him that night, so that when they did a drug screen they'd think he was me, since I had *the* problem. But somehow he got out of the house. When Tim woke up in rehab and figured out I'd killed our parents, I gave him a choice. Take the rap or die. I told him I'd never go to prison, that they'd find me insane, that I'd get out, and I'd get him. He was afraid to cross me."

"You forced him to pretend he was you. How clever," she said, hating his pleased smile.

"I couldn't stick around, though. What if he changed his story?" He leaned closer. "Now come the fun times."

Expertly he sliced her wet black dress from neck to thigh. And then her damp bra, exposing her breasts.

"I used to love these. After all, I created them, didn't I?" When he bent and bit each nipple, she flinched at the pain.

"You'll be wet in no time, and I don't mean from the rain."

There was a telling bulge in his jeans. She twisted at her ropes and felt the left pipe groan and give a little. When he looked up at the wall, she moaned to distract him.

"I told you you'd get hot."

"So, you took the insurance money and vanished. Smart," she said, hoping to keep him talking.

"Tim used to be a wimp. He was scared of me. But he's taught me a valuable lesson about loose ends. I should have killed the son of a bitch. Prison hardened him. He came after me. Oh, it took him awhile to find me. I'd changed my face and my name, but he'd known my interests and ambitions. When he found me, he demanded money, for all the wasted years, he said. Over time, he got greedy and demanded more.

"Then there was the problem of his mouth. Who would he tell? I realized I was going to have to kill him and Pierce Carver, too, and assume an entirely new identity. I would have to change my face again and my name, and perhaps my country."

Pierce gave a humorless smile. "People think I'm broke, but I had money saved in offshore back accounts, just in case something like this should happen. And lucky for me, I had a bitter ex-girlfriend."

"So, you invited me over to your house the night you planned to kill Tim."

"Yes. I will tell you that I tried to kill him a couple of weekends earlier without involving you, but he was too clever. So, the next time I knew he was dropping by my house for a payment, I called you. And you came running." His sneer was coldly contemptuous.

"You didn't want me back?" She remembered stripping for him.

Again he laughed. When she notched up her chin, he smiled.

Well, at least she hadn't gone to bed with him that night.

"I made pretty work of Tim's face, don't you think? I slashed it up, but I was careful to leave the eyes. Because plastic surgery hadn't changed me that way."

"And I—I thought it was you! I couldn't believe you were dead until I saw those crime scene photos. I actually felt sorry for you...."

"Poor Tim. He was so stunned when I stuck him the first time. Did he really think I'd let him call the shots forever?" Pierce paused. "You deserve this, you know. Because of Anita."

"Anita?"

"You turned her against me with all your questions. She was going with me when I left Austin."

"She knows you murdered your brother?"

"She thinks you killed him by mistake, that you were after me and maybe her, too. But you got her really thinking that maybe I was the bad guy and not you, and she got scared again and ran away and hid. But I found her. So, tonight she pays, too."

"She's here?"

"With your precious Alexis. People will think you killed her in a jealous frenzy because they know you chased her out of Morgan's office."

"And Alexis?"

"Who cares what they think when I'm gone? You've been such a fool."

"The cops were going to arrest me tonight. Why did you have to take Alexis?"

"Loose ends, remember? You'd seen the Johnson files. I didn't know what you'd spill to that cop. I meant to get rid of that box years ago, but I lost track of it. I'd forgotten about it until Tim showed up. Then I thought it might be in your warehouse. You should have given me the key."

"How'd you get in here tonight?"

"I stole your key out of the lock the last time you and I had so much fun here. I was panhandling across the street." He smiled. "It's been fun, Rosie."

The finality in his low tone sent a chill through her. "Where are you going after tonight?"

"There are a million places where one can simply disappear and enjoy lots of beautiful, young women."

"You hate women. You destroy them."

"Not when they're obedient."

Rosie wondered how she could have been blind to who he really was.

Pierce leaned down and opened a large red can she hadn't seen before. Then he turned it over.

Oh, my God! As the liquid streamed across the ground, the stench of gasoline fumes mingled with bat guano and stung her nostrils.

"I advised you against buying this place. You should have listened. It's going to prove to have been a most unwise investment. Old buildings in bad neighborhoods frequently are."

"Where's Alexis? You've got to let her go."

He laughed. "Loose ends."

"No!"

"You're so naive. That's what I loved about you once.... I don't *have* to anything."

"I was naive to ever think I loved you," she whispered.

"Or to think I could ever love you, a trashy, fast thing from East Austin. *Me?* The elegant Dr. Pierce Carver?" He laughed. "You were a hottie, though." When he chuckled at some memory, she wanted to claw him. "An amusement. Useful, too. You served me. That's all you ever were. Anita, on the other hand, is from an aristocratic family in Guatemala. I never loved you the way I loved her."

Rosie seethed at his insults, which was probably what he wanted.

"Before I light the match and send you straight to hell, I'm going to have one for the road."

"What?"

"A final fuck." His face was contorted, his eyes insane. "*Your* final fuck."

With his knife, he slit the waistband of her black lace panties, so that the flimsy, damp material sagged beneath her belly. Then he dipped the point of his knife into her navel. When he deliberately pricked her, she screamed.

"You used to go for the bondage bit. I bet you're wet just thinking about it."

No, she wasn't wet; she was shaking violently. She'd never been so mad.

Tim's death, her own death. Alexis's death.
Anita's death. Everything was all her fault. She'd
been so blindly determined to believe herself in love
and to marry him and have a sparkling life that
other people would envy, she hadn't seen what a
sham he was, any more than she'd seen what a sham
her own values had been.

She *had* to live. She *had* to save Alexis. And
Carmen... Rosie had so much to make up for.

When Pierce's hand went to the zipper of his
jeans, her vision clouded and all rational thought left
her. Using all her strength, she writhed against the
ropes like a wild animal caught in a trap, pulling at
them. Her wrists began to feel raw as the left pipe
came loose. Still tied to both pipes, she lunged at
him. When she jammed a knee into his crotch, he
yelped. Then he twisted and crumpled, bending
double, and she hit him in the head with the loose
pipe. As he toppled toward her, she yanked Harry's
gun out of his waistband with her left hand.

"If you move, I'll shoot."

Even as she said it, she wondered if she could shoot
with that hand. Maybe the same thought crossed his
mind, too, because he looked up, his nostrils flaring.
His eyes crazed with hate, he lunged toward her.

She screamed again and aimed for his chest. With
her left hand extended, she shot him twice, quick
and tight just like her father had taught her. Her
right arm was still tied to the pipe.

Pierce looked surprised when he jolted backward from the bullets' impact. The gun's recoil threw Rosie against the wall. As if amazed, he raised his hand to his chest, where twin blotches of blood were slowly spreading across his shirt.

Terrified he'd leap at her again, she kept the gun pointed at him. Gradually, the crazed light went out of his eyes. His pupils widened.

She knew the look of a dying man.

"Where's Alexis?" she yelled.

"In hell," Pierce said, his voice no more than a murmur.

He died with a smile on his lips and his eyes wide-open, still staring at her with that look of amazement.

She glanced up at the gray skylights where bat wings flickered, but her mind couldn't seem to focus. She was a little girl again, out hunting with her father. She remembered shooting a little bird, watching it fall, watching it tremble on the ground, and feeling horror.

She'd cupped its body and had vowed never again to touch a gun or take another life.

Oh, God…

Slowly Rosie's adult mind reentered her body, and she looked down and met Pierce's unwavering, slightly startled stare once more.

He wasn't the only one who'd died today.

That little girl who'd shot the bird with her father was gone forever. So was the woman who'd wanted to be young forever, who'd thought other people lived charmed lives in sparkling train cars, who'd thought being rich and well-married would solve all her problems.

Michael jumped out of Keith's car into deep pools of water. He heard a woman's screams and then two gunshots. In the silent aftermath, he heard no sound other than the pounding of his heart and the beating of the rain.

Was he too late? Fear froze the blood in his veins as he raced for the warehouse door.

No matter how rejected and angry Rosie had made him feel, he wanted her alive. He wanted to work things out.

If she were dead, he'd go on, but there would be a void in his heart. Years ago she'd claimed a piece of his soul. She was special to him as no one on earth had ever been or would ever be again.

He hoped to hell he wasn't figuring this all out after it was too late.

His gun was already in his hand as he wrenched the big door upward a foot or two. Then he crawled under it and inched forward on the filthy, wet floor in a crouch.

The place reeked of bat shit and gasoline. All it would take was a spark, and this place would go off like a bomb.

"Michael," Rosie sobbed. "Michael."

He ran to her. Tied to the wall by her right wrist, she sagged there, as white as snow. She was half-naked and her eyes were glazed. Blood streaked her body, but Pierce lay at her feet in a pool of his own blood. She held a Glock in her left hand.

"It's okay. Everything's going to be okay. Just put the gun down," Michael said softly, soothingly, because she looked like she was still in shock.

Slowly, she drooped against the wall. When the gun fell to the floor with a clatter, he yelled for Keith.

Then Michael ran to her, ripped off his shirt and wrapped her in it. She expelled a sigh of relief.

The warehouse door crashed upward, and suddenly cops were everywhere, their guns raised, their flashlights bouncing off walls.

"I said no cops," she whispered as he cut her loose and cradled her in his arms.

"I know."

She clung to him, still sobbing. "He was going to kill me."

"Where's Alexis?" Michael whispered.

"You've got to find her."

And then he knew it wasn't over.

Thirty-Two

High above them on the second and third floors, brilliant cones of light bobbed in the dark rafters. The bats were in an uproar as police shouted Alexis's name.

So far, the little girl hadn't answered.

Michael saw the panic building in Rosie's eyes. Suddenly she switched on her own flashlight, grabbed his hand and ran toward the back of the warehouse.

"What is it?"

"Alexis," she screamed hoarsely. "She's got to be here."

His men were still shouting upstairs.

"They've looked everywhere," he said.

"No." She closed her eyes. "The basement. I almost forgot. There's a basement, too."

She tightened her grasp on his hand and led him through a narrow door that he hadn't noticed before.

Before he could summon Keith, she let go and disappeared into the black hole. He heard wooden steps groaning as she descended them. Racing after her, he felt like he was following her down into hell.

He would've called for backup, but he sensed her impatience. Down, down they went, into utter blackness. She led him through another narrow doorway and then down another short wooden flight. Each step sagged nearly to the breaking point from his weight. He heard scuttling sounds on the walls. Something furry brushed his leg. Rats?

When they finally reached the bottom, the black space was tight, the air damp and musty.

"Seems like nobody's been down here in years," he said.

A rat squealed, and Rosie threw herself into Michael's arms.

"It's okay," he whispered, holding her close.

She began shaking as he flashed his light around the shadowy basement. There was nothing but dozens of brown cardboard boxes.

When she realized the little room didn't hold her granddaughter, she began to weep.

"Don't give up," Michael muttered, even as he felt his own hope die.

"Alexis, darling, answer me, please…." Rosie cried.

When no one answered, he went cold. He let her go and began to pace the small, square room, shining his light on every surface again and again. The light bobbed, and the cardboard boxes cast dancing shadows against the walls.

Rosie had quit sobbing, and stopped calling to Alexis. His heavy footsteps were the only sounds. Suddenly, he stumbled on something uneven in the flooring. His light fell and rolled. He cursed and then grabbed it and flashed it on the ground where he'd tripped.

She gasped. "It's a little handle."

He raced to it. The handle was attached to a small, steel door about two feet square.

"What the hell?" Excitement charged his voice.

Rosie knelt beside it. "I thought this was the bottom floor."

Michael's skin crawled as he grasped the handle and yanked the little door upward. A gust of cold, foul-smelling air brushed his cheek as he stared down into the horrible black hole that yawned into nothingness.

When he shone his light into it, he saw that a ladder led down into an even smaller room. Bending cautiously, he peered inside, but it was much too dark to see anything.

"Alexis?" he whispered, his voice breaking.

The only answer was blackness and silence.

All hope gone, and icy terror ricocheting through his arteries as he thought of the little girl down there murdered, he lowered himself into the awful hole and climbed down.

When he got to the bottom and flashed his light again, something soft and coppery shone in a dark corner.

"Alexis?" he called, focusing the light in that direction.

Enormous, dilated blue eyes blinked tearfully. Alexis was bound hand and foot, and her mouth was crisscrossed with duct tape.

"Alexis?" Rosie screamed, hysterical above him. "Is she—"

"She's alive," he yelled.

"I'm coming—"

"No. Stay up there—in case the ladder gives."

Rosie groaned and bit her lips, but stayed put.

"It's me, little princess," Michael said as he set his light down. Gently he cut her hands loose and then her feet. "It's okay. It's okay."

When he removed the duct tape from her mouth, she began to cough and sob and cling to him.

He held her close. "Everything is going to be okay," he repeated, smoothing her hair out of her eyes.

"Mmmmm. Mmmmm."

Thrashing sounds came from a dark corner opposite them. When he whirled with his flashlight, Anita's black head bobbed at him weakly. She was lying on her side in a fetal position, her mouth duct taped, her legs and arms bound.

Carrying Alexis, he crawled to her. He cut Anita's hands loose and then her feet. When she was too weak to remove the duct tape, he did it for her. Her lips were cut, and she had a black eye.

Taking a deep breath, she pushed the hair out of her eyes and tried to smile, but her mouth quivered instead. When he saw more bruises and cuts on her cheek and neck, he swore viciously.

"You're going to be okay," he said.

"Alexis?" Rosie called, peering anxiously down at them.

"Mimi!"

His body taut, Michael cradled Alexis close as he climbed the ladder.

"Mimi!"

When Rosie held out her arms, Alexis held out hers, too. But since she didn't let go of Michael, he circled both Alexis and Rosie with his own arms. Pressing them tightly against his chest, he knew he'd never let them go again.

The rain had stopped, but the street was like a lake. A feeble sun lit the warehouse, which was surrounded by ambulances, stretchers, police radio cars with their flashing lights, dozens of uniformed officers, paramedics and the press.

Rosie gulped in long breaths of fresh, humid air as she sat in one of the ambulances beside Alexis and watched the paramedics take her vital signs and start an IV.

It felt wonderful just to be out of that airless, reeking hole, to be alive and to know Alexis was alive. To know Alexis was in competent hands.

"You can have your real life back now," Michael said.

"As long as it includes you."

"Have I ever been able to resist you?"

"I'm sorry," she whispered as even she observed the EMTs with a critical eye.

"It's okay."

The paramedics had Alexis's IV going. She was on oxygen, too. Her color was good. She seemed stable.

Rosie stiffened when she saw uniformed men carrying a body bag out of the warehouse.

"It was all my fault," she said. "All of this… And it goes way back. I never thought I was good enough or that you were. I never believed in you or…us. And I was such a lousy mother. I was too young. I was always too busy doing *my* thing, and it wasn't a smart thing. I never saw what I really had…until it was almost too late."

"As long as you've learned your lesson," Michael said with a grin. "You just fixed on an idea and wouldn't let go. You've got to quit beating up on yourself, Rosie. You're okay just the way you are."

"I'm forty."

"And cuter than ever."

"I think I'd rather be smarter than ever." She was about to kiss him for saying she was cuter than ever when a motorcycle gliding slowly up the wet street caught her attention.

The big bike stopped, and Carmen slid off the back and handed Xavier her helmet. She was dressed modestly again, in jeans and a leather jacket.

As the EMTs slammed doors, and the driver revved the engine, Carmen ran toward them. When she saw Alexis on the stretcher, tears filled her eyes. Wiping them away, she leaped into the ambulance.

"Wait!"

"Ma'am, we've got to go."

Carmen ignored the medic. When she reached Alexis, she knelt and went still. Swallowing hard, she took another deep breath.

"She's going to be okay," Rosie said.

"I'm sorry I was mean to you, Alexis. When I got back to the car and you were gone… I've never been so scared."

"Ma'am."

Alexis struggled to sit up. Carmen slowly put her arms around her. For a long moment the little girl clung to her. "Me, too. Oh, me, too. I was so scared. He was real mean. Way meaner than you. They're going to take me to the hospital…because my cough is really bad."

"I know. Believe me, I know," Carmen said. "I'm sorry I got so mad about it. It's just that…"

"Ma'am! We need to get her to the hospital."

"You're always angry," Alexis said.

"I'm going to work on that. I promise." Carmen let her go and backed out of the ambulance.

As the ambulance sped away, Rosie squeezed Carmen's hand. When she hugged her, her daughter didn't try to pull away. Slowly, her gaze drifted questioningly to Michael.

"I have something to tell you," Rosie said, "after we see about Alexis at the hospital. Something I should have told you a long, long time ago. But not now." She paused. "When we're alone," she promised.

Carmen nodded. Then she stole another shy glance at Michael. As she held on to Rosie's hand even more tightly, her luminous eyes kept devouring him. When she blushed, he smiled down at her gently. His dark brown eyes, so like hers, were alight with pride and joy and hope.

Watching them in that first tentative moment, Rosie felt giddy, exhilarated.

As her mother, Rosie owed her a long, confidential talk—the whole, unvarnished story. Maybe telling her the facts that she'd been so ashamed of wouldn't be as difficult as she'd always feared. Maybe it would be.

But wasn't getting started always the hardest part of any challenge? Only when the truth was out would they have a chance at a real relationship. Maybe then they could all start to heal.

As if he read her thoughts, Michael threaded his

hand through Rosie's free hand and pulled her closer until an old Dodge pulled up and Hazel and Carlo Castellano got out.

"Hazel," Carmen whispered. "Pop."

Carlo's big blue eyes lit up when he saw Rosie.

"Daddy…." Rosie didn't know how she got there, but she was in her father's arms.

Rosie winced when she saw all the candles on her birthday cake. Chocolate, of course, because Yolie had baked it.

I shouldn't have let them do this.

"Forty candles for the birthday girl, plus one to grow on," Yolie said, smiling at Rosie, as she carried a huge tray that looked more like a torch than a cake to a small wrought-iron table by her pool. "Get over here, sweetie, and face the music!"

As soon as she'd seen the news bulletin about Pierce's death, Yolie had rushed to Alexis's hospital room. After she'd apologized to Rosie, and quite contritely, on bended knee even, she'd said, "Carmen did me a favor, of course. I might never have accepted Vicenzo's dinner invitation if she hadn't slept with Xavier."

"Vicenzo?"

"I told you about him. Italy. The Vespa. Tuscany. He'll be at your birthday party."

"My birthday party? Excuse me, did I miss something?"

"He's a year older than Xavier."

"Hello? Back to my birthday, which was over, weeks ago. I don't do birthdays, remember?"

"I think we all have a lot to celebrate," Yolie had said. "For one thing, you finally killed Pierce, and best of all, you're going to get away with it."

"That's not funny."

"Then think sparkling train car and sparkling candles. Think beautiful people giving you a party at my mansion."

And that had been that. After all, Yolie was a very forceful woman, and once she made up her mind, it was almost impossible to say no to her, especially when it involved chocolate.

So here Rosie was, blowing out forty-one sparkling candles.

"A black cake! My favorite!" Alexis cried in delight. Springing out of the pool, she ran up to the table, making wet splatters on the concrete as she grabbed a paper plate.

"Double-fudge, Italian-cream chocolate cake, young lady," Yolie corrected. "Hey, sweetie, I told you to get over here."

"Wait, I take family picture of you all!" Vicenzo held up his tiny digital camera.

Vicenzo had extended his stay in Austin indefinitely after Yolie had invited him to her house the first night he'd been in town.

"After all, I was used to having a cool

roommate, sweetie," Yolie had explained to Rosie. "Plus, we're in lust."

"Did you have to give him my old room?"

"Why not? You won't be needing it now that Michael's moved in with you. When are you going to marry him?"

"I don't know. He hasn't asked me."

"He will."

"Smiles, everybody!" Vicenzo said.

Carmen, her face radiant, was cuddling close in Xavier's arms. Carlo and Hazel were holding hands, and it didn't bother Rosie at all. She shot her father a loving smile, and he returned it. When he'd shown up at the warehouse that night after they'd found Alexis, she'd thrown herself into his arms and wept for all the lost years.

She'd never even asked for his forgiveness. She hadn't had to.

She'd wasted so many years by being stubborn and determined to see things one way. There were always many sides to a story. She'd clung to one.

"Big smile again," Vicenzo said.

As if in a dream, Rosie let Michael fold her hand in his and lead her toward her smiling family. Yes, everybody was smiling. Well, almost everybody. Carmen wasn't really smiling, but she wasn't frowning, so Rosie thought maybe that counted.

Alexis stood in front in between Beth and Nan

because she was five and dripping wet, and her grin was the biggest and brightest of them all.

"Hurry," the little girl cried, "so Mimi can blow out her candles. I'm starving!"

Vicenzo's flash went off, and Rosie leaned over her forty-one candles.

So many, she thought. Hopefully, there would be more cakes with many, many more.

"Make a wish," Michael said against her ear when she knelt even lower to blow them out.

"I don't have to," she whispered, smiling up at him. "My wish has already come true."

"Yes! Yes!"

Rosie was still screaming when she climaxed. Michael pulled her hot, sweaty body even closer. Watching every nuance of her expression, he spilled himself inside her.

"Yes," she whispered, opening her eyes and staring into his. The shuddering moment lengthened and grew sacred and then passed, as so many precious moments pass in a lifetime.

But he knew he was changed somehow, as if vows had been exchanged. Feeling closer to her than ever, if that were possible, he relaxed and rolled slowly off her.

"You're better than chocolate," she said. "Way better. I don't think I can ever get enough."

"Of chocolate or me?"

"Do I have to choose?"

"No. You can have me anytime, all the time."

"I'm sorry," she said, "for all the wasted years. I was such a stubborn little fool."

"I wish you'd quit apologizing."

"Someday."

"Soon, I hope," he whispered.

"I just can't believe you can forgive—"

"I can and I have. And I'm not all that great at the sport either, am I? So, believe it. I know it took me awhile to forgive you in middle school, and this has been an even bigger deal...."

"I know. I'm sorry."

"I really want you to quit apologizing and asking for my forgiveness. I love you. That says it all."

"I've been a bad girl," she whispered. "A very bad girl. Maybe you should punish me...." She smiled rather too coyly for his liking, because he was exhausted and wasn't at all that sure he could live up to her expectations. And he hated the thought of disappointing her—especially in bed.

When her hand moved under his pillow, he heard something jingle.

"Oh, my gosh," she said, feigning innocence. "Look what I found. Handcuffs. Is this an omen or what?"

Playfully, she locked a cuff around her right wrist and then winked at him.

He grabbed her and pulled her underneath him.

"You have been a bad girl. A really bad girl."

"What are you going to do about it?"

"Kiss you until you're breathless, maybe."

She giggled.

His kiss was long and hard. "I love you," he said. "Kinks, warts, mistakes, lies and all. I love you just the way you are."

"And for the good sex, too?"

"Lucky for you, you're good in bed, damn good, and I'm the kind of guy who'd probably stick around just for the sex alone."

"I'd rather have your love."

He leaned down and kissed the lacy palm fronds above her heart. "The two are like chocolates and orgasms, princess. You don't have to choose."

Without waiting for her reply, he hooked the other cuff to the bedpost. When she yanked at it and pretended to try to escape, he seized her free wrist and held her down. Then he climbed on top and slowly buried himself inside her. His body began to move with hers in a familiar, erotic dance that made him hotter and hotter.

He wanted her forever, all of her—her mind, her heart and her soul. Oh, yes, her body, too, definitely her forty-year-old body, forever and forever and forever until they were both really old.

As it turned out, he wasn't nearly as exhausted as he'd thought. His body took over, or maybe hers did. All too soon, they were doing a tango that made thought impossible.

The Crystal Rose

New York Times bestselling author

REBECCA BRANDEWYNE

London, England, 1850: Rose Windermere is nearly knocked to the ground by a man who whispers a dire warning…and presses a letter into her hands before fleeing. The mark with which the letter is sealed recalls Rose's idyllic childhood in India and a world that was destroyed when an uprising left her friend Hugo dead.

Pulled back into the exotic land of her youth, Rose must now unravel the strange machinations of a man whose lust for power will threaten a monarchy—and Rose's own heart.

"Intriguing tale (à la Dickens) that will captivate gothic fans."
—*Romantic Times BOOKreviews*
on *The Ninefold Key*

Available the first week of December 2006,
wherever paperbacks are sold!

MIRA®

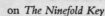

Don't miss this
Aurora Teagarden mystery
by *New York Times*
bestselling author

Charlaine Harris

Aurora Teagarden never forgot
her first case: a serial killer
who terrorized suburban
Lawrencetown. Now that
story is about to hit the small
screen, and Aurora can't help
getting involved. Her ex, Robin,
wrote the screenplay and her
stepson, Barrett, has a starring
role. Then there's Celia, the
catty actress portraying
Roe—who also happens to be
Robin's latest squeeze.

But when Celia is murdered
and Barrett is accused, the real-
life script takes a deadly turn.
Between threatening letters,
deranged fans and renewed
feelings for Robin, Aurora has
one goal: catch a killer and
make it to the final scene alive.

Last Scene Alive

"Best of the series to date."
—*Publishers Weekly*

*Available the first week of
December 2006, wherever
paperbacks are sold!*

REQUEST YOUR FREE BOOKS!

2 FREE NOVELS
FROM THE ROMANCE/SUSPENSE
COLLECTION PLUS 2 FREE GIFTS!

YES! Please send me 2 FREE novels from the Romance/Suspense Collection and my 2 FREE gifts. After receiving them, if I don't wish to receive any more books, I can return the shipping statement marked "cancel." If I don't cancel, I will receive 4 brand-new novels every month and be billed just $5.24 per book in the U.S., or $5.74 per book in Canada, plus 25¢ shipping and handling per book plus applicable taxes, if any*. That's a savings of at least 10% off the cover price! I understand that accepting the 2 free books and gifts places me under no obligation to buy anything. I can always return a shipment and cancel at any time. Even if I never buy another book from the Reader Service, the two free books and gifts are mine to keep forever.

185 MDN EF3H   385 MDN EF3J

Name _____ (PLEASE PRINT) _____

Address _____ Apt. # _____

City _____ State/Prov. _____ Zip/Postal Code _____

Signature (if under 18, a parent or guardian must sign)

Mail to The Reader Service:

IN U.S.A.
P.O. Box 1867
Buffalo, NY
14240-1867

IN CANADA
P.O. Box 609
Fort Erie, Ontario
L2A 5X3

Not valid to current subscribers to the Romance Collection,
the Suspense Collection or the Romance/Suspense Collection.

Want to try two free books from another line?
Call 1-800-873-8635 or visit www.morefreebooks.com.

* Terms and prices subject to change without notice. NY residents add applicable sales tax. Canadian residents will be charged applicable provincial taxes and GST. This offer is limited to one order per household. All orders subject to approval. Credit or debit balances in a customer's account(s) may be offset by any other outstanding balance owed by or to the customer. Please allow 4 to 6 weeks for delivery.

BOB206

By the Way, Did You Know You're Pregnant?

After twenty-five years of wedlock and
three grown children, starting over with the
diaper-and-formula scene was inconceivable
for Laurel Mitchell. But between her tears
and her husband's terror, they're waiting
for a bundle of joy that's proving life's
most unexpected gifts are the best.

The Second Time Around

by Marie Ferrarella

ANN MAJOR

32088 THE GIRL WITH   ___ $6.99 U.S.   ___ $8.50 CAN.
       THE GOLDEN GUN

(limited quantities available)

TOTAL AMOUNT	$ _____
POSTAGE & HANDLING	$ _____
($1.00 FOR 1 BOOK, 50¢ for each additional)	
APPLICABLE TAXES*	$ _____
TOTAL PAYABLE	$ _____

(check or money order—please do not send cash)

To order, complete this form and send it, along with a check or money order for the total above, payable to MIRA Books, to: **In the U.S.:** 3010 Walden Avenue, P.O. Box 9077, Buffalo, NY 14269-9077; **In Canada:** P.O. Box 636, Fort Erie, Ontario, L2A 5X3.

Name: _____
Address: _____ City: _____
State/Prov.: _____ Zip/Postal Code: _____
Account Number (if applicable): _____

075 CSAS

*New York residents remit applicable sales taxes.
*Canadian residents remit applicable GST and provincial taxes.

MIRA®